'A harrowing and horrific game of consequences'
Val McDermid

'Margaret Kirk's brilliant Inverness series is atmospheric and gripping. She goes from strength to strength . . .'
Cass Green

'Told with an admirable grip on police procedure and an unerring feel for character . . .Tartan Noir at its very best'
Daily Mail

'A harrowing tale of two murders set in Inverness.
Be prepared to hear more from DI Lukas Mahler and his talented creator'
Good Housekeeping

'Dark and compelling'
Sun

Margaret Kirk is a Highland Scot and a graduate of Glasgow University. She is the winner of the *Good Housekeeping* Novel Competition 2016, and author of the DI Lukas Mahler crime series.

To find out more, follow Margaret on Twitter or visit her website.

🐦 @HighlandWriter
🌐 margaretmortonkirk.wordpress.com

Also by Margaret Kirk
Shadow Man
What Lies Buried

IN THE
BLOOD

MARGARET KIRK

ORION

An Orion paperback
First published in Great Britain in 2021 by Orion Fiction,
an imprint of The Orion Publishing Group Ltd
Carmelite House, 50 Victoria Embankment
London EC4Y 0DZ

An Hachette UK Company

1 3 5 7 9 10 8 6 4 2

A CIP catalogue record for this book is
available from the British Library.

ISBN (Mass Market Paperback) 978 1 4091 8870 4
ISBN (eBook) 978 1 4091 8871 1

Typeset by Input Data Services Ltd, Somerset

Printed and bound in Great Britain by Clays Ltd, Elcograf S.p.A.

MIX
Paper from
responsible sources
FSC® C104740
www.fsc.org

www.orionbooks.co.uk

To Alison and Janet, and all the nameless victims.
'They Wur Cheust Folk'

Some places speak distinctly. Certain dark gardens cry aloud for a murder; certain old houses demand to be haunted; certain coasts are set apart for shipwreck.

Robert Louis Stevenson

I

Sandisquoy, Orkney
At the End

He opens his eyes to darkness.

Not the near-instant totality of black, whose suddenness is the last thing he remembers. This dark is faded, uneven patches of light bleeding through it like sun through cheap linen, and it smells of sweat and ozone. There's something wrong with his face, some odd shrouded heaviness against his skin, and a smell like rotting vegetation. He's cold, too, colder than he's ever been. And why can't he move his hands? Or his legs?

Fear, bright and sudden, like a signal flare igniting in his chest. It closes around his heart and squeezes. Hard. And bit by bit, as memory returns, he starts to understand the reality of what's happened to him.

A noise at the door he'd stupidly left unlocked, breaking the habit of a lifetime. Footsteps in the hallway, so stealthy-quiet he'd failed to register them at first. Half turning, then, too late, as a hard and heavy something smashed down onto his neck. And as he sank to his knees, a . . . a hood, he thinks. Dragged down over his face, held in place and weighed down somehow, so that when the next blow came he was already blinded.

That's why he can't see, isn't it? Can't move his hands either, can't even feel them, so he can't wipe away the sticky wetness trickling down the right side of his face. And now he can hear the footsteps again, this time on . . . gravel? Shingle?

He tries to turn his head towards the sound, but the weight moves and tightens, slamming his head backwards. He strains to listen as the footsteps come closer. Closer. And stop.

'You're awake, then? Good, I thought I saw you moving.'

A wheeze of fear, forcing its way up through his bruised throat. This is beyond bad, beyond anything he'd imagined. The voice is muffled, obviously disguised, to the extent that he can't be sure if it's male or female. But it's familiar, too. Like someone—

'Hold on, let's get that off you.'

More movement; closer to him this time. Hands on his shoulders, the tightness round his neck loosening momentarily as the hood's yanked upwards and off. Then there's brightness blinding him. Making him blink and screw up his eyes against the glare as a sun-blurred figure bends towards him.

It glances at the throbbing area above his left ear. Nods. Steps back a little, bends to place what looks like a small rucksack down on the shingle. Then moves to stand in front of him again, silhouetted against the light. Unwinds the scarf around its neck. And raises a hand in greeting.

'Hello, Billy. How're you doing there?'

He blinks the blood and tears out of his eyes. Runs his tongue over his cracked lips, tastes the copper and salt tang of blood. Because what he's seeing . . . it can't be. It just can't.

No.

He tries to shake his head, tries to say that's not his name. But his tongue feels thick and stupid in his mouth, and he can't get the words out. And the figure in front of him keeps shifting in and out of focus. Christ, what's happening to him? Why?

'Not . . . not real.' His voice a rasping whisper, forcing the words out through the creeping numbness in his throat and mouth. 'Can't be . . . real.'

'Afraid it is.' The figure bends closer, lets him get a good look. 'But I'm guessing it's a little hard to trust what you're seeing right now.' A mock-pitying sigh. 'You can run, but you can't hide. That's what they say, isn't it . . . and didn't you run a long way, in the end? Well, this is your time to settle up.'

Wind; sudden ozone-sharp gusts of it, cutting through the sun's heat. Whipping across his face as the panic starts to scrabble at his insides. He jerks his head, feels something tear in his neck as he tries to pull away from whatever he's been tethered to, and grits his teeth against the bright flare of pain it produces.

This isn't going to happen, not to him, not today. He's slowed a little, yes, but he's better than this. So much better. If he can just get a hand free . . .

'Come on, this is crazy! Whatever the problem is, we can talk it over, can't we? Sort it out between us—'

'Sorry, no can do.' A bright, dismissive smile, cutting across his words. And a glance over one shoulder. 'Need to wrap this up. Time and tide, you know?'

'What . . . what are you going to do?'

'Me? Nothing. I won't have to.' A smartphone is held out in front of him. 'This is where you are. No place like home, right?'

At first, all he can make out on the screen is the tumbled dry-stone wall where his scrubby garden slopes down to the shore. Then the camera pans out, showing him the jetty's rotting timbers . . . and the trussed-up figure tied to one of the posts, just above the waterline.

He's not aware of his bladder letting go as he watches, just a momentary lessening of the chill around his groin. And then the panic takes over and he's straining every muscle, fighting the numbness invading his body in a desperate attempt to get away from what's waiting for him.

'You don't need to do this.' Words tumbling out of him now, clamouring to be heard. 'Please! I've got money—'

3

A starburst of pain across his face, slamming his head back against the wooden jetty post.

'You're offering me money? Seriously?' A wintry, disbelieving anger in the face that's looking down at him. 'Trust me, this can get worse. A lot worse.' One hand reaches into the rucksack. Takes out a plastic container and unscrews the cap. Holds it close to his face, close enough for the knowledge of what's in there to turn his bones to water.

'Please.' Sobbing now, tears and snot tracking down his face. 'They'll find you. They'll know—'

'I doubt it.' His killer repacks the rucksack, glances at the now-darkening sky. Gives him a quick, malicious smile before hefting the rucksack and raising a hand in farewell.

'Tide's coming in, Billy. Be sure and don't catch a chill.'

2

Mainland, Orkney
Late October

Black rainclouds hanging above the sullen grey sea. Dark huddles of cattle along the shoreline, hunched against the early-morning chill as Etta's post van heads along the A965.

It had been shaping up to be a decent day when she left on her early-morning drive to Kirkwall. A glint of sun on the water as she headed up over the Churchill Barriers, not much wind to speak of; with autumn well and truly on its way in the islands, always something to be thankful for. But by the time she'd got to the sorting office the sun had dimmed, dulling the waters to a murky grey, and now there's a rising wind battering the van as she heads for Finstown and the north coast.

Still, she's got a light round today, even by Orkney standards. After this stop, she's only got a couple of QVC parcels to drop off. A quick run to Dounby, then it's back to Kirkwall and a bacon roll with Callum in the sorting office. Who happens to be a fine-looking man for his age – fit, the youngsters would say – and just the right kind of cheery to take her mind off having to stop here in the first place.

Bloody heater's on the blink again. Etta zips up her fleece a little higher, slips her hand into the pocket to find the chocolate caramel she knows is hiding there, and pops it into her mouth.

Tells herself she's daft for wishing Callum was sitting there beside her as the van climbs the long slow hill that leads to her destination.

Daft or needing a holiday, maybe. What's got into her today? She likes Callum fine, but she's never wanted his company on her round before. Never needed to have people around her all the time like some folk do; frankly, most days Etta can take them or leave them. Not that she's uncaring, mind; she keeps an eye on the older folks on her rounds, spends a bit of time with them if she can. Still, there are places Etta doesn't feel the need to linger. And Sandisquoy is one of them.

Partly, it's the bay itself. From a distance, it looks scenic enough; the kind of place tourists might take windswept selfies to show their pals back home, though the stink of decomposing seaweed at low tide means they tend not to hang around too long. But there's an odd, overlooked kind of feel to the place that Etta can't explain, one that makes you glance over your shoulder if you walk down to the shore. And then, of course, there's Sandisquoy House itself. Even in midsummer, when the light seldom fades beyond a muted grey into the night's smallest hours, the old stone-built manse keeps its place in the shadows. Some sort of gallery, supposed to be, though Etta can't remember seeing it open more than half a dozen times, even in peak tourist season.

She pulls in off the road, kills the engine. Picks up the couple of bits of junk mail it's hardly worth delivering and sets off to the battered mailbox at the top of the track. She's only done this run maybe a dozen times, but there's no way she'd forget the routine she's supposed to follow, even if the instructions weren't taped to the box. Mainly, because it's just too bloody weird:

POSTMAN
Get the mailbox key from the key safe (combination under the fourth whitewashed stone to the left). Unlock the box and put the post inside. If an item is too bulky for the box, lower it over the drystone wall by the gate.

NO NEED TO CALL AT THE HOUSE

No need, eh? Aye, no worries on that score, pal. Even without that bloody rude note taped to the mailbox, there's nothing about Sandisquoy House that would make Etta want to hang around the place. Nothing—

A hint of movement as she turns to go back to the van, parked by the derelict jetty. Seal? It's breeding season for grey seals, but this looks bigger. Darker. And there's something about the motion, something about the way the shape is clinging to the furthest jetty timbers that looks . . . not right.

She opens the gate and makes her way down the rutted track. Maybe the seal's got tangled up in a fishing net? Wouldn't be the first time. She can just about make out a line of sleek dark heads bobbing out at sea as the rain begins to fall. Watching her as she clambers over the sagging fence and heads down to the shore.

And then the smell is everywhere around her, a high, throat-burning stench that makes her want to gag. Etta takes off her glasses, wipes them on the hem of her fleece before replacing them. Pulls a tissue from her pocket and holds it to her nose as she goes closer to the slumped dark thing beside the jetty. Telling herself it isn't, it *can't be*—

Bending over. Retching. The phone she'd reached for to call the SSPCA dropping from her fingers as a crab, disturbed by her approach, scuttles out of one eyeless socket and down the man's grey-green mottled cheek.

7

3

Police Scotland Divisional HQ
Old Perth Road
Inverness

'At least we've got a decent-sized room this time.' DS Iain 'Fergie' Ferguson puts down the box he's been carrying, looks round the Major Investigation Team's new home. 'You've got to admit, Burnett Road was getting a wee bit cramped for us. And there's a canteen too – might even have that posh coffee you like, eh? Could be worse, boss.'

'Tempting fate, Fergie. Tempting fate.'

Lukas Mahler crosses to the window, looks out at the less than inspiring view of the staff car park. And tries to shake the uncomfortable feeling that's been dogging him ever since the MIT's move to HQ had been announced.

Fergie's right about the conditions they'd been working in at their old home, he supposes. This move had been coming for months, and only Detective Chief Inspector June 'Braveheart' Wallace's determination to stay in her eyrie at Burnett Road had delayed it until now. But with June on sick leave, the Chief Super had lit a fire under Facilities Management and pushed the move through in record time.

Now, less than four months after June's departure, Chae Hunt has got his wish. The entire MIT has moved across the city into divisional headquarters at Inshes, with all the advantages and disadvantages that entails.

On the plus side, there's no denying their new home is physically more comfortable. It's less prone to leaking after a spell of heavy rain, for one thing. And weekend shifts are certainly calmer without the possibility of encountering Friday night revellers tanked up on cheap booze and desperate for 'a square go' on their way to the cells.

In fact, if you didn't know the Armed Response Unit's glory boys lurked behind toughened glass in one corner of the ground floor, North Div HQ could easily be the home of some prosperous city business; Mahler half expects to be greeted by piped muzak when he walks through the foyer of the sandstone and smoked glass building each morning. Even so, if June Wallace had made the move along with her team, he knows he'd be feeling less out of place right now.

June Wallace had been more than his immediate boss; tough as tempered steel but fair and well respected, the DCI had been the MIT's shock absorber, a welcome buffer zone between the team and Hunt's determination to micro-manage them. Now, with June on long-term sick leave and Mahler temporarily promoted to June's old post, Chae Hunt is seizing the opportunity to flex his muscles. And the entire MIT is developing an uneasy shoulder twitch in response.

'Right enough, you never know what's around the corner,' Fergie agrees. 'Look on the bright side, though, eh? Like that "Managing Change" wifie was telling us on her course the other week, there's always positives.'

'The course you had to leave halfway through because you got that urgent phone call from Zofia?'

'Aye, well. I got the gist of the thing.' Fergie takes a file out of the box, frowns at it and dumps it in his in-tray. 'And look at it this way – Pete and Naz have more room for the techie stuff they need, Donna's only five minutes away from her dad now, so she can look in on him if there's a problem, and Gary . . . ach, that one's not bothered where he works as long as he can slope off for a crafty ciggie when no one's looking.'

Fergie glances at his watch, then at Mahler. 'Did you want to stay for the morning briefing? We're waiting for an update on that stabbing in Nairn and the hit-and-run at Culbokie, but . . .'

Mahler does want to. But Chae Hunt is expecting him upstairs in fifteen minutes with the latest on the ongoing investigations into Kat Williams and Patrick Grey, the murderous couple who'd preyed on young children across the UK for fifteen years before an apparent cold case had uncovered the secret of their vile past.

And this is Fergie's show now, anyway; as a DI, Mahler had taken a more active part in the MIT's investigations than his job description strictly warranted. As long as he'd done the necessary admin more or less on time, June Wallace had let him get away with it. But with Chae Hunt breathing down his neck, Mahler knows those days are over, at least for the foreseeable future.

He shakes his head. 'I won't hold you up. I've a meeting with the Chief shortly, so—'

Footsteps coming down the corridor towards them. Email alerts pinging into his and Fergie's mobile at the same instant that Dave Christie, the duty crime-scene manager, puts his head round the door.

'Good, I've caught you both.' He nods at their mobiles. 'Just flagged up a report on STORM for you – unexplained death, called in by Kirkwall Police.'

'Orkney?'

Christie nods again. 'You'll want to take a look at it before the morning briefing. Wee road trip and a ferry ride for me on the cards, I'm thinking.'

Mahler exchanges glances with Fergie. Whatever's come in, it's bad enough to put that grim, closed-down expression on Christie's normally cheerful features. Bad enough for the tension to build across Mahler's shoulder blades, even before he's fired up his laptop and logged into the System for Tasking and Operational Resource Management.

He calls up the incident summary and reads through the details. Deceased male, tied to one of the posts of a disused jetty, called in by a luckless postie who'd made the grim discovery during her daily round. Mahler's seen enough bodies recovered from water to hope it hadn't been there too long.

He turns the laptop towards Fergie, angles the screen so he can read it too. 'Do we have an ID?'

Christie shakes his head. 'Nothing confirmed, but the jetty belongs to a nearby property, Sandisquoy House. Owner's one William Spencer, who's a bit of a recluse by all accounts – and there's no sign of him at the property.'

'Not sounding too good, that.' Fergie peers at the screen. 'Local guy?'

'No, a Londoner,' Christie tells them. 'Lived on Orkney since 2013, but you know what it's like up there. If you're not three-quarters Viking on your granny's side, you're an incomer for the next three generations.'

'London?' Mahler reads through the details again. Frowns as the name hovers on the edge of his memory. 'Not known to us by any chance, is he?'

Christie shakes his head. 'Artist. Why?'

'Doesn't matter.' Coincidence, he tells himself. It has to be. 'Right, if you sort out your arrangements, I'll bring the Chief up to speed. Fergie, I'll need you to—' he breaks off as Fergie scrolls to the end of the report, and an image appears on screen. 'What's that?'

'When the first responder entered the house, Spencer's wallet

11

was sitting on the hall table,' Christie tells him. 'It was empty – no cards, no cash, nothing – but his driving licence was on the floor beside it. Fallen out unnoticed, at a guess.'

'And that's definitely him? The owner of the property?' Mahler tries to convince himself he's mistaken. The name's wrong, for one thing, and the face he's looking at is older than it should be, even allowing for a gap of ten years. But that tightness across his shoulders is digging in, refusing to let go. And there's only one way to make sense of what it's telling him.

'Okay.' Mahler turns to Fergie. 'I need you to sit this one out, I'm afraid. I'm going to try and get a flight to Kirkwall, but failing that I'll drive up to Gill's Bay and take the Pentalina ferry after the morning briefing.'

'You're going yourself, boss?'

Confusion on Fergie's face, and rightly so. Fergie should be the one to go, of course he should; DCIs don't normally attend initial crime scenes. Their role is managerial, allocating resources and directing lines of enquiry. Normally. But if Mahler's right, if the face on that driving licence is an older, wearier version of the one he remembers . . . He forces down the gathering sourness at the back of his throat and turns to Fergie.

'I have to. We need a confirmed ID for him, and I . . . I can do that.'

'You know him, boss?'

Mahler takes a final look at the image on the screen. Nods. 'The name threw me at first, and the licence photo isn't the best. But yes, I know exactly who he is.'

4

Apart from the lingering smell of fresh paint, Chae Hunt's office at Divisional HQ is a near-perfect reproduction of his former one at Burnett Road. No family photos, no personal touches of any kind, apart from the set of framed commendations on his wall. That, and the near-arctic room temperature Mahler encounters each time he walks through the door.

As always, Hunt looks as though he's just got back from a Caribbean holiday, the result of weekly spray tans and regular sunbed top-ups, according to the gossip-mongers. But by the time Mahler's passed on Dave Christie's report and told Hunt what he plans to do about it, there's a distinctly pallid tinge to the Chief's caramel complexion.

'Tied to a jetty on Orkney? Christ on a sodding bike. And you're convinced the victim's this former boss of yours?'

'If you compare the two images I sent on to you, there's a strong resemblance—'

'There's *a* resemblance,' Hunt concedes. 'At this stage, I'm not prepared to go further than that. And I'm certainly not prepared to send you off on a jaunt to Orkney on the strength of it. Supposing it *is* your boy – why the hell would he be living up there under an assumed name in the first place?'

'Alex Fleming retired early from the Met on health grounds,

sir. A heart condition, I believe.' Though Alex's drinking would have had a part in that decision, he suspects. 'Perhaps he wanted a completely fresh start? A new name for a new stage of his life?'

Hunt's eyebrow twitches upwards. 'Most folk just buy a bloody sports car.' He skim-reads the rest of the report Mahler's forwarded to him. 'Do we know how long the body's been there?'

Mahler shakes his head. 'The jetty's semi-derelict, on the northernmost tip of the main island. If it hadn't been for our unfortunate postie, it might have lain undiscovered for longer.'

'Wonderful. So, we're talking two scene examiners and a van on the next ferry?'

'Plus a biologist for samples if we can get one from Aberdeen,' Mahler confirms. 'According to Kirkwall police, the body's in pretty poor condition, so the sooner we can set things in motion—'

'I'm aware of that, thank you,' Hunt snaps. 'That's not at issue here – the budget's well and truly screwed for this quarter, of course, but that can't be helped. But if you think I'm authorising you to spend time out of the office on something any good DI is perfectly capable of handling—'

'Normally I'd agree, of course. But with Andy Black still . . . still unavailable, I've only got one DI at the moment,' Mahler points out. He watches Hunt's face darken with the mention of Black's ongoing suspension, then plays his trump card. 'And if I'm right about our victim's identity, the Met are going to be all over this. We'll want to be on top of things from the outset, sir.'

A twitch of annoyance disturbs the botoxed serenity of Hunt's forehead, before he gives a grudging nod. 'Yes, well. With June Wallace still on sick leave, we're all having to manage our expectations, aren't we? But if you *are* right, we'll need to make sure your former colleagues understand who's running the enquiry from the get-go.'

'Of course. So you're happy to authorise my journey, sir?'

'I'm nothing of the kind. But in the circumstances, I'll allow it.' Hunt gives him a bilious look. 'Go on, get your flights booked – one night's accommodation, but only if it's absolutely necessary. Is that clear?'

'Perfectly.' Mahler's about to leave when Hunt's tablet pings with an email alert. Hunt glances at it and gestures to Mahler to wait. Hunt opens the email, glances at it. Smiles a thin-edged smile as he looks across at Mahler. And delivers the last news Mahler had expected to hear so soon.

'Well, at least the MIT will be back to full complement shortly,' Hunt tells him. 'The investigation into DI Black's conduct has concluded. He'll be returning to duty next week.'

5

Kirkwall
Orkney

The rain is falling when Mahler's Loganair flight comes in to land at Kirkwall; fine but relentless, turning the Orkney landscape into a featureless grey blur. Smaller even than Inverness Airport, the tiny concourse is semi-deserted apart from a tour group ordering lattes at the café, so it's easy to spot the nervous-looking young officer in Police Scotland black who's been detailed to pick him up. Even if he does seem to be looking straight past Mahler and scanning the half-dozen passengers waiting by the baggage reclaim.

Mahler walks over, makes himself known. And watches the officer's expression cycle from relief to mild panic as he looks down at the pair of takeaway coffees he's holding.

'DI Mahler? Yes, sorry, I—'

'He's a DCI, Colin. Aye, they're making them younger these days – just like bobbies, eh?' A woman's voice, cheerfully Doric and loud enough to make the group of latte drinkers turn and stare.

Mahler looks round to see a tall, business-suited woman with close-cropped ice-blonde hair making her way towards him. 'Don't worry, he's my nephew so I can say that to him.' She grins, holds out her hand to Mahler. 'Cath McAvoy, the Fiscal.

We've spoken on the phone, haven't we? About that malicious wounding in Stromness last year?'

'Of course.' No wonder she'd sounded familiar. Since returning to Scotland four years earlier, Mahler's worked with a number of procurators fiscal, a uniquely Scottish amalgam of local coroner and public prosecutor offices that are separate elsewhere. And Cath McAvoy's establishing a growing reputation as one of the very best. 'I'm sorry, if I'd known we were on the same plane—'

The fiscal pulls a face. 'I'd have been back last night, but had to switch a couple of meetings round – right, let's get going. Your scene examiners took the ferry from Gill's Bay, I'm guessing, so if we head off to Sandisquoy now we'll be able to meet up with them and Tony Armstrong – he's the local inspector who's taken on the crime-scene manager role for this one.' She grins at her nephew. 'Those our coffees, Colin? Good lad.'

She takes them, passes one to Mahler. 'I'd get it down you now if I were you.' Her face tightens, losing its cheerfulness. 'From what I've heard, you'll not be fancying much after we've had a look at our poor dead mannie.'

The road to Sandisquoy Bay takes them to the northernmost coast of Mainland, Orkney's largest island, past clusters of small, weathered cottages and lush jewel-green fields. An old, old landscape, layer upon layer of history lying on the land where people have lived and farmed since Neolithic times.

Somewhere to be at peace, Mahler thinks, surprising himself with the thought because peace has never come easily to him. But this place has an otherness to it, a feeling of being not quite part of the modern world in spite of the scattering of new housing developments and the occasional tour bus they meet on the road.

They've been driving for almost an hour since leaving

Kirkwall when they crest another of the island's long unhurried hills. Almost immediately afterwards, the land slopes away towards a long, sheltered bay. A gaunt Victorian building sits near the shoreline, with the scene examiner's van parked next to it.

Their forensic tent has been erected almost on the water's edge, beside the broken spine of a crumbling wooden jetty. But it's the building itself that catches Mahler's attention as they turn off the main road and onto a narrow dirt track. Built from dull grey stone so dark it's almost black, it squats alone on the shoreline like a huge carrion bird, its stepped gables disturbingly like vast folded wings.

'That's Sandisquoy there. Named after the bay, and—' The fiscal breaks off, throws him a sharp glance as they follow the track down towards the house. 'Aye, can't say I'm a fan of the place myself.'

'You've been there?'

'Just walked around the headland a couple of times,' she tells him. 'Apparently Sandisquoy was an old manse once upon a time, though it's miles from the nearest kirk. Not exactly dream home material, is it? Not the kind of place you'd run an art gallery from either, I'd have thought. Are you sure this William Spencer's really your former boss at the Met?'

Mahler shakes his head. Perhaps it's the way Sandisquoy House sits in a natural depression in the landscape, so that even on sunny days, he suspects the light would struggle to reach it. Or the odd lack of windows, particularly on the upper floors. But the closer they get, the more he's starting to dislike the place. And the harder he's finding it to imagine the Alex Fleming he knew living somewhere like this.

'It was Alex's photo on that driving licence,' he tells the fiscal. 'Right now, that's the only thing I'm sure about – believe me, if this turns out to be a case of identity theft, I'll be delighted.'

'Aye, well. Let's hope that's what we're looking at, then.'

She leans forward, taps her nephew on the shoulder. 'Colin, you're fine to let us out here. I can see Tony waiting for us down by the tape.'

They walk down the track to a cordoned-off area, marked by Police Scotland blue and white incident tape. McAvoy introduces Mahler to the local police inspector and crime-scene manager, a big, weather-beaten man with a shock of iron-grey hair who was among the first responders. A couple of years off retirement, Mahler estimates, Armstrong's expression speaks volumes about what's waiting for them down by the shore.

Dave Christie appears as they're struggling into their protective suits. The scene examiner looks them up and down, sighs and holds out two pairs of bright blue bootees.

'Here, I knew you'd forget them – not that there's much more contamination you could bring to the scene, frankly.'

'That bad?'

Christie gives the fiscal a sombre nod. 'Body's been in the water for at least a couple of days. Tide's been in and out, crabs and the like have got curious, so overall . . . well, you'll see for yourself.'

'He's still in situ?'

Another nod. 'Will be for a while, while we work out how to move him. It's down this way.'

The approach path runs parallel to the dirt track for a couple of hundred yards before dividing in two a little short of the house. Mahler and McAvoy follow the scene examiner down the left-hand fork, through the yellowing marram grass to the sand and shingle foreshore.

This close to the jetty, Mahler can see it's in even worse condition than his first view of it had indicated; the walkway has completely fallen away, and the pilings that remain jut crookedly upwards, like the ribs of an ancient sea creature. Those that he can see, at least. The forensic tent covers the right side of the structure's final section . . . and if he hadn't already known what the tent concealed, the smell being carried towards him on the rising wind is ripely, stomach-churningly unambiguous.

Christie glances at Mahler. Reads something in his face, perhaps, that he thought he'd managed to keep hidden. 'Lukas, we've got plenty of images we can send on – 360-degree panoramics, close-ups, the whole shebang. You don't need to physically see—'

'I do. Are the features intact enough to be identified?'

'I'd say so, yes. But . . .' Christie shrugs, nods. 'Okay, then.' He walks down to the tent, motions to Mahler and McAvoy to follow, and pushes open the entrance flap.

As soon as they enter, the smell hits them. Bad enough in the open air, once inside, there's nowhere to escape the blast of overheated, sweet-sour ripeness that rises to meet them.

'Jesus Christ.' The fiscal coughs, puts an instinctive hand up to her face. The masks they're wearing are no protection against what's assaulting their nasal passages right now. Or the sight of the grey, misshapen thing lashed to one of the jetty uprights. 'That's after just a few days?'

'About that, aye,' Christie tells her. 'Though we'll need to get him back to Raigmore for the PM to confirm that. Talking of which, the tide will be coming in soon, so we need to start moving him as soon as we can. Lukas, if you're ready—'

'Yes.' Not the face, though. Not that. Not yet.

Mahler closes off the clamminess of the tent, the unrelenting smell of death hanging in the tainted air. *Concentrate.* Closes off the look of concern he'd glimpsed on Christie's face. *Focus*, he tells himself. He clears his mind of anything but the need to evaluate the scene in front of him, and walks over to the wooden upright.

The corpse's hands and feet have been bound with cable ties, and there's an obvious wound to the base of the skull. But

Mahler can't see any sort of restraint around the victim's torso, so what's holding him in position?

Christie glances at Mahler, nods. 'Aye, it took me a minute to work it out too. Look there.' The scene examiner lifts a section of the victim's thick grey hair, points to a dark leather band encircling its mottled neck. Roughly three centimetres wide, the band passes through the rotting slats of the jetty and loops round the wooden upright, forming a type of noose.

'That's just a normal leather belt, as far as I can tell. Did the job, though – together with the cable ties, someone wanted to make damn sure there was no way out for . . . well, whoever he is.'

'That's the question, isn't it?' Mahler points at the belt. 'Any chance you could get something from that buckle?'

'Latent prints? Aye, maybe. Have to see once we get him off there.'

Mahler checks the position of the body in relation to the wooden upright. Frowns. 'That's the only thing holding him in place? Could he have been killed somewhere else and placed here post-mortem?'

'We've got drag-marks leading here from the house,' Christie tells him. 'So he'll have been incapacitated, at the very least. Again, we'll have a clearer idea once we move him.' Christie glances at Mahler, hesitates. 'If you're ready to take a look?'

At his nod, the scene examiner pushes back the hair still obscuring the corpse's features. Mahler bends closer, makes himself look at what remains of its face. And reconstructs it in his mind until he's certain there's no mistake.

He straightens up, unclenches his jaw. Releases a long, slow breath. And turns to face Christie and the fiscal.

'Yes,' he tells them. 'Yes, that's Alex Fleming.'

6

'Okay, folks, that's it.'

Fergie finishes the morning briefing and watches the team file out. No daft questions from Skivey Pete or Big Gary for once; the hit-and-run at Culbokie has just turned into a murder enquiry, and no one's in the mood to give him a hard time this morning.

But God, it still feels weird to be taking them through the investigation strategy as their detective inspector. *Acting* DI, he reminds himself; nothing permanent about this promotion. At least, he damn well hopes not. The boss isn't too happy about having to step into June Wallace's shoes while she's on sick leave, but at least Mahler had the skills to hit the ground running. Right now, Fergie's not even sure where the damn ground is.

Zofia knows he's not happy about it, but she thinks all that's wrong with him is a bad case of impostor syndrome. But Zo hasn't seen him standing in front of their bedroom mirror in his new suit, sucking in his gut and tugging at his collar. Feeling like a kid wearing his big brother's hand-me-downs on his first day at the big school. Impostor syndrome? No bloody syndrome about it, as far as Fergie's concerned. He *is* an impostor, and sooner or later someone's going to find him out. He just hopes he doesn't mess up too badly when it happens.

Oh, he's had his chances to go for promotion in the past; had the nod from June Wallace a few years back a couple of times, in fact. But by then he'd seen the job changing, paperwork breeding paperwork until it seemed like you had two choices. You could be out there keeping folk safe and bringing in the bad guys, or you could climb the ladder and find yourself writing reports and filling in spreadsheets about it. And right from the start, he'd known which route he wanted to follow.

True, the boss manages to balance both sides of the job, but the boss . . . well, the boss is a bit different to most coppers. And Fergie's not sure even Mahler will manage to pull it off for long. The whole MIT's exhausted after the horrors of the Child Snatcher case a few short months ago. They're still dealing with the fallout from what they'd found at the old steading at Culloden, and by Fergie's reckoning, the boss is pretty close to running on empty after that one.

At least the MIT will be back to full strength once Andy Black's back at work; there'll be two DIs to do the damn admin, for one thing. Though looking back, he can't remember Andy ever pulling his weight in the paperwork department, even before his suspension.

Not what you'd call a team player at the best of times, Andy. He blames the boss for the reprimand he got for messing up in the Child Snatcher case, and if there's one thing Andy's good at, it's holding grudges. Then there's wee Nazreen Khan: whip-smart, ambitious, good-looking. Pushing all of Andy's buttons since the day she joined the team.

Fergie worries there may be something truly rotten behind Andy's attitude, some sort of disgusting mix of prejudice and misogyny he doesn't even want to think about right now, not with everything else they've got going on at the moment. But he can see a time when they'll have to go there, him and the boss, and—

His mobile lights up on the desk, a tinny little jingle announcing yet another bloody email's arrival. Fergie squares his shoulders and walks over to take a look, wincing as he scrolls through what looks like an endless list. Some with red flags, some with red flags *and* attachments.

Christ, he *hates* attachments; they're usually forms, or spreadsheets, or some other impenetrable guff that's guaranteed to make his brain feel like it's slowly catching fire inside his head. Either that or it's one of those daft *'Tell us how satisfied you are in your role so we can ignore everything you say'* surveys that HR sends out every so often. Sometimes Fergie wonders if they're really some sort of psychological testing method in disguise, to see how much crap folk like him are willing to put up with.

He sits at his desk, opens up his laptop to take a closer look at the notification that's just come in from the Crown Office. And almost wishes it *had* been one of those daft survey things that landed in his inbox.

There're no attachments with this one, and it's only a couple of paragraphs long. But the name in the subject header is enough to give him a bloody headache, just the same: James Douglas Gordon.

Hack writer.

Z-list celeb.

Triple murderer.

7

Sandisquoy
Orkney

By the time the contracted undertakers arrive, the weather is starting to turn again. Ponderous black clouds are gathering over the bay, and there's a rising wind whipping the sides of the forensic tent.

Mahler watches from the house's porch as the hearse makes its way down the track; moving faster than the norm, this one. But there are no distressed relatives here to be mindful of, he supposes. And every need for urgency.

'Does he have family, do you know? Anyone we need to inform?'

Mahler turns to the fiscal, shakes his head. 'No siblings, as far as I'm aware, and his mother died some years ago. As for relationships, I've no idea.'

'You didn't know him that well, then?'

'Apparently not.'

A sharpness in his voice he hadn't intended. But Alex Fleming had been Mahler's first DI when he'd joined the Met; a big, genial man with a laugh you could hear from one end of Charing Cross nick to the other, he'd shown more kindness to the young detective with the foreign-sounding name and non-existent social skills than Mahler suspects he'd probably deserved.

It was down to Fleming and Raj Lal, one of the few friends he'd made during his training at Hendon, that Mahler had got through those early days in the Met. In different ways, the job had destroyed them both within a couple of years. But Raj's death had at least made an appalling sort of sense. Nothing about Alex Fleming's death currently makes sense to Mahler. Nothing at all.

The hearse pulls up and waits just shy of the police cordon. With high tide due in just over a couple of hours, David Christie's team have been working against the clock to record every scrap of information at the scene. When they leave Sandisquoy, the locus will have been photographed from every conceivable angle, and a 360-degree panoramic video taken to ensure nothing is missed that could be vital to the investigation's progress. And now, there's only one final task left for them to accomplish.

Movement from inside the tent. The flaps open, and Christie looks out. Retreats. And reappears, carrying one end of something long, bulky and unmistakable. Mahler's told himself this is part of his job, steeled himself not to think of the thing that lies inside it, extremities bagged, wrapped in plastic sheeting and sealed like a macabre Christmas cracker. But Christie's colleague, who's carrying the other end, stumbles briefly on the uneven ground as they exit the tent, causing the load they're carrying to shift slightly. And Mahler finds he can't make himself stand and watch, after all.

He tells the fiscal he wants to take a look at the interior of the house now the scene examiners have finished there, and goes inside.

The cold hits him as soon as he's over the threshold. Not just the chill of an old house left unoccupied for a day or so; this is a deep, multi-layered cold that feels as though it lives within the fabric of the building itself. Mahler zips up the parka he's thrown over his suit jacket. And tries to imagine living somewhere like this for any length of time.

'Jeez-o, and I thought it was freezing *out*side.' Cath McAvoy follows him down the hall, past an ornate wooden dresser and into the kitchen. 'How long has he been here?'

'Three years, according to the electoral roll.' Again, though, he's listed under the name of William Spencer. How could Alex have taken over another identity so successfully? And more importantly, *why* had he done it?

Mahler looks round at the dark, old-fashioned kitchen. A traditional Orkney chair with its high wicker back sits next to an iron range, angled towards the back door. On the drying rack next to the sink, there's an upturned saucepan, together with a single mug, plate and set of cutlery. Other than that, there are no other items of crockery, no cooking implements at all that he can see.

'Not a foodie, then.' The fiscal pulls open a cupboard door and peers at the empty shelving. 'Can't even see a fridge in here, can you? Man living on his own, you'd think there'd be somewhere to keep a couple of beers. But it looks like he hardly set foot in the place.'

Mahler shakes his head. Wherever Alex Fleming had spent his time, it certainly hadn't been in this room. 'Let's take a look at the rest of the house.'

There are two more rooms on this floor: a sparsely furnished living room with maroon velvet curtains, smelling faintly of mildew, and a back parlour which looks as though it might have been used as a dining room at some point. In this second room, a row of cardboard boxes have been pushed against the far wall, mouse-nibbled and sealed with duct tape.

Both rooms have the same dusty, neglected air, and Mahler can't help wondering if Alex Fleming had spent much time at Sandisquoy. There's no sign here of his prize record collection, no sign of the stack of Stephen King paperbacks he'd hoarded. Had this soulless house really been somewhere Alex had called home? Or had something made him invent an entire new personality to go with his new name?

'I thought you said he ran an art gallery?'

The fiscal shrugs. 'The William Spencer Gallery is listed in *Creative Orkney*, yes. Could have given it up, I suppose – don't remember seeing his name on anything recently. Let's see if upstairs is a wee bit cheerier.'

She goes to the foot of the stairs to look for a light switch. Finds one and flips it, frowning when nothing happens. 'Power was working earlier, wasn't it?'

'Must be a fuse.' The light fittings look like the original Bakelite, and Mahler's willing to bet the wiring's similarly ancient. 'Watch your footing, the carpet's coming loose in places.'

By the time they reach the half-landing, they're in semi-darkness and the chill is becoming more intense. The only natural light comes from a scratched and pitted stained-glass window high on the wall, its colours so faded they merge into a uniform grey. Why so few windows in a house this size?

There are two bedrooms on the first floor, both as empty and uncared for as the downstairs rooms had been, neither looking as though anyone had ever spent a night in them. So where had Alex Fleming slept?

Mahler takes the next flight of stairs to the top floor. He opens the door to a small, spartan bathroom, takes a quick look round. And comes out to see the fiscal standing in the doorway of what he'd assumed would be another bedroom.

'Cath?'

'Come and look at this.' She steps aside, giving him a clear view of the room's interior. 'Might want to put your sunglasses on, though.'

He walks over to where she's standing, takes a look inside. And puts his hand up to his eyes to shield them from the brightness that's suddenly all around him. Everything in this room, from the brickwork walls to an enormous antique wardrobe standing in one corner, has been painted white, and a massive picture window occupies most of what would have been the upper floor's gable end. After the gloom of the rest of the house, the concentrated brightness in this one room is startling; if sunlight ever did penetrate this far into Sandisquoy, Mahler suspects the effect here would be almost overwhelming.

'Looks like this is where he slept.' The fiscal walks over to a mattress on the floor, covered with a jumble of bedding. She pokes at an odd mound in the centre, and an empty bottle of Highland Park rolls out. 'And had a wee nightcap or two, apparently.' She wrinkles her nose, sniffs. 'What's that smell?'

'Some sort of solvent, I think. For cleaning paintbrushes.' Mahler walks over to the stack of artists' canvasses propped against one wall, turns one round. And hears his own hiss of shock echoed in the fiscal's voice as she comes over to take a closer look.

'Bloody hell.' She looks up at Mahler and back at the painting. 'That's meant to be the bay here, isn't it? What are those things in the water that look like they're on fire?'

Mahler looks at the slashes of black and red, the sweep of gunmetal sky and molten sea. If this represents how Fleming had felt about the place he'd made his home . . . 'Some of them are seals, I think.' Though there's something disturbingly human about the writhing creatures, something that looks more at home in a medieval vision of hell. What had been going on in Alex's head to make him produce something like this?

The fiscal pulls out another canvas. And another. Apart from a few minor variants, they're almost indistinguishable from the first.

She looks up at Mahler. Shakes her head. 'Well, there's no denying the mannie had talent. But I doubt the tourists would have been flocking to his door to buy much of this stuff.'

8

Procurator Fiscal's Office
Kirkwall

The wi-fi has gone down suddenly and catastrophically at the police station in Kirkwall, so the videolink strategy meeting Mahler's arranged with Chae Hunt has been reconvened to Cath McAvoy's office, in the grounds of the ruined seventeenth-century palace of the former earls of Orkney.

The Chief listens impassively to David Christie's report on the samples recovered at the scene and the likely costings for the forensic tests. Only the slight pulse of a vein below his jaw suggests to Mahler his internal budget calculator is shifting into overdrive.

'What about the media?' Hunt asks once Christie's finished. 'Any sign of interest from the local press yet?'

Mahler shakes his head. 'Nothing so far, but we'll need to release a holding statement as soon as possible and issue an initial appeal for information.'

It will almost certainly be fruitless; Sandisquoy lies in a remote area of the island, so far from the usual visitor attractions that the chances of someone coming forward with any kind of meaningful information are minimal. And with the nearest neighbour miles away, they can forget about the usual door-to-door enquiries. But Dave Christie has estimated Fleming's body could have been tied to the jetty for anything up to four days, so they need to get the investigation moving as quickly as possible.

He nods at Armstrong, the local police inspector. 'If Tony issues something this evening, I can deal with the rest first thing tomorrow.'

'You're coming back tonight?'

'Most efficient use of available resources, sir. We'll need a full search of the property but that will take several days, and Inspector Armstrong's officers are best placed to undertake that.'

An unconvincing cough from Armstrong as he mentions the 'e' word. Rumour has it there's a Chief's Lingo Bingo game circulating with a bottle of twelve-year-old Talisker as the prize, and Mahler suspects he's just gifted the local inspector a winning line. But Armstrong knows the island, knows the people, and Mahler doesn't; it makes sense for Armstrong to continue the initial stages of the enquiry up here. And the text from Fergie that's just flashed up on his phone means he needs to get back to the mainland as soon as possible.

'Makes sense, I suppose,' Hunt concedes. 'If your identification's correct, we'll need to liaise with the Met, make sure we're on top of this one from the outset.' He turns to the scene examiner. 'Any pointers so far – anything at all we can work with?'

'Nothing particularly helpful,' Christie warns. 'We've found no evidence of forced entry to the house, no signs of a struggle taking place there. There are contusions on the victim's face and neck—'

'Involved in a fight?'

'A reasonable guess at this stage, aye. Lukas has made a preliminary identification of the victim as the man who lived at Sandisquoy under the name of William Spencer. He looks to have been a recluse, and his living conditions were . . . unusual, let's just say. So how you're going to identify potential persons of interest . . .' Christie shrugs. 'It's a weird one, this. Everything about it's weird.'

'Weird or not, we need to get on top of it.' Hunt's chemically enhanced forehead attempts a frown. 'We're late to the game already – four days late, sounds like. Let's make sure we don't lose any more time.'

Mahler had planned to fly back to Inverness immediately after the meeting, but as they're finishing up, the news comes through that the airport's been hit by the knock-on effect of an air-traffic controllers' strike down south. With nothing likely to be moving from there until the following afternoon, all he can do is hire a car at the ferry terminal in St Margaret's Hope and take the Pentalina back to the mainland.

'Drop you off, if you like,' the fiscal offers. 'I need to call in on someone there, and you'll make the earlier ferry that way.'

The weather's clearing as they drive south, enough for Mahler to glimpse the scuttled wrecks of the First World War fleet as they cross the Churchill Barriers, the causeways linking Orkney's main island with North Ronaldsay. Again, Mahler's struck by the intense green of the landscape they're driving through; combined with the wide skies and expanse of dark blue water everywhere he looks, it offers a tranquillity he hadn't expected to find here.

'Planning a transfer?' Cath McAvoy glances at him as they turn onto the approach road for the ferry terminal. 'I know, it's tempting. How do you think I ended up here? Met an Orkney guy when my parents took a holiday cottage for the summer, and that was it – never wanted to be anywhere else.'

'I can see how that could happen.'

'And it's a great place to live, it really is. You need to have the right mindset, though – there's no dark in the summer, none

33

at all. And the winters . . .' she shakes her head. 'The isolation can get to you sometimes, that's all I'm saying. And if you cut yourself off the way your boss did . . . well, you're not making life easy for yourself, are you? You said he retired early?'

'A few years ago, I think. He had a heart condition.'

Cath frowns. 'And he chose to move all the way up here? Don't get me wrong, our local hospital's first class. But for anything major, he'd need to travel to Aberdeen or Edinburgh.'

'Perhaps he didn't think it through.' Or perhaps the need for isolation had outweighed all other considerations. But why? And why the need for an alias?

They've reached the ferry terminal. The fiscal pulls over, turns to him. 'Like I said, this is a great place to live. But it seems to me, folk who move huge distances for no apparent reason are either running to or from something.'

'Like Alex.'

She shrugs. 'Not always easy for ex-cops to leave it all behind them, is it? And whatever problems the guy had, looks like he brought them with him. Those paintings weren't done by a well man, Lukas. And that house . . . If my head was full of the sort of things that went into those paintings, Sandisquoy's the last place I'd have chosen to live.'

9

Dornoch
40 miles north of Inverness

It's a fast crossing from St Margaret's Hope back to the mainland, but a much less calm one than Mahler had been hoping
for. The storm that had abated briefly during the drive from
Sandisquoy to the ferry terminal is back in full force now. Rain
batters the hire car's windscreen as he follows the A9 down the
stark east coast, through Caithness villages with Norse-derived
place-names like Thrumster and Lybster before passing into
Sutherland.

By the time he's reached Berriedale Braes and its notorious
hairpin bends, the weather's deteriorated further; even more
reason to turn off at Dornoch until the rain eases a little, and call
in to see Anna. She would tell him he doesn't need a reason, of
course. That she's seen him at the lowest of his bleak, despairing
lows and hasn't walked away. Isn't going to walk away.

On good days, he lets himself believe that; even on bad
days, sometimes. Right up until he'd read the Crown Office
email about James Gordon, he'd kept that thought in his head.
Now . . . Christ, what is he supposed to tell her? What words
can he use to try to make sense of this travesty of justice?

He parks in the main square, opposite Anna's block of flats.
It's barely a five-minute walk to her door, but there's no

response to his first two rings. He's about to leave when the buzzer sounds and the communal entrance door swings open.

By the time he reaches Anna's flat, she's waiting for him. She's wrapped in a vast white dressing gown and wearing those peculiar furry boots she loves, so he's guessing the heating in her flat is playing up again, but she looks genuinely pleased to see him. No one's told her what's happened, then. Mahler tells himself that's a good thing.

'Anna, buzzing me in like that wasn't wise. I could have been anyone—'

'I saw you getting out of the car. Honestly, Lukas, don't fuss – and for goodness' sake, come in! You're dripping all over the hall.'

She takes him through to the living room, picks up a pile of papers from the sofa and dumps it on the table. 'Deadline for this in less than a week, and I'm getting nowhere fast. How hard can it be to get an abstract together for . . .' She looks across at him, and her smile dies. 'You're not just visiting, are you? What's happened?'

'Anna, sit down. Please.' He takes a seat next to her, reaches for her hand. 'It's about James Gordon's appeal hearing. The one scheduled for January.'

He watches her face change. Watches the tightening of her jaw, the pulse beating in the base of her throat at the mention of the man who'd killed her sister and come within a hair's breadth of killing her too.

'He isn't withdrawing, is he? If he was planning to withdraw his appeal, you wouldn't be looking at me like that.'

'I'm sorry, no.' Mahler makes himself meet her eyes. 'There's ongoing renovation work at the High Court, so a number of cases have been rescheduled. Some have been put back several weeks, others have been bumped up the list. His appeal's going to be heard in four weeks' time.'

36

'And there's nothing we can do? No way of fighting this?'

'I'm sorry.'

'Yes, so you said.' She pulls her hand away, pushes her hair back from her face. 'Christ, what a mess. Does my mother know? I should ring her—'

'I'd leave it for tonight. Maxine from Family Liaison will be in touch first thing tomorrow, and you can talk it through with her then.'

'Maybe you're right.' She gives him a quick, angry glance. 'Not like it's going to change anything, is it?'

'Anna, I don't . . .' He shakes his head, lets the sentence die. All he can offer is another worthless apology, and she doesn't want to hear that. She hasn't moved away, not physically. But the room seems to have expanded, tripling the distance between them. 'There will be media interest,' he tells her. 'I just . . . I wanted to prepare you for it. If there's anything you need, anything at all—'

'A time machine, maybe. To go back to that day on the cliffs at Badbea, and hit him over the head again. A damn sight harder this time.'

'You don't mean that.'

'Don't I?' Anna glances at Mahler, sighs. 'Look, thanks for trekking up here to tell me. You didn't have to do that.'

'I did. And I was on my way back to Inverness anyway. There was an incident on Orkney I was called to.'

'A bad one?' She glances at him again. 'Yes, I can see it was. Look, you can stay over, if you want – you know you shouldn't drive with those headaches, right?'

Mahler shakes his head, starts to tell her he's fine. And feels the first hooks of pain dig in behind his right eye. She's right, he shouldn't drive. But there's no way he can stay here tonight.

It's two years since the brutal murder of Morven Murray. Two years since Mahler and Anna had tracked down her sister's killer and seen him brought to justice. Two years, in which Anna had returned to San Diego and her lecturing post at UCSD before coming home for good.

And something had been taking shape between them, some cautious, uncertain thing they'd only recently acknowledged. Then the news had broken that Gordon was preparing to appeal his sentence.

Anna's dealing with the news better than he might have done in her place, Mahler suspects. But it's taking its toll. He can read it in the darkness under her eyes, the new gauntness of her face. And he can't be around her tonight. Not with the sight of Alex Fleming's bloated corpse seared into his brain. And the memories it's forcing him to relive.

A slumped, dark shape, painted against the light; his friend Raj's body, hanging from a beam in his garage. Sirens wailing, and a rising scream behind him . . .

'I need to get back. But thanks.' Too abrupt. Too cold. But what is he supposed to do, burden Anna with the images playing in his head? 'I'll call you tomorrow. As soon as I have more details.' He puts his arms round her. Realises too late he should have done it as soon as he walked through the door. 'Anna, I'm so sorry. If there's anything I can do—'

She looks at him. Sighs. Touches his cheek with more kindness than he deserves. 'Jamie can't . . . there's no way he could somehow walk free, is there?'

Mahler shakes his head. On that at least, he can reassure her. 'The appeal's against the length of sentence, not the actual conviction. So no, I can't imagine any way that could happen.'

'No.' Her mouth drawn into a grim line, Anna walks with him to the door. 'No, neither can I. Safe journey back, Lukas.'

10

Sandisquoy
The Beginning

Without the storm, he might never have found it.

God knows, after three years on this bloody island he should be used to how the seasons work here. Spring doesn't exist, for one thing; not an English spring, with daffodils and tulips and trees getting ready for the warmer weather. The cloudless, ice-blue skies here can take you by surprise, can make you think about heading out somewhere, maybe getting away from the damn bay and the damn seals and your own damn thoughts for a while.

But all of that's just trying to fool you. Because the wind . . . even in spring, the wind is always there, always waiting. Waiting to rip the front door out of your hands, to pin you flat against the house's gable end as you turn away from the lee-side and into its full fury. Waiting for you to chance that walk along the cliffs to clear the worst of your hangover and get your head together . . .

No, by now he's learned not to trust the cloudless, ice-blue sky and the momentary lift of warmth the sun provides. The dark half of the year, he's found, is just that. A dark and brutal contest with the world in darkness, counting down the days for winter to be done and summer to finally arrive.

But this year has been a mild one, at least by Orkney standards. Only minor floods in at-risk areas, nothing around the Churchill

Barriers so far. So when the storm blew in from nowhere, he'd been in the walled garden, axe in hand, squaring up to the thick, dark tangle of overgrown greenery that might have been an orchard, once upon a time.

Not his favourite place, this, truth be told. More trees than he'd expected on an island whose capital boasts about a stunted sycamore in the middle of its high street. Which should have been a bonus, he supposes.

He's never liked enclosed spaces much, though, and even when the sun's out, the light seems to struggle here; one of the reasons he'd left things alone for so long, maybe. Even when he'd stopped pratting about and made a start on the scrubby bushes by the far wall, he'd achieved less than half of what he'd set out to do.

It was the lightning that had finally got him moving. Jagged flares of white, splintering the sky as he raced back to the house. Wind screaming in his ears, driving fierce, slanted rain against his face. Slamming him against the lichen-covered lump of grey-green stone that might have been an angel or a goddess, once upon a time. And the axe had fallen from his grip, coming to rest with a grating metallic clang by the statue's base.

Metal striking metal. Why not stone? Weird. Bloody weird. But there was no time to investigate, not then; his shoulder was sending bright bursts of pain down his arm where he'd hit the stone. He'd dragged himself back to the house, secured the doors and windows against the storm and got what the locals call a good dram inside him.

It wasn't until the next morning that he ventured back into the garden to retrieve the axe. The debris from the storm was everywhere he looked, branches and foliage ripped from the tangle of bushes and strewn across the mossy grass. The axe was lying a little away from the statue, the blade half buried in a clump of storm-exposed roots.

He walked over to retrieve it, bent to pull it free . . . and again, heard the distinctive scrape of metal on metal as the blade made contact with something by the statue's base. Something there. Something buried?

Crouching, he'd laid the axe aside and started to clear the area around the statue. After a few minutes, he could see a dull glint of metal. He reached down, probed the area with a cautious hand and found a smooth, man-made surface less than a foot below ground level.

Tank. You've found the frigging septic tank, moron.

Only he's pretty sure the tank's on the other side of the building, and surely it would be buried deeper than this? Anyway, this place is way too overgrown; nothing's been disturbed here for years, he's sure of it.

He carries on working, getting a feel for the shape of whatever it is; definitely man-made, roughly rectangular, about six foot by two . . . his stomach gives a disturbing lurch as he realises what those sort of dimensions usually mean. But Christ, who'd bury a coffin this close to the surface? Then his fingers find what can only be a rusted bolt. And below that, a lock.

He stares down at what he's uncovered. What the fuck's this, the start of a sodding horror film?

He worries at the bolt a couple of times, but it's rusted shut. The lock is massive, the kind he's seen in old films or museums, and if he wants to take a look at what's inside . . . He sits back on his heels, wipes his hands on his jeans. Asks himself if that's really what he wants.

Because whatever this is, it hasn't just been left to get overgrown. Now that he looks closely, he can see that the roots of scrubby gorse and heather mingling with the mossy grass form a sort of sequence, as though they've been planted rather than grown up naturally.

Which means someone, a long time ago, decided they needed to bury what he's just found. Decided it was worth doing quite a decent job of it. If it hadn't been for last night's storm, he'd never have known it was there. And digging around in the past, raking through hidden things . . . well, he knows how that can turn out, doesn't he?

And yet . . . and yet. It's there, in front of him. Something no one's seen for years, maybe decades. Maybe longer. Maybe much longer. On his land. On his property. So whatever's there, it's his now, isn't it? It belongs to him.

He gets to his feet. And goes back to the house to get the tools he needs.

I I

Raigmore Hospital Mortuary
Inverness
10 a.m.

'Oh my.' Marco McVinish, masked and swathed in green scrubs, glances up at Fergie as he arrives in the viewing gallery. 'Sure you want to stay for this? Because I can tell you now, it isn't going to be pretty.'

'It never is.' Fergie knows he's not exactly *Mastermind* material, but he's worked that one out for himself, thank you very much. And no, he doesn't want to stay and watch what's going to happen next. He's attended enough post-mortems for bodies recovered from water to know roughly what condition this one's going to be in, and given the choice, he'd be out of that room and heading back to HQ faster than Lewis Hamilton late for an appointment.

But someone's got to be here with the scene examiner to witness the samples being taken, and Fergie's sure as hell not going to land it on someone like wee Nazreen Khan or Skivey Pete. He squares his shoulders, nods at McVinish. 'Let's just get it done, eh?'

'Fair enough.' McVinish turns away, signals to the pathology technician who's assisting him.

Before any physical examination of the body can take place,

its clothing will have to be cut away; it's the least invasive procedure the pathologist will carry out during the post-mortem, but somehow it's the one Fergie finds hardest to watch.

Stripping away the poor sod's dignity, he always thinks; removing one by one the things that made him a living, breathing person, just going about his business . . .

'Subject appears to be in his mid-fifties, well nourished with a heavy build. Outer clothing consists of a parka-type jacket, jeans and walking boots. All items appear in good condition – boots are unfastened, so—'

'He was on his way out somewhere? Or had just got back, when someone jumped him? Dave Christie's report said there was an injury to the back of his neck.'

'Two minor injuries, in fact, and one to his jaw, which I'll examine in due course. Without jumping to conclusions about where they came from. In the meantime . . .' McVinish frowns, bends to take a closer look at the outer clothing, and nods at his technician. 'Craig, can we investigate the bulge in that pocket, please? I'm wondering if – oh, bollocks. What are you doing here?'

A blast of cold air on Fergie's neck. He turns to see the boss standing in the viewing gallery doorway. His face is . . . well, he's not quite as ghost-grey as the man on the pathologist's table, but he's not that far off it.

'Boss, I don't think—'

'What have I missed?'

McVinish shakes his head. 'Lukas, for God's sake—'

'I'm attending a post-mortem on a suspicious death. My potential connection to the victim is immaterial. Where have we got to, Marco?'

For a man wearing a mask and glasses, the pathologist manages to give the boss an impressive side-eye. 'All that time you spent down south, and you've still got a streak of Highland thrawn a mile wide. Fine, then – don't say you weren't warned.'

McVinish runs through his initial comments again as the technician continues to cut away the corpse's clothing. 'As I explained to Fergie, the head trauma is minor, and may not—'

A muted, clattering sound as the corpse's jacket, now unfastened, falls open. McVinish turns at the noise, frowns. 'Craig, let's have a look at those pockets, please. Sounds as though there's something in there.'

The technician slices open the right-hand pocket and takes a quick step backwards as the contents burst out. The pebbles roll everywhere, the metallic clanging as they hit the steel table amplified by McVinish's mic. And in amongst them, what looks like a pouch of some dark fabric.

'What's that? Is there something inside it?'

'Hold your horses, gentlemen, and we'll find out.'

The pathologist nods at his technician, who records its weight and dimensions while McVinish continues his observations. 'Object is a rough bag of some sort, remnants of decorative stitching visible in places. It should be possible to make an incision along one of the seams – yes, there, thanks, Craig – so preserving the original drawstring fastening, and . . . bloody hell!' He bends to take a closer look at what's slid out of the opening. 'Okay. Excuse the unprofessional language there, folks, but that was . . . unexpected.'

Fergie stares at the bleached white objects the technician's cut has scattered across the table. 'Are those what I think they are?'

'Finger bones?' McVinish picks one up and shows it to the scene examiner while his technician photographs the rest. He examines it for a moment before shaking his head.

'Almost certainly animal, with cut marks on the larger ones. If I had to guess, I'd say—'

'Seals.' An odd look on the boss's face. 'There were seal . . .

seal-like things in all the paintings he'd done at Sandisquoy.'

McVinish frowns. Turns the thing between his fingers a couple of times, nods. 'Could be, yes. Okay, Craig, we'll take a look at the other side now.'

This time, they're ready when the stones burst out. No bones this time, just a slew of grey and ochre pebbles.

No need to voice the thing out loud; they've all got the same scene playing in their heads right now. A man tied to a crumbling jetty on the edge of the bloody world, his pockets full of stones and seal bones. Waiting for a cold, inevitable death.

Fergie glances at the boss. Wonders if it's such a great idea for him to be here, staring down at the body of someone he knew, someone he used to work with—

'How? How did they do it, Marco?'

'Lukas—'

'He had a leather belt – a ligature! – around his neck. Some-one overpowered him, tied him to that damn jetty, filled his pockets full of stones and he just . . . let it happen? How is that possible?'

'If you let me proceed without interruption, I'll attempt to find out.' McVinish looks up at the viewing gallery. Shakes his head. 'Lukas, this isn't working – go away, and let Fergie and me do our jobs.'

Before Mahler can say anything, his mobile beeps a text alert. He pulls out his phone, glances at it. And shoves it back in his pocket with a curse Fergie's never heard him use before.

'Apparently the Chief agrees. I'm being summoned back to HQ.' Mahler turns to go, looks back at the pathologist. 'Alex Fleming was an ex-cop, living on Orkney under an assumed name – am I the only one who's hearing some bloody big alarm bells right now? We can all see what happened to him, Marco. I need you to tell me *how*.'

12

The first clue that something's going on at North Division HQ is sitting in the staff car park as Mahler pulls in.

The sleekly anonymous Mercedes parked next to the Chief's Range Rover doesn't just look out of place among the lines of unremarkable family saloons and scruffy run-arounds; it looks showroom-pristine, as though it's just rolled off an assembly line. Top brass, then. *High heid yins,* as Fergie would say, from Police Scotland's crime campus at Gartcosh. Or it's the organisational movers and shakers based at Tulliallan Castle paying the Chief an unexpected visit. But what's either scenario got to do with Mahler?

Voices coming from Chae Hunt's office as he knocks and waits. And then he gets the second hint that something's way off kilter as the Chief comes to the door himself. Mahler would have said Hunt doesn't do nervous, but right now he looks more ill at ease than Mahler's seen him in a long time.

'Good of you to drop in. Eventually.' Hunt waves him inside, closes the door behind him as the man standing at the window turns around. Mahler sizes him up: around his own age, dark, sharp-featured. Watchful. Not wearing a uniform, but looks like he'd prefer to be. Interesting.

Hunt introduces him as DCI Harkness from the crime campus

at Gartcosh. He attaches a string of acronyms to the rank, but one of them jumps out at Mahler right away.

'You're with OCCT? What brings Organised Crime and Counter Terrorism to Inverness?'

Harkness look him up and down, offers a thin smile. 'You've heard of Operation Absinthe, I take it? I'm here on what you might call mop-up duty.'

Which makes Chae Hunt's twitchiness a lot more understandable. Run jointly with the National Crime Agency, Absinthe was the biggest, most successful of a series of operations mounted against organised crime groups in Scotland's Central Belt. Over the course of a week in early July, the teams had pulled in a massive drugs haul with a street value just shy of two million pounds – and lifted half a dozen well-known gangland 'names' into the bargain. Not top tier, perhaps, but definitely a significant result.

'I see. And you're here to mop up a spillage on our patch, is that it?'

'Just a minor one.' The Chief motions at them to sit down, slides the folder on his desk across to Mahler. 'But it does involve an old friend of ours.'

Mahler opens the file. Glances at the mugshot clipped inside, scans the first few lines and looks at Hunt. 'Cazza MacKay? Sir, Cazza's an ageing small-time villain with a couple of sleazy clubs. Are we really linking him to serious organised crime here?'

The Chief starts to say something, but Harkness gets there first. 'We think he merits taking a closer look at, yes. It seems a couple of the Manchester gangs have been testing the water up here over the past year. That recovery of Class A drugs on the A9 in March? Word is, the Styles boys are behind that.'

Boys. An interesting expression to describe Jake and Barry, the thirty-something Mancunian twins who could moonlight as Orcs in any future *Lord of The Rings* reboot. With minimal intervention from the make-up department.

They'd already been making a serious name in the Moss Side area of their home city as extortionists and racketeers by the summer of 2010, when their father and uncle were gunned down in a drive-by shooting by a rival gang. Following the shooting, the Styles brothers had gone to ground for several months before emerging with a smaller, tighter outfit. But over the last year or so, they've been breaking out of their usual stamping ground.

'And you think they're looking for new business opportunities?' Mahler nods. 'Okay, I'll buy that – we've certainly noticed increased levels of activity in that area over the last few months. But the link with Cazza MacKay . . .' He leafs through the file again, shakes his head. 'Not seeing that anywhere here. You're aware that following his stroke, Cazza no longer has a hands-on role in any of his businesses – legit or otherwise, as far as we can tell?'

Until some months ago, MacKay had been the closest thing Inverness could point to as a local former crime lord. But an attempt on his life some months ago – organised, he'd insisted, by a shadowy underworld figure called Hollander – had taken a huge physical and mental toll on the man. Unless MacKay's pulling off some kind of bizarre con trick, Mahler can't see him going anywhere near the sort of operation Harkness is suggesting.

'A minor stroke, by all accounts,' Harkness points out. 'But while establishing a direct link between MacKay and the Styles brothers remains a work in progress, we've been hearing some very interesting stuff about the way he set up his operations. Including the kind of people he picks to work for him.'

Harkness leans across, turns to two further images clipped

inside the file. 'This guy, for example. And this one. Cousins who just happen to hail from Manchester. And who've both been inside for possession with intent to supply, amongst other things. Interesting to find a stint as MacKay's bar staff on their CVs, huh?'

Bar staff? When Mahler's team were investigating the murder of a petty criminal called Kevin Ramsay a couple of years ago, they'd been fed some intriguing intel about Working Girls, MacKay's tacky 'gentlemen's club' on the edge of the city's industrial estate. Trouble is, neither the information nor its source turned out to be reliable. And Mahler's got a good idea this latest instalment's come from the same source.

'Let me guess – Liam Gerrity's been in touch. What does he want this time, a move to Castle Huntly?'

Harkness raises an eyebrow. 'Open prison? Where do you think he's been for the last three months? Gerrity's up for release on licence in a few days' time – and he's very jittery indeed about who might be waiting for him on the outside.'

Mahler turns to Hunt. 'Sir, we spoke to Gerrity two years ago, when we were looking into Kevin Ramsay's murder. Gerrity had nothing concrete to tell us then, and I seriously doubt that's changed.'

In answer, Harkness turns to the final page of the file. It's an extract of a report following an assault on Gerrity in Perth Prison; it only runs to a single paragraph, but the brutality detailed in two short sentences makes Mahler wince.

'Two days after Gerrity's lawyer indicated he'd be up for a chat, that happened. His hearing's permanently damaged, and he's lost most of the sight in one eye.'

'Which suggests he does know something,' Mahler concedes. 'But why talk now – and what's he hoping to get out of it?'

'It got him moved to Castle Huntly, for one thing,' Harkness points out. 'But now he's due for release, he's clammed up. Which means we need to do a bit of digging – and that's where your team comes in.'

Harkness outlines a couple of small-scale operations he's got planned, one in Inverness and the other further north, sketches a few details of where the MIT's resources are likely to be needed. There's nothing that feels exactly wrong to Mahler on the face of it; trouble is, it doesn't feel exactly right, either. But if OCCT *does* have good reason to link Cazza to the Styles twins . . .

Harkness glances at his watch. 'Another meeting I need to be at, gentlemen.' He rises, heads for the door. 'Thank you for your time today. I'll be in touch later to finalise details of what's required.'

Hunt's genial expression switches off the moment the door closes. 'Aye, I'll bet you will.' He closes the file, pushes it back across the desk to Mahler. 'Yours. Get a strategy together, and make sure you've got the resources on hand to deal with whatever he's going to throw at us.'

'Could be tricky, given he hasn't actually told us that yet. Sir.'

Hunt gives him a sour look. 'Welcome to senior management. Bet you thought it was all rounds of golf and funny handshakes, eh? In case you weren't paying attention, I'll spell it out for you – this operation is being coordinated at a national level, and we'll be cooperating fully with DCI Harkness in its final stages. Understood?'

There's a tightness to the Chief's voice that Mahler doesn't miss; he wouldn't have thought it possible, but he suspects Harkness may have nudged him off pole position as Hunt's least favourite officer.

'Of course, sir,' Mahler acknowledges. 'But Cazza only got out of hospital a couple of months ago, and word is, he's making moves to relocate to Spain – Working Girls is up for sale, and we're pretty sure he's pulled out of his other interests over here. Unless we assume he's planning some sort of last hurrah before he leaves—'

'Fine, assume that.' Hunt's eyebrow twitches irritably. 'Assume Harkness, for all that he's a smug git, might just know what he's talking about – and just for once, *don't* damn well assume your posh Oxbridge degree means you know better than everyone else around you. Are we clear?'

'Sir.' What else is he supposed to say to that? He and Hunt have what you might call a history; with June Wallace on sick leave, the buffer zone between them she'd occupied is growing thinner by the day. Mahler picks up the file, gets up to go, but Hunt holds up a hand.

'Running late? That'll be down to this morning's little detour to Raigmore, I assume. Oh yes, I know about that. What the hell did you think you were doing, man?'

'I called in briefly while the PM was taking place. We'd discussed the need for me to be on top of the situation, if you recall, and—'

Hunt gives him the kind of look June Wallace would have been proud of.

'On top of it meant you going up to the scene and checking it out. "On top of it" meant you making an initial identification, liaising with the Fiscal and the local guys, then getting back down here and leaving everyone to do their jobs – and that includes Marco McVinish.' He glances at Mahler. Shakes his head. 'How bad was it?'

The slumped, misshapen thing tied to the crumbling jetty. That gaunt grey house looming over the deserted bay, where Alex had lived like a squatter, painting those bizarre, unsettling pictures. The small, pale bones, spilling across the mortuary table—

'Pretty much as expected, sir.'

Hunt nods. 'Aye, I saw Dave Christie cleaning out the van this morning. He gave me the gist of it.' A glance at his tablet as an alert flashes on screen. 'Right, Tony Armstrong's got his press statement out. Let's see what that brings in. There's no chance you've got it wrong, I suppose – our victim is definitely your ex-boss, not some guy called William Spencer who just happened to look a bit like him?'

'It's Alex, sir. I'm sure of it. As to why he'd be using an alias . . .' Not just any alias, either; the name is whispering a link to him, some tenuous, floating *thing* he should be able to grasp, but can't.

Mahler shakes his head. 'We're still waiting for the official confirmation from the Met. I'll chase it up—'

'*Fergie* will chase it up,' Hunt corrects him. 'Fergie leads on the Orkney scenario, and Andy Black works with Harkness. You'll oversee both enquiries, and direct as necessary. Oversee, not take part in. Is that understood?'

'Sir—'

'Enough. We've got eyes on us already because of this Absinthe stuff – important eyes, some of them. So if this *is* your ex-boss, you'll keep a safe distance from the nuts and bolts of any potential investigation.'

What? How the hell is *that* going to work? Mahler swallows the first response he's tempted to make, forces a conciliatory tone into his voice. And tells Hunt the first outright lie of his career.

'Alex Fleming was my ex-boss, sir, not a personal friend – and even if Fergie is nominal lead on this, he's still going to need my input. And you said yourself, the delay in finding the body means we're on the clock with this one.'

Hunt gives him a disgruntled look. 'You said you were a wee, wet-behind-the-ears DC back then. How far do you think your input's going to get us? And a personal connection to the victim, even a remote one—'

'Is the only advantage we've got right now,' Mahler tells him. 'I know who's worth talking to, and who's a waste of time and resources. And if we're going to make up the ground we've lost on this enquiry—'

Hunt waves an irritated hand at him. 'Fine, you stay on board for now. But *only* on the periphery – and you keep me informed every step of the way, is that clear? Because anything you get involved in . . . it ends up complicated, Mahler. Like Kevin Ramsay's murder. Like the Child Snatcher clusterbourach. Like James Gordon going ahead with his appeal, and all the crap *that's* going to open up again – and if there's one thing we don't need right now, it's any more bloody complications.'

13

7.45 a.m. A grey October Monday, the early morning damp-ness still hanging in the air. When Mahler pulls into the car park, Fergie's decrepit Audi is skulking in its customary spot by the commercial waste container; an impressive display of bravado on bin collection day, Mahler always thinks. And as far from the Audi as it's possible to get, a gleaming black and silver motorbike straddles two spaces next to the fitness centre.

Mahler parks, goes over to take a look. Close up, it's less immaculate than he'd thought: the chrome is pitted in places and there are scuffs along one side, as though it's kissed a couple of road surfaces in its time. But it's a powerful machine, all the same. One intended to make a statement. The question is, who's doing the talking? Harkness, or the Chief?

He scans the messages on his phone as he heads upstairs. No summons from Chae Hunt, nothing from Harkness. But there's a familiar, leather-jacketed figure lounging in the MIT's open doorway, a motorcycle helmet tucked under one arm. And the arrogance of that double-space parking suddenly makes perfect sense to Mahler.

'Thought I'd come in early. Find my way around, like.' Andy Black offers him a micro-nod of acknowledgement before turning back to Fergie. 'Landed on our feet here, eh? Posh canteen, decent fitness centre. And an MIT room that can take more than three bloody laptops plugged in at once.'

Andy Black, back from suspension. He's dropped some weight and his eyes are less bloodshot than usual, suggesting he's cut down on the booze. Plus, he's in the office before eight-thirty.

All good signs, on the face of it. Beneath the customary swagger he looks a little edgy, but Mahler can't blame him for that; if their situations were reversed, he'd be struggling with the thought of Black as his superior officer, even temporarily. He ignores the tightness gathering at the base of his skull and tells himself not to go looking for trouble.

'Good to have you back with us, Andy. We've got a fair bit—'

'Morning, all.' The smell of takeaway coffee accompanies Nazreen Khan along the hallway. She passes one to Fergie and Mahler, shrugs at Black. 'Didn't think you'd be in yet, Andy. Boss, there's a couple of things—'

'Sorry, Nazreen, it'll have to wait for the morning briefing.' Message alerts beep on his mobile, but they'll have to wait too; he needs to bring Black and Fergie up to speed on what they'll be handling, and he needs to do it quickly.

Mahler takes them through to his office, summarises his meeting with Harkness and the Chief. Black slouches in his chair, uncharacteristically quiet, until Mahler mentions Operation Absinthe.

'Not seriously buying this, are you?' Black leafs through the file Mahler's passed him, puts it back on the desk. 'Cazza MacKay doesn't have the *cojones* to play with the big boys, you know that.'

'Andy's right,' Fergie puts in. 'And last I heard, Cazza's fair had the stuffing knocked out of him by that stroke.'

Mahler nods. 'All good points, all of which I passed on to the Chief. But Harkness is pretty sure of his sources, so let's see what we can dig up. Andy, get a draft strategy together – Harkness is due in later this morning. I'll introduce you, and you can fine-tune things with him.'

'Better make a start, then.' Black gets to his feet, picks up the file and heads for the door. 'Let me know when this Harkness guy puts in an appearance. Fergie, I'll see you downstairs, aye?'

Fergie watches the door close behind Black, turns to Mahler. 'In good form today, our Andy. Very team-spirited.'

'Let's keep it that way. Cut him a bit of slack while he settles back in, yes? It can't be easy for him.' Open scepticism on Fergie's face. For which Mahler can hardly blame him. 'I know, I know. Just keep an eye on things for now. What's happening with our Orkney victim? Marco got anything for us yet?'

'Give him a chance, boss. I had to leave when I got the call about the Nairn stabbing, and he was nowhere near finished by then. Said he'd get his report over to us by lunchtime, though.'

Not the news Mahler had been hoping for. 'What about the Kirkwall end – any update from Tony Armstrong?'

Fergie brings Mahler up to speed on the local police's investigations. Searching Sandisquoy had turned up council tax bills and bank statements, even a passport, but everything had been in the name of William Spencer. And no one had responded to the team's appeal for witnesses.

'What about his online presence? Have we looked into that?'

'Non-existent, Pete says. And no reports of a laptop or tablet, anything like that at his address. Not even a smartphone. Guy really didn't want those PPI calls, did he?'

Mahler shakes his head. 'That's more than just a desire for privacy. That's deliberately dropping off everyone's radar. Tell

Pete to do more digging. Look for any mention of the name Alex Fleming in connection with Orkney, anything at all. And . . .' he catches the look on Fergie's face, and scrubs the rest of that sentence. 'Go on, spit it out.'

'I *saw* the body, boss. Aye, the photo on that driving licence looked like Fleming. Sort of. But the state it was in . . .' he shrugs. 'Look, you've had a hell of a time recently. We all have. Now that bastard Gordon's going ahead with his appeal, and your mam's not well again—'

'She's doing better now. And if you're suggesting my judgement's been affected—'

Footsteps outside his office. On their way past? Probably. But taking just that second or so too long to move away.

'I didn't say that. Look, if I was out of line—'

Mahler holds up his hand, listens as the footsteps continue along the corridor. Shakes his head as Fergie starts to say something. 'I know how it looks. How it sounds. But that man *is* Alex Fleming. We just need to prove it.'

'Without the medical records from the Met? And Media Liaison are nipping at us for more details – we have to do a full statement soon, and we need more than the "unidentified male" guff we've been giving them.'

'No, we don't. We double down on what we've got, and see what happens.'

Fergie gives him a look. 'We can't do that, boss. We've got a name—'

'The *wrong* name. For a dead man no one cares about. No one's even come forward to say, I knew him, Fergie. *No one*. It's as though he's fallen from the bloody sky!'

'It's weird, right enough. But—'

'It's more than weird, it's unbelievable. So, we put everything we have out there – the driving licence photo, his age, where he was found – everything *except* a name. And we wait to see who bites. In the meantime, I light a fire under my contacts at the Met to come up with the goods.'

'You can't, boss. You're not supposed to get that involved, you said so yourself.'

Mahler briefs Fergie on his conversation with Chae Hunt; the gist of it, at least.

'Once we know for sure it's Alex, I'll reduce my role in the enquiry. Until then, I'm the best person to liaise with the Met and get that confirmation. Before we lose any more time.'

Fergie gives him a doubtful look. 'Sailing bloody close to the wind there. If the Chief finds out you're going full hands-on—'

'I'll keep him fully briefed.' Even if, inexplicably, there turns out to be a small delay in getting those briefings to him. 'If there's nothing from Marco by noon, chase up that report. And get Nazreen to look at when Sandisquoy was sold – where did the funds come from? Who handled the sale? Follow the paper trail, there's got to be something for us there.'

'Will do.' Fergie gets up to go. 'So, the press statement—'
Mahler shakes his head. 'I'll do this one.'

'I'm leading the enquiry, boss. Supposed to be.'

'And I'm overseeing it. Which means taking the decisions . . . and the flak, if necessary.' Fergie starts to say something, but Mahler holds up his hand. 'Not up for discussion, Iain. Not this time.'

Silence. Followed by the kind of look Mahler's more used to receiving from June Wallace. 'Aye, well.' Fergie takes his phone out, makes a point of checking something. Stuffs it back in his pocket. 'Like you say, you're in charge.'

He crosses to the door. And turns to look back at Mahler. 'I'll keep a shovel handy, though, will I? To get you out of that bloody great hole you're digging for yourself.'

14

Mahler waits for the door to close behind Fergie before pulling out the blister pack of painkillers from his pocket and tossing a couple into his mouth.

He closes his eyes and leans back, waits for the meds to dull the migraine trying to claw its way into his optic nerve. And tells himself again it's just coincidence his headaches are returning, now he's finished the gift Ella Kirkpatrick had pressed on him the last time he'd seen her. *A little herbal tea to help with the pain. Just feverfew and valerian, picked by moonlight.*

Ella, who'd saved a child's life at the expense of her own at the farmhouse near Culloden that had earned a place in his nightmares. Ella, who'd been—

Mahler shakes his head. Just because he hasn't come up with a rational explanation for everything Ella had been, everything she'd known, it doesn't mean there *isn't* one. The herbal potion the old woman had pressed on him was something to help him sleep, that's all. Something to deal with the insomnia, keep the flashbacks at bay; the worst of them, at least.

Until last night. Until the small quiet hours, when he'd given into the hope that sleep might come. He'd unplugged his headphones, cutting off Julie Fowlis's *Òran nan Ròin*. Closed his eyes. And seen Alex Fleming's slick grey corpse, stretched out on Marco McVinish's mortuary table, waiting for the bone saws and the scalpels to do their work.

It doesn't matter that he'd left before that happened; the image is in his head now, lodged in the dark place inside his brain—

A series of angry-wasp whines, coming from somewhere in front of him. Mahler opens one eye, slides his mobile towards him. And sees the screen fill up with alerts at the same time as he hears the footsteps hurrying along the corridor.

He's already on his feet when the door opens. Fergie's breathing heavily, as though he's been running. And the look on his face has Mahler reaching for his car keys before Fergie's got a word out.

'What is it? What's happened?'

'Been an incident up in Crown.' Fergie leans against the doorframe to catch his breath, scrubs his hand across his sweating forehead. 'Serious assault, sounds like. And the address . . . Boss, it happened at your mam's.'

No blues and twos, no sirens. No ambulance, and thank God, no duty undertaker standing by to give the gaggle of bystanders something else to gawp at. But there's a cordon of incident tape running from the pavement to his mother's front door, and a brace of uniforms in hi-vis jackets standing guard outside.

Mahler pulls in by the café, races across the road. Whips out his ID as the younger PC steps forward, hand raised, to challenge him.

'Sorry, sir, you can't—'

'Lukas, is that you? With you in a minute.'

Lisa Barker, Burnett Road CID, standing inside the doorway. Glancing up and down the street as she talks into her mobile, as though she's waiting for someone to arrive.

She ends the call, aims a glare at the small but growing crowd

61

across the road, and nods at the officer on the gate. 'Donnie, get that lot shifted. Tell them there's a traffic warden coming up Ardconnel Street, that ought to do it. And let me know the minute this Fiona Lomax shows up.'

She turns to Mahler, grimaces. 'Mental health care manager, apparently. Supposed to be on her way to us, but—'

'I know who she is. This is my mother's address.' He watches her expression change, watches her confusion change to under-standing and the inevitable embarrassment. None of which he has time for. 'Where is she? What's—'

'Lukas, is that you?'

His mother's face, peering over Lisa's shoulder; not seriously hurt, then. Relief fills his throat, hard and tight enough to choke on. Lisa turns to her, says something Mahler doesn't catch, and waves him round to the flat's back entrance. When he gets there, she's pouring tea into mugs and putting them onto a tray.

'I've taken her through to the sitting room to wait with Jim until the care manager gets here,' Lisa tells him. 'We've tried to get the doc for her, but she's not having any of it.'

'I don't need a doctor. I'm not ill.'

His mother's standing in the doorway, frowning at the tray as though she can't remember what it's for. She's ghost-pale, worrying at the scar lines on the inside of her wrist, but it's the dazed expression on her face that alarms him most.

'Mum, what's wrong?' His mobile's buzzing in his pocket. He ignores it, guides her to one of the kitchen chairs and tells Lisa to call the other officer through; they'll need a statement from his mother, and this feels like the simplest way to do it. 'Can you tell us what happened?'

She swallows. Nods. 'It's . . . it's Mina. I was baking when I heard a noise outside. It was like a . . . a loud moan, then a thud, like something heavy slamming against the door. I thought maybe it was a delivery, so I came through to look.

62

And when I opened the door . . .' her voice falters, breaks. 'She was just lying there, and her face was all blue. Lukas, I . . . I thought she was dead!'

She's crying now. Mahler powers off his mobile without looking at it, and crouches beside her. 'Mum, it's okay.' He puts his arm round her shoulders. 'You phoned for an ambulance, yes? So you did the right thing for her. And Mina's being looked after right now.'

He glances at Lisa, gets a shrug in response to his unspoken question; better than the headshake he'd half expected, but not by much. 'I didn't know you were still in touch with Mina.'

'I wasn't, not really. But I met her outside the post office the other day, and . . .' she gives him a weary look. 'I know, Mina steals things. And she drinks too much. I *know* what she does with her money, okay? I'm not stupid. But she looked so ill, so miserable. So I . . . I gave her a few pounds. Said she could come and see me if she needed help.'

She scrubs her eyes, looks up at him. 'I know what you think of her. But what else could I do?'

Several answers to that, none of which will make it past his mother's profanity filter. Mahler summons a reassuring smile from somewhere. 'Nothing,' he tells her. 'Absolutely nothing.'

The sound of a car pulling up outside and someone getting out. Footsteps hurrying up the path to the back door.

Fiona Lomax bustles in, breathless and full of apologies. Mahler leaves his mother talking to her care manager and nods at Lisa to follow him into the garden.

'Doubt Mina's going to make it,' she tells Mahler as soon as they're out of earshot. 'Paramedics were working on her in the ambulance, but it wasn't looking good.'

'What happened to her? Control passed it on as an assault.'

'Looked that way at first, I'm guessing. But the paramedics thought it's more likely she's had some sort of seizure – she's hit her head on the front step, blood all over the place. She'd been sleeping rough down the Islands, and at this time of year . . .' Lisa shrugs. 'Back on the booze, God knows how many benefit sanctions hanging over her, with that sodding universal credit thing they've brought in. What a way to end up, eh?' A curious sideways look at him. 'She a relative of your mam's or something? Mina doesn't seem like . . . well, the sort of pal I'd expect Grace to hang about with.'

Mahler shakes his head. 'They were at school together. And later, they met up again in hospital. In New Craigs.'

'Ah, okay. I didn't know.' She looks away, gives an embarrassed nod; the usual reaction to any mention of the local psychiatric hospital, he's found. As though the kind of trauma his mother had suffered, the lasting aftermath of what his father had done, was something to be ashamed of.

And normally Mahler would let it pass – because what's he supposed to do? Challenge every thoughtless comment, every throwaway remark he overhears about loony bins and funny farms? But what he'd seen at Sandisquoy is still burning in his mind, stripping away the layers of composure he forces on the furnace of his anger.

He opens his mouth to say something scathing about attitudes to mental health, something Lisa probably doesn't deserve. But Fiona Lomax is hovering in the doorway, frowning at something on her mobile.

'Lukas, are you free for a chat with Grace? It's about tonight. She says she's fine to stay here, but I'm not sure it's a great idea.'

It's a terrible idea; one look at his mother's gaunt, unhappy face is enough to confirm it when he follows Fiona back into the kitchen. But when he suggests she stays at his flat overnight, she refuses to even consider it.

'We agreed when you came back to Inverness, that was never going to happen.' She reaches for his hand, covers it with hers.

'You're not going to be my carer, Lukas. I won't let you.'

'Only for a night or two, until you feel ready to come back . . .'

'No. If Fiona can get me a respite bed at the Recovery Centre, I'll go there.' Enough determination in her voice to tell him it's pointless arguing with her. 'I've been meaning to go over anyway to choose my photographs for the exhibition.'

She glances at him, sighs at the blank look on his face. 'The ones I took for mental health week, don't you remember? I showed you one of Mina's friend Archie doing that terrible Frank Spencer impression when you and Anna . . . Lukas, what is it? What's wrong?'

'Yes. I remember now.'

And there it is, laid out before him, courtesy of a scruffy old man in a filthy beret: the link between Alex Fleming and his chosen alias. The link that tells Mahler he'd been right all along.

A white forensic suit. A man called Billy Spencer who photographed the dead. A cheerful, gangling sort of man whom everyone called by his nickname.

Frank.

'Mum, I need to go, I'm sorry.' He arranges to call the care manager later to check what's happening, powers up his mobile. And watches the display fill up with missed calls as he walks back to the car.

Fergie. Andy Black. The Orkney fiscal's office. And twenty minutes ago, the call from Marco McVinish he's been waiting for.

Mahler listens to the message he's been left. Swears briefly but satisfyingly. And heads over to Raigmore Hospital to catch the pathologist before it's too late.

15

'He didn't drown, Lukas. Though the sea did kill him, in a way.'

Marco McVinish pours Mahler a coffee, takes a report folder from the pile on his desk and leafs through it. 'No fluid in the lungs, you see. But the North Sea in October? A young, fit man in good shape would have lasted maybe fifteen minutes, and our unidentified friend was anything but that. His liver was enlarged and showed signs of severe fatty cirrhosis, probably as a result of ongoing alcohol abuse. And his heart—'

'His heart didn't kill him, Marco. Being tied to a jetty and left to die killed him. What else is in that report?'

'Briefly?' McVinish flips over a page, scans the first few lines. 'I'll spare you the pretentious Latin terminology, but basically, we're looking at a cocktail of no less than three separate toxins: belladonna, henbane and aconite.'

'Alex was *poisoned*?' Mahler had assumed some sort of fast-acting incapacitant – ketamine, maybe, or Rohypnol, both infamous date-rape drugs. 'How? Did you check for possible injection sites?'

'No, because I've only been doing my job for twenty-odd years and would never think of such a thing.'

'I didn't mean to imply—'

'I should damn well hope not.' The pathologist closes the folder, dumps it back on top of the pile.

'For the record, I checked every inch of a four-day-old corpse in which decomposition was already—' He catches Mahler's expression and lets the rest of that sentence die. 'Sorry. Briefly, there was no evidence of habitual drug use, and I couldn't determine with any certainty how the toxins were administered. I say with certainty, because the condition of the body made it difficult—'

'Understood.'

'Aye.' McVinish drains his coffee, pushes the mug aside with a grimace. 'Well, as it happens, I doubt they played a significant part in the man's demise, even with his underlying conditions – probably wouldn't have been sufficient to knock him out for more than a few minutes, perhaps just long enough to secure him to the jetty. Though given what happened to him—'

'Hold on.' Mahler rewinds the pathologist's last couple of sentences. 'You're saying he was *awake* with all of that inside him?'

'Looks that way, yes. I found an additional injury to the back of his head, others roughly corresponding to minor but repeated impacts against the wooden upright he was tied to. My guess? He saw death coming for him. And he tried to fight against it.'

The pathologist gives Mahler a weary look. 'Someone wanted him to know exactly what was happening to him, Lukas. Maybe he had a good reason for using an alias, eh?'

He saw death coming for him. Mahler lets his mind slide away from the image that conjures up. 'Alex was a copper for a long time. He'd have made enemies, the way we all do, but this—'

'Doesn't feel right?' McVinish nods, scrubs his hand across his face. 'Aye, well, join the club. Nothing connected with this case feels right to me either – and I'm still waiting for the files I need to finally confirm our friend's identity, by the way. If you can chase things up with the Met—'

'They've still not come through?' Mahler shakes his head. 'That's ridiculous. I'll get on it right away.'

There's no way a simple inter-force information request should be taking this long; some sort of bureaucratic hold-up, Mahler suspects, potentially above his pay grade. Luckily, he knows exactly what to do about it – if there's one thing Chae Hunt's good at, it's moving things along.

He gets up to leave and catches an odd wariness on Mc-Vinish's face. 'There's something else? Marco, if it'll get this investigation moving—'

'I doubt that. It's just . . .' The pathologist glances at him. Shrugs. 'What the hell. Seeing we've landed in "gut feeling" territory, take a look at these.'

He opens a file on his laptop, angles the screen towards Mahler. 'You remember the animal bones our victim had in his pocket? The ones with what appeared to be cut marks? I was documenting the images for addition to the file when I noticed something.'

Mahler studies the screen. Frowns, turns to McVinish. 'I don't—'

'There's more.' The pathologist scrolls to the next image. And the next. And then Mahler's looking at something so obvious he can't believe he missed it the first time around.

'The marks form a pattern. Some sort of embellishment?'

McVinish shakes his head. 'More like a script, I think. Hiero-glyphs, or a runic alphabet – given the Viking influence on Orkney, I'd say that was more likely.'

'Viking?' Mahler takes another look at the image on screen; the marks are uneven, darker in places but hardly visible in others. And yes, he concedes, there is a sense of age about them. 'You think they could be that old?'

'Why not? Makes about as much sense as anything else to do with this bloody case. And old bones . . . there's a feel to them, sometimes. Nothing logical, nothing quantifiable, but somehow it's there.' The pathologist gives him an odd, sideways look. 'You could still be wrong, you know. About it being your old boss.'

Mahler shakes his head. 'I'm not wrong, I know it's him. Because the man whose name he used was a crime-scene photographer with the Met – and William Spencer died back in 2008.'

Billy, he'd insisted on, not William. And they'd nicknamed him Frank anyway; too young to get the reference to *Some Mothers Do 'Ave 'Em,* an ancient BBC sitcom, Mahler had only half listened when it was explained to him. Listened, and forgotten all about it . . . until his mother had made that chance comment about one of her former lodger's disreputable friends.

Another odd glance from the pathologist. 'You're sure?'

'One hundred per cent. I've no idea what's holding up the files, but I'll get that confirmation for you.'

'Okay,' McVinish nods. 'Then you step away from the investigation – you step away, Lukas, and you let Fergie do his job. Because it's *his* job now, not yours. You know that, don't you?'

'Of course.' And he *will* do it, of course he will. Just as soon as he's made the calls he needs to make. Tracked down the people he needs to get in touch with. Because Marco's right, nothing about this bloody case makes sense; Alex Fleming taking on a dead man's identity least of all.

McVinish starts to say something, and his phone lights up with a text. He glances at it. Sighs. 'Reminder from Duncan to get my arse in gear. No rest for the wicked, eh?'

The pathologist takes the files out of his desk tidy, dumps them in a drawer and locks it with a flourish. He turns to Mahler, makes a shooing gesture.

'Out. I've sent you the full report – I'm not back from Aberdeen until tomorrow lunchtime, though, so any queries will have to wait till then.'

Mahler's on his way out when McVinish calls him back. 'Just a thought. Those bones – they're not the sort of thing you find just lying around, even on Orkney. Find out what they are and where they came from, Lukas. Maybe that'll tell you how they ended up in a dead man's pocket.'

16

'Great report there from Callum on those gorgeous wolf cubs at Kincraig Wildlife Park.'

The TV presenter adjusts the folds of her black net skirt and flicks a stray cobweb from her shoulder. 'Now for our Halloween edition of *Highland Happenings* live from Inverness Town House – be prepared to be scared! My next guest is Anna Murray, from the University of the Highlands and Islands' Centre for History in Dornoch – and she'll be chilling our blood tonight with tales of spooky goings-on right across our area.'

She turns to Anna with a mock-shiver. 'So, *Wise Women, Witches and Warriors* was a fantastic series – and with the second one due to be filmed in January, you're set to put the Highlands on the paranormal map. But witchcraft is a bit . . . well, it's a bit Hogwarts, isn't it? So tell me – what makes a serious historian turn to the dark side?'

Anna curves her mouth into the best smile she can manage. And promises never to let her boss talk her into something like this again. Ever.

The 'seasonal' backdrop to the set – giant pumpkins and artfully draped cobwebs adorning the Victorian Gothic surroundings of

71

the Town House – had been startling enough. But during the run-through, the interviewer had seemed genuinely interested in the background to the History Centre's new online modules. Until the cameras had started rolling for the 'live' recording, that is.

'Well, that's not quite how I'd put it,' Anna tells the interviewer. 'And I'm sorry to disappoint Harry Potter fans, but witchcraft definitely *isn't* one of the new courses we'll be offering at UHI. What we'll be looking at is the changing social and political circumstances in seventeenth-century Scotland.'

'James VI, right. He was obsessed with witchcraft, wasn't he?'

Anna can't quite repress a sigh at that. Yes, she thinks, let's focus on one man, not the victims of his paranoia. *Plus ça change* . . . On the other hand, it's a fair-enough assessment. By the time he reached adulthood, Mary Stuart's clever, tormented son was a rag-bag of neuroses looking for something to fixate on. And an ill-fated Danish visit in 1589 had gifted it to him.

'James wasn't alone in that,' she tells the interviewer. 'Though you're right, he was a bit more hands-on than most. But what we recognise as the persecution period in Scotland ran for over a century. And killed between four and six thousand people.'

A murmur from the audience. Anna stops to let the figure sink in.

'Think of that, in a small country like ours. From the North Berwick witches in 1589 to poor Janet Horne in 1727, we murdered those women – and yes, they *were* mostly women. Disadvantaged ones, mainly.'

Interested looks there. *Good.* Anna leans forward, talks directly to the audience. 'We murdered them for so many reasons. For being healers who sometimes failed. We murdered them for being argumentative, for being a bit odd, for getting older and becoming confused . . . in short, we murdered them because

72

they didn't fit the mould Scotland's intensely patriarchal society thought they should. Live and let live, it's safe to say, was not a phrase our witch-burning ancestors would have had much time for.'

The interviewer nods. 'You mentioned Janet Horne, but this was happening right across the Highlands, wasn't it?'

'Across the whole country, yes, from Orkney to Berwick. In fact, researchers at Edinburgh University are talking about an interactive map—'

'Wow, that's fascinating!' The interviewer glances at her notes. Leans closer. And Anna realises that, yes, in spite of everything she's said, in spite of everything they'd talked about beforehand, she's going to be asked *that* question. Again.

'So, tell me, Anna – how many of them do you think were *really* witches?'

She'd hoped just to slip away afterwards, but there are more people waiting to speak to her than she'd realised. And one in particular that she definitely hadn't expected.

'That went well, I thought.'

Lukas Mahler. Holding a copy of her book like an admission ticket. Looking exhausted. Looking . . . *grey*, as though whatever he's working on is draining the life from him.

'Well, no one fell asleep. At least, I don't think they did.' Anna nods at the book in his hand. 'You didn't need to buy one, you know. Not that I don't appreciate the gesture, but I've still got a few author copies left.'

He shakes his head. 'This one's for my mother. Maybe you could sign it for me, though? Then there's something I need your opinion on, if you're free – it's in connection with an enquiry.'

'Of course, if I can help.' She takes the book from him, writes a message for Grace. 'Though if you need a historian's input—'

'I don't know what I need right now. I'm probably chasing shadows, but . . .' He breaks off to stare at her left shoulder. 'I think you've acquired part of the scenery.' He reaches out, picks a red-fanged plastic bat off her jacket and hands it to her. 'Unless this is part of your outfit?'

'More your style, Goth Boy.' A faint smile at that, enough for her to see the new lines at the corners of his eyes. Enough for her to question what this job is doing to him. What it's taking from him. 'Lukas, are you all right? You don't—'

He's looking at someone behind her, someone near the entrance. Switching into full policeman mode suddenly, eyes narrowed. Frowning. Anna turns to see what's wrong, but then her mother appears by her side, clutching a couple of flyers.

'I got Sheena to sign these for us, Anna. She's lovely, isn't she? A real professional.' A dismissive nod at Lukas. 'Not working tonight? I'd have thought you'd be at your desk. Working out how to stop James Gordon making fools of all of us.'

'It's not a police matter, Yvonne. I don't like it any more than you do, but Gordon's got a right to appeal his sentence. And—'

Her mother's eyes widen. 'I can't believe you're defending him. The man who killed my daughter? Call yourself a policeman. What's wrong with you?'

She starts to cry, her voice full of angry tears. As heads start to turn in their direction, Lukas raises a placatory hand.

'I'd never do that. I'm sorry, but there's nothing I can say—'

'No, there really isn't. Anna, I need a lift home, please. Now.' When Anna doesn't move immediately, Yvonne's mouth acquires a bitter twist. 'Oh, I see. As soon as you've said good- bye to your fancy man, then. I'll be waiting outside.'

Anna watches her mother make her way to the exit, sweep- ing her way through the gradually thinning crowd. When she'd made the decision to move back to Inverness following her father's death, Anna had hoped their relationship might finally move to a better footing. Now she can't remember the last time they'd even had a civil conversation, and tonight looks as though it's going to follow the same pattern.

'She blames me, doesn't she?' Layers of weariness in Lukas's face when he turns to her. 'Anna, I was as gutted as you were when I heard about Gordon's appeal. If there was any way to make him change his mind—'

She shakes her head. 'None of this is down to you. The appeal's just too much for her to deal with sometimes. Listen, that thing you needed me to look at? If you can put it in an email for me, I'll get back to you as soon as I can.'

Anna turns to go. Catches something in his expression, something she worries it'll take more than a few nights' decent sleep to put right. She puts her arms round him, catching them both by surprise, and reaches up to touch his cheek.

'Thanks for coming tonight – it's good to know at least one person in the audience doesn't think I'm planning to turn the Centre for History into bloody Hogwarts. Let me know if you get a definite date through for the appeal hearing, okay? I'll need a bit of notice to arrange some leave.'

'You're planning to attend?' He shakes his head. 'Anna, it's a hearing, not a trial – you won't be called as a witness, and you won't be able to make a statement. And the memories it will bring up . . . This isn't a good idea. Believe me.'

'You make it sound like I have a choice.' More irritation in her voice than she'd intended, but somehow she'd expected him to understand. 'I can't *not* go, Lukas. If my sister's killer has a chance of getting out of jail early—'

'That's not going to happen.'

'You don't know that!'

A few stragglers on their way to the exit turn at the sound

of her raised voice. Anna gives them a bland, *nothing to see here* smile until they've moved on. 'You *can't* know that. And those memories? They're right here with me, Lukas – I live with them every bloody day.'

17

Sandisquoy
The Uncovering

He'd thought it would be easy. Crowbar off the bolt, cut out the lock; bash the hinges with a sledgehammer if absolutely necessary. But twenty sweat-filled, grunting minutes later he's getting nowhere. The bloody bolts aren't shifting, he's growing a decent crop of blisters on his palm and the hinges aren't moving anywhere near as much as he'd expected. What the hell are they made from – reinforced titanium?

He glances up at the rapidly darkening sky. Rainclouds gathering, and a chill haar rolling in from the bay. There's a heaviness in the air, too, that makes him think there's another storm coming. And he could give up now, could tell himself to leave it for another day, because God knows, his days are not exactly filled with purpose from dawn to sodding dusk. But he's got the bit between his teeth, now; the damn thing's bugging him too much to let it go. Time to get this done.

He picks up the hammer again, swings. And the bolt shudders apart, showering him in a hail of rust flakes. He squats down to examine the results of his handiwork; there's still the lock to deal with, but . . . or you could just try the handle, fuckwit.

He glances at the dark metal ring latch. Estimates the chances of the rusted mechanism turning as less than zero, but gives it a twist anyway. And hears a grinding metallic wail as the thing starts to turn. It moves less than half an inch, but that's all the encouragement he needs. He gets the coil of rope from his pile of tools and attaches it to the ring. Then he walks back to his van, and reverses it down the side of the house, until he's got a roughly straight line of sight to the underground cellar, or store room, or whatever the hell it is.

By the time he's secured the rope to the trailer hitch, the haar has thickened, moving in faster than he's known it before. If he's going to get this done, he needs to get a move on.

He gets in the van, starts her up. Feels the engine complain as he pulls forward and the rope tightens; the van's on its last legs, but it's got enough guts for what he needs. He hopes.

A whine of gears as the van struggles for purchase on the soft grass. He puts his foot down, hears metallic screams from behind him, just audible above the labouring engine . . . Not going to work. It's pulling the bloody latch off, that's all. Then the van shoots forward, so unexpectedly he has to stamp on the brake to stop it ploughing into his decrepit timber garage.

He kills the engine and walks back to the statue. One of the door hinges is hanging at a weird angle, but his plan's worked. The door is—

He stops short. Peers down the flight of stone steps leading into what he'd assumed would be a disused store room. It's mostly in darkness, but it looks bigger than he'd expected. In the half-light he can just about make out a sort of pit, roughly oval in shape, in the centre of the space.

Old. Older than the house. He doesn't know where the thought's come from, but somehow it fits; the air smells stale, as though no one's been down here in decades. Maybe longer? The estate agent guy certainly hadn't mentioned it, and it hadn't been on any of the paperwork.

He takes out his mobile, flicks on the torch function, and starts down the steps. They've been well used at some point; the treads dip unevenly in the middle, and his foot slips a couple of times, enough to make him grab the rough stone wall to keep himself upright. Cold. Christ, it's cold down here. Like a bloody dungeon or something. Or—

He doesn't see it until he's almost at the edge of the pit. Doesn't see the scraps of fabric, or the pale gleam of what lies within them. Doesn't see the shape they make, until his eyes adjust to the light, to the shadows cast by the torch, and—

The next moment, he's backing away; doing it slowly, because his heart is thumping like a bloody sledgehammer in his chest, and he's damn sure he's not going to pop his clogs here, in this damp forgotten place. Not alone, not in sight of . . . of whatever that is.

Move. Now. *His heel hits the bottom step and he half falls backwards, righting himself at the last minute. He makes himself stand still, makes himself catch his breath and take another look, make sure the half-light and the damp, unpleasant smell aren't messing with his head, showing him things that make no sense, things he knows can't possibly be—*

A faint scurrying in the darkness, beyond the circle of light. And then he's scrambling up the steps, running up the final few, and sinking to his knees on the churned-up grass beside the statue. Mice, he tells himself. Mice, or maybe rats – an old house like this, of course that's what it is. Odd that he hasn't heard them before, though.

When his breathing's calm again, when his heart has stopped trying to batter its way out through his rib cage, he gets to his feet. He wipes his filthy hands on his jeans, turns to look back at what his excavations have uncovered. Lets himself take in the full significance of what he's seeing here. If he was a man who believed in fate, right now he'd be quaking in his boots.

No booze tonight, he tells himself, not even if the cries of those damn seals on the shore feel like rusty nails being driven inside his skull; he needs to think this through, and he can't do it wrapped inside his usual whisky haze.

He doesn't like leaving the place exposed overnight, but he's not in any state to deal with it right now. Tomorrow, he'll need to heave the door back into position, conceal what he'd stumbled into unawares; another good reason for laying off the booze for the rest of the day. After that, he'll take a trip into Kirkwall. See about something to deal with those bloody rats. And other things.

Skirting the entrance to the store room, he walks slowly back to the house.

18

The rain is battering down in Mahler's nightmare, driving needle-sharp against his face as he lies stunned and motionless on the cliff at Badbea. And James Gordon is bending over him, holding a wheel wrench.

Anna's managed to damage Gordon, that much is obvious; he's swaying slightly, and his face is a mess. In spite of everything, Mahler raises a faint smile. But the look of satisfaction on Gordon's face . . .

No, this isn't how it happened. Something's wrong.

He tries to shape the dream to make it stop. To turn things back to how they ought to be. But the words stick in his throat, half formed, as Gordon squats beside him. Smiling.

'So here you are at last. The cavalry. Is this really the best you could do for her? I think she was expecting better.'

'Where is she? Where's Anna?'

'Too late, Lukas.' Not Gordon's voice, not the one he remembers. The contours of the face looming over him changing. Sharpening.

Gordon stands, points to a bloodied, motionless heap beside the memorial cairn. Smiles as he raises the wrench. '*Schade, Lukas. Kommst doch immer zu spät an—*'

He wakes up moments before the scream inside can tear

itself free. Shivering, sweat-drenched, Mahler sits up, slides his phone across the nightstand. Groans at the time the lock screen's showing him. Too early to call it morning. Too late to do anything but give up on any hope of getting back to sleep, even supposing the adrenaline coursing through his system wasn't urging him to get up. To move. To *do*.

He gets out of bed, goes across to the window and opens it. Breathes in the silent city. Three years since he's left the Met and moved back to Inverness, and still the city's night-time calmness manages to surprise him. It's an illusion, of course. Criminality doesn't stop when darkness falls; like vampires, criminals are mainly creatures of the night. But without the wail of sirens that had serenaded his North London nights, Mahler can almost make himself believe the city is as peaceful as it looks.

He pulls on his running gear, stuffs his phone and keys into his pocket and heads out along Island Bank Road. Crossing the first bridge across the river, his breath pluming out in the sharp, clear air as he makes for the canal. Longer than he'd usually take on before work, but he needs something hard, something physical to shake the fog inside his head.

Not difficult to work out where this particular combination of nightmare had come from; James Gordon's pending appeal is weighing on Mahler as much as it is on Anna. Perhaps she doesn't blame him for those final moments at Badbea, when Gordon had come close to killing her, but God, he blames himself. Will *always* blame himself.

And at the end of his nightmare, the way Gordon's voice had morphed into his father's . . . He shudders, forces the memory away. An older guilt, this one. But just as dark. Just as corrosive.

Along by the river, and Mahler's moving fast. Pushing himself, deliberately, as he waits for the motion to take hold, to lift him out of himself the way he needs it to. But as he approaches

82

the Archive Centre there's a stitch building in his side, and he knows he's going to have to turn back soon.

Too many days spent at his desk, too much time juggling teams and resources. Too many nights like this. How long has it been since he's had a proper break? He'll do it, he promises himself. Even if it's only a few days on Skye, or the west coast, he needs to take some time—

Movement in the darkness ahead, where the river bends just before the weir; just a hint of it, a barely glimpsed something he'd probably have missed at any other time.

'Hello?'

No response. Mahler calls out again, takes another couple of steps towards the bank. The trees are denser here, their mingled branches bent towards the water by successive Highland winters. And although it's mid-October, the leaf cover is mostly still in place. But he can just about make out a shape, a darker outline against the grey pre-dawn light . . .

No. The sound of his own heartbeat filling the world as he backs away from what's in front of him. Because no matter what his mind is telling him, what he's seeing there can't be real, *can't be*—

His back slams into a thick, low-hanging tree branch at the water's edge. It catches him squarely in the kidneys, the unexpected impact hard and brutal, but Mahler barely notices. He's staring at the perfectly empty, perfectly calm stretch of water in front of him.

Whatever he'd seen – *thought* he'd seen – is nothing more than an arrangement of shadows. No slumped and tethered thing, given a pretence of movement by the current, no grey and bloated shape that had once been human. Had been a friend.

Sweat, ice-cold, pooling in the small of his back. Mahler scrubs his hand across his mouth. Nothing there. *Nothing.* Alex Fleming's restless presence exists inside his head, nowhere else.

Well, he'll have company enough in there; there are victims who have never quite left him, years after their killers were jailed and their casefiles closed. But Alex's murder . . . Sometimes, in the dark, small hours of the night, Mahler wonders how many more deaths lie in his future. How many more putrefying corpses, how many more white and gleaming bones—

Enough. He closes down the images, forces them away before his mind can add more grisly details from his mental gallery of horrors. There's just one death he needs to focus on right now: a friend's death, despite the lie he'd told Chae Hunt.

For once, Mahler concedes, the Chief's instincts are absolutely right. He *shouldn't* be involved in this case, shouldn't be anywhere near it. But four years ago, Mahler had been forced to stand on the sidelines as the investigation into his friend Raj's death had been mismanaged. There's no way he's letting history repeat itself, no matter what it ends up costing him.

A low rumble in the distance, as the early morning traffic begins to flow. Mahler turns his back on the river and heads towards the slowly stirring city.

19

UHI Centre for History
Dornoch

'It can't happen, Anna. I'm telling you. The numbers just don't stack up.'

Her last student of the morning, an intense postgrad on an exchange from Seattle, pulls up another newspaper article on his tablet, shows it to her. 'Sure, there are issues with Hillary, but Trump's a con man, pure and simple. It'd be like you electing that Boris bozo, or the other one, that Farage guy that looks like a used car salesman. Come on, you've lived in the States – San Diego, wasn't it? You know how it works. The primaries—'

Anna's eyes slide longingly towards her coffee mug as Bryce expands on his theory that Donald Trump will never make it to the White House. He's not mansplaining, not exactly, because she actually *doesn't* know how it works; despite the years she'd spent lecturing in the US, its complicated political system remains a mystery to her. But today's conversation feels subtly different. As though she's not the only one he's trying to convince.

'I guess we'll just have to wait and see.'

She picks up her coffee mug and shepherds him gently towards the door. Not mentioning the B word, the UK-wide Brexit vote that had confounded every one of the pundits who'd insisted a Leave victory was out of the question. The B word forcing the History Centre staff to contemplate a future that suddenly seemed a lot less certain.

Anna forces a smile onto her face, holds the door open for him in case he's tempted to launch into another mini lecture. 'In the meantime, see what you think about exploring those other angles we talked about today, okay? Try the Fraser-Mackintosh collection at Inverness Library, or the Archive Centre – their staff are incredibly helpful.'

A muted buzzing from the desk drawer where she keeps her mobile during tutorials. He nods, raises a hand in farewell and heads downstairs as she goes to get her phone out. She usually has it set to silent when she's with a student, but she's keen to hear what her friend Gudrun makes of the email Anna had forwarded on from Lukas. The images had looked vaguely runic to her, at least at first glance, but Gudrun's the expert in Viking history, and—

'Anna, do you have a minute?' Màiri, the departmental secretary, is hovering in the doorway. 'It's just that there's a man downstairs asking for you, and he seems a bit . . . well, agitated.'

'Agitated?' A whisper of coldness settles on the back of her neck. Anna puts the phone down. 'Do you know who he is?'

Màiri shakes her head. 'He said his name was Alan. He doesn't look . . . you know, weird. But I can tell him you're not in yet, if you don't want—'

'It's fine. Ask him to wait downstairs for a moment. I'll grab a coffee, and—'

'Anna?'

The man who's just appeared behind Màiri looks to be in his sixties; a hard, beaten-down kind of sixties, the kind Anna suspects might make it into his seventies, but only just. He's a small man, slump-shouldered and grey-featured in a dark tweed overcoat, but there's something familiar about the set of his mouth, the way he carries himself. Something that cranks up the chill at the base of her neck as she realises why he hadn't given his full name.

'Alan. You're Jamie Gordon's father, aren't you?'

A gasp from Màiri. 'I'm calling the police—'

'No, wait!' The man holds up his hand. 'Just hear me out. Please? I promise I'm not here to . . . to rake anything up. Five minutes of your time, that's all I'm asking.'

It's five minutes more than he deserves. But there's a dogged determination on Gordon's gaunt features that tells Anna he's not going to give up easily. And better she talks to him here than have him turn up at her flat one day. Or, God forbid, at her mother's.

'Five minutes. Then you leave. After that, if you're not on your way downstairs, Màiri will be making that call.'

'Trust me on that.' Màiri pushes back her sleeve and makes a show of looking at her watch. She throws Gordon a parting glare over her shoulder before making her way downstairs.

Anna nods at Gordon to come in. She closes the door behind him, motions him to a chair. When he starts to thank her, she shakes her head. 'Really, don't. Whatever you've come to say—'

'I'm sorry.' Enough bleakness in his voice for her to feel a twinge of pity, in spite of everything. 'The things I heard at the trial . . .' he sighs, looks down at his hands. 'It doesn't make sense. You knew my boy. How could he have done those awful things?'

'Your boy killed three people. You'd have to ask him that.'

Part of her is sorry when he flinches. But she's spent two years dealing with the aftermath of James Gordon's actions. There's no way she's opening up those wounds again.

She glances at her watch. 'I've got a webinar in fifteen

87

minutes, and you've used up two of your five. I don't know what it is you want from me—'

'I need to ask you something.' For the first time, he looks directly at her. 'You want to know why he did it, don't you? You want the pictures in your head to go away. Just like I do.'

Is that what she wants? Her mouth dries. 'Does Jamie know you're here?'

Gordon nods. 'I told him I wanted us to . . . to talk things through. Maybe see if we could make sense of things together.'

'After all this time? I don't understand . . .' Then suddenly, she does. 'This is because of his appeal, isn't it? That's why you've come here now.'

'Not just that.' But his eyes slide away from hers as he says it. 'Jamie didn't want me to come, not at first. But when I said I was determined, he asked if I'd talk to you. Ask if you could find it within yourself to go and see him.'

'After what he did? How dare he.' Anger burns the back of her throat, a quick bitter tide of it that threatens to rise up and make her scream her rage at him. 'How *dare* he.'

She crosses to the door, throws it wide. 'I'm sorry, you've had a wasted journey. Now, if you don't mind—'

'He said that's what you'd say.' Gordon takes a crumpled envelope from his jacket pocket, holds it out to her. 'And then he asked me to give you this.'

20

The body recovered from the jetty at Sandisquoy *is* Alex Fleming – the official confirmation Mahler's been pushing the Met for arrives early the following morning. When Fergie puts his head round the door to say he's sent through the monthly overtime figures, Mahler's finalising a list of former colleagues his former boss might have kept in touch with.

It's not a long list – having grown up in care, Alex had been as much a natural loner as Mahler himself – but it's a start.

'Jack Gillan's our best bet,' he tells Fergie. 'Alex was his best man, I think.'

And even if they'd only kept in touch for a while after Fleming retired, there's got to be *something* Gillan can tell them about Fleming's movements after leaving the job. 'His old number just rings out, but I've emailed him and Matt Shawcross, his former DS. I'll get the rest of the list over to you before the morning briefing, and – what?'

Fergie gives him a look. 'The path report's come through, and we've got a positive ID on our victim – I think the team can handle things from here, boss. And you told the Chief you'd take a step back.'

'I've laid a bit of groundwork, that's all.' The expression

89

on Fergie's face tells Mahler he isn't buying that. And frankly, Mahler doesn't blame him. 'And while we've got Andy tied up with Operation Absinthe, we need to make the best possible use of all the resources at our disposal – currently, that includes me.'

He winces at his lapse into Chae Hunt-speak, but after a moment, Fergie gives a grudging nod.

'Aye, well. At least we're about done with the Nairn stabbing for now.'

A sideways glance at Mahler. 'Look, about those overtime figures. Boss, I need to let you know . . . well, the thing is, I had help.'

Mahler raises an eyebrow. 'I should hope so. I know Andy's been on the road a lot with Absinthe visits, but he still needs to take his share—'

'Not Andy. Naz.'

Mahler stares at Fergie. Tries to tell himself he's misheard that. 'Naz. *Detective Constable* Nazreen Khan, who's only been with the team for a year, and shouldn't be anywhere near managerial level accounting records, let alone—'

'I can't do it, boss.' There's a look of utter misery on Fergie's face. 'I'm doing my best to get my head round this Excel stuff, I swear I am – but compared to me, Naz is like bloody Superwoman. And it's not like she inputs the figures for me. She just tells me what the hell I'm doing wrong, and how to fix it.'

'Even so, it's . . .' Mahler shakes his head. Skating on thin ice, procedurally, he'd been going to say. But hasn't he been doing exactly the same thing himself? 'Andy should be stepping up while you find your feet – in future, I'll make sure he does. In the meantime, just do what you need to for this month. *Discreetly.*'

'Understood.' Fergie gives him a grateful nod and gets up to leave. 'And if the Chief wants an update from me—'

'We've a briefing scheduled for this afternoon – I'll bring him up to speed, then make it clear I'm stepping back from now on.' Though Mahler's pretty sure he'll be hearing from Hunt long before that. 'Update the team that our Sandisquoy victim is definitely Alex, and send me the latest from Kirkwall. I'll pull something together we can feed Media Liaison at short notice.'

'Boss.' At the door, Fergie turns. 'I've been thinking. Your DI Fleming . . . he was on the level, right? As far as you know?'

'Completely. Alex was one of the good guys.'

'But he changed his name and moved to the other end of the country – and it took us a hell of a long time to get that confirmation from Met HR. Makes you wonder just how "retired" he was, doesn't it?'

'Undercover?' Mahler nods slowly. He'd thought about it, briefly, then dismissed the idea. A London cop working undercover on Orkney? No, he isn't buying that. What would be the point? On the other hand, supposing Fleming had been involved in something that had ended badly. Something he'd needed a new name and a new identity to escape.

'It's worth exploring,' Mahler concedes. 'Look, leave it with me – I know, I know, I said I was stepping back. But if that's what's going on here, we need to tread carefully. There's a couple of people I can talk to, but it might mean calling in a few favours.'

When Fergie heads back to the MIT room, Mahler puts a call through to Special Ops, and leaves a message for Bea Colgan, a former colleague. Bea's an asset whose goodwill he doesn't want to squander, but she's helped him out once before. And if Fergie's right about Alex Fleming's real reason for moving to Orkney, Bea's one of the few people with enough clout to find out the truth.

Harkness's number flashes up on his mobile. When he

answers, the din Mahler hears in the background sounds like a cross between a zombie apocalypse movie and one of the city's sports bars during an Old Firm match. Which is enough of a clue to Harkness's location before he's said a word.

'You're at Burnett Road? Is there a problem?'

'There's what you might call a developing situation.' Harkness sounds as if he's fighting the urge to add at least one four-letter word to that sentence. 'DI Black and I have Liam Gerrity sitting in Reception at this end, and we're very keen to speak to him.'

'Good, I hope the feeling's mutual. But I don't understand—'

'It isn't bloody mutual. The slippery little bastard's refusing to say anything unless he talks to you.'

21

Burnett Road Police Station
Inverness

Burnett Road has had a spruce-up for a forthcoming visit from
the Justice Minister, but it's strictly on the surface; beneath the
smell of hastily applied institutional beige paint lurks the reek
of body odour and stale smoke that haunts the lower levels of
every police station Mahler's ever been in.

There's no sign of Andy Black when Mahler arrives, but
Harkness is waiting by the custody desk. Pacing by the desk,
inhaling a takeaway espresso so darkly bitter Mahler can smell it
as soon as he enters the building.

Harkness gives him an irritable look. 'I called you almost
forty minutes ago.'

'Traffic was appalling. And it won't have done Gerrity any
harm to have been kept waiting for a while.'

Mahler signs in, checks where Liam Gerrity's been parked
and sets off for interview room one, leaving Harkness to follow.

Turns out it's just as well he checked which room they'd
be using. Because if he'd passed Gerrity in the street, Mahler
doubts he'd have recognised him as the cocky chancer he'd in-
terviewed two years ago in HMP Porterfield. Prison doesn't do
anyone any favours, but Gerrity looks bleached, like a child's
toy that's been left out in the sun too long. And his damaged

eye is milky, turned slightly inwards and sunken in its socket.

'You took your time.' Gerrity looks Mahler up and down, makes a show of leaning back, apparently at ease. But he's using two hands to hold the paper cup, and even then, he's making a terrible job of it, the tremble in his fingers threatening to make the murky brown fluid spill over the lip.

'Not interested in what I've got to say? You should be. You and your sleekit-looking pal here should be hanging on every fucking word.'

'Why's that, Liam?'

Gerrity gives up on the paper cup, puts it on the table. 'I was made up when I got sent to Perth. Too many guys up here wanting a piece of me, ken? I've a big mouth sometimes. Gets me into trouble. But I knew if I got to Perth, no one would bother me. I could keep my head down and do my time, like.'

'And drip-feed us bits of intel until you got a move to Castle Huntly.' Harkness nods. 'Didn't work out like that though, did it?'

Gerrity shakes his head, scrubs a pale scrawny hand across his mouth. 'There was a guy there – a big guy, built like a fucking tank, man – and every time I turned around, he had his fucking eyes on me. Couldn't work out what was going on with him for ages. Then I remembered where I'd seen him before. One of King Spice's boys, wasn't he? Used to do the east coast run, taking the messages for him from Dundee to Stonehaven and Aberdeen.'

King Spice? Before Mahler can query the nickname, Harkness leans forward. 'Worked for "Glasgow Phil" McMonagle, did he? Who was he?'

Gerrity shakes his head. 'Folk called him Frankie, that's all I know. Because he looked like a fucking monster, ken?' His mouth sets in a bitter twist. 'Turns out he wasn't the biggest monster in there at all.'

'What happened, Liam?'

Gerrity glances at Mahler. Shrugs. 'I was doing a wee bit of business. Nothing big, just enough to top up my spends a bit, you know? Bit of buying and selling.' Through sheer bad luck, he'd been dropping off an order for one of his regulars when he'd overheard Frankie arguing with someone.

'Something was going down, I could feel it. Frankie was backed into a corner, he was telling the guy Phil had a new route and everything was cool . . .' He shakes his head, swallows. 'Guy didn't look like he was buying it.'

Gerrity had fled, abandoning his order. And when no one had come after him, assumed he was safe.

'Thought I'd got away with it,' he tells Mahler. 'Thought they hadn't seen me. Two days later I was making another delivery when I got this.' He points to his ruined eye, which is starting to water, and wipes it with his finger. 'Fucking dead man walking, aye? Well, I can take a hint. Told my brief I needed to get out of there or I'd fucking top myself.'

'And Mr Gerrity let slip a couple of things he'd picked up in the course of his retail activities, which smoothed his path a little.' Harkness's smile is ice dipped in acid. 'Only now he seems to be suffering delayed memory loss. He's backtracking on statements he's already given, and dropping vague hints about more huge revelations he claims to have up his sleeve – only if the price is right, of course. But if you think—'

Mahler sees Gerrity lunge a fraction of a second too late. Before he can react, Gerrity grabs Harkness's shirt front, pulls him forward so that their faces are almost touching.

'See this face, pal? Aye, take a good look – this is what I got as a fucking *warning*. Pretty, isn't it?' He lets go of Harkness, slumps back into his seat. 'You think I'm scared of anything you can do to me? When this is the face I wake up with every morning?'

'That can't be easy.' Mahler glances at Harkness, warning him not to react. 'I'm sorry. But my friend here's just being honest. We're going to need something concrete from you, Liam. Something we can work with.'

'All right for you to say.' Gerrity swallows, nods. 'Fine. There's a route up north McMonagle uses sometimes. A wee scenic trip for goods coming in from Europe, ken? One the Feds don't keep that close a watch on.'

'From Europe? What's the route?'

Gerrity shrugs. 'Boats from Holland, that's what I heard. Boats with a *lot* of merchandise.'

Movement from Harkness. Gerrity's mouth stretches in a knowing smile. 'Aye, got your interest there, didn't I? But that's all you get for free – you want more, you need to do something for me first. Sort me out a new place, give me a wee bit of cash to help me get started. You've done it for other folk, haven't you? See me right, and I'll do the same for you.'

'You know we can't make promises like that.'

'You can. And you have to. I need to get right away from here, man. Somewhere down south, maybe. Seaside sounds nice, eh? Don't fancy another freezing Scottish winter.'

Mahler shakes his head. Gerrity's a professional chancer, but there's real panic beneath the flippancy.

'Why's it so urgent, Liam? Has something happened?'

'Aye. Maybe.' Gerrity's damaged eye is watering again. He takes out a tissue, dabs at it. 'I was coming into town on the bus, but the fucking routes are all different now and I got on the wrong one. It took me past that new housing estate they're building at Slackbuie and down through Culduthel. And that's where I saw Frankie and the other guy.'

Mahler exchanges a glance with Harkness. 'They were to-gether? What were they doing?'

'Standing at the entrance to a block of flats, talking. Then they met a third guy and walked off. But before they left, Frankie turned back and took a photo – did it super-fast, so you'd hardly know what he was doing if you weren't watching.'

'You saw him do it, though.'

Gerrity's bleached-linen face loses even more colour as he looks up at Mahler. 'Yes, I saw him – why do you think I need to get out of here? Because he fucking saw me too, that's why.'

22

Mahler's phone is lit up like a Christmas tree, text alerts flashing onto his screen as he makes his way back from Burnett Road to Police HQ.

He heads down Academy Street and along past Johnny Foxes before looping back up Castle Street. The traffic is building at the usual bottlenecks, adding more time to a journey that's longer than it should be, thanks to the convoluted route he's taking back to HQ; when Chae Hunt's name appears on his phone twice in quick succession, Mahler knows he's living dangerously.

But there's a pull between his shoulder blades, a tightness that's been gathering there since he and Harkness had talked to Liam Gerrity. Harkness had mishandled the man, had pushed him too hard about McMonagle's northern supply route, and in the end Gerrity had clammed up completely and walked out. And the tightness between Mahler's shoulders, that little twist of instinct he's learning not to mistrust, had warned him not to let this go.

No point in chasing after Gerrity, not yet; he's spooked enough to run if they push him any more right now. But that doesn't mean Mahler can't follow up on what Gerrity had told them he'd seen. So now Mahler's on his way to Culduthel, following the routes of the buses Gerrity might have taken, checking out the houses as he drives. Looking for something – anything – that catches his attention, any hint of wrongness.

Another text alert, and two more emails. Mahler mutters a curse, glances at the previews and draws a quick, sharp breath – whatever is going on with Liam Gerrity will have to wait. Mahler turns the BMW round and heads back towards Perth Road.

It's raining by the time Liam gets to the city centre, raining hard enough to start leaking through his thin Primark jacket. He walks down to the bus station past the Rose Street car park, his feet half frozen inside his knock-off Puma trainers. And finds out he's missed the half-past bus, meaning he'll have to hang around for another bloody hour.

Fuck. When he'd got out of the cop shop at Burnett Road, he'd thought about taking a taxi. But who takes a taxi for a ten-minute walk? He's not bloody made of money. And there's no way he was letting Mahler send him off with one of the Feds from CID to keep an eye on him until he got his bus. Like *that* wouldn't attract attention? Polis look like polis, in or out of uniform.

He'd had a bad moment, though, walking past the old Nessie garage. For a minute, he'd been sure someone was following him. He'd turned, convinced he'd heard footsteps behind him, but all he'd seen was a guy in a black sweatshirt talking on his mobile; having a good ding-dong with his girlfriend, sounded like, and not paying him any attention at all.

Christ, he needs to get a grip. No one knows he's been to see the cops, how could they? He just needs to keep his head down, and hope Mahler meant what he said about seeing what they could do for him. There's more he could have told Mahler – a *lot* more – but he's giving none of it away for free.

Liam glances at the bus station café, thinks about going in for a coffee and a wee rest somewhere warm and dry. Coming back here had been a fucking stupid decision, he knows that now; one of the stupidest in a life piled high with truly shite decisions. But what was he supposed to do – hide himself away in that manky hostel and watch folk shouting at each other on daytime TV talk shows? He's seen enough tanked-up nutters get in each other's faces in HMP Perth, thank you.

The rain's really coming down now, fat icy droplets dripping down the neck of his jacket. Liam takes a couple of steps towards the café, pauses at the entrance. And an old man with a walking stick barges past him, pushing the door hard enough for it to swing back and nearly catch him in the face.

Liam grabs the door, starts to yank it open and go after the guy. Then asks himself what the fuck he thinks he's doing. Beating up old guys now, eh? Real hard man stuff, that. Anyway, he's only out on licence. Get into any sort of trouble, and it'll be straight back inside for him. And there's no way he could deal with that, not after Perth.

He zips up his jacket, turns the collar up against the wind and rain, and heads down Academy Street to McGregor's. It's not his usual kind of place – too full of tourists and crusty fiddle players for his liking – but it'll be quiet at this time of day, enough for him to get a drink in peace. And right now, keeping well away from his usual kind of place makes sense.

Inside, the bar's all but deserted. Liam gets his pint and wanders over to a table by the fire. He unzips his jacket, moves his chair a bit closer to the warmth . . . and looks up as a pint glass clunks down onto the table in front of him.

'Hiya, Liam.' The man he'd seen outside the bus station gives him a smile that turns his guts inside out. 'Mind if we join you?'

We. Christ. Liam looks round for the bar staff, but there's no one around. Not a fucking soul, like in one of those old westerns his old man used to watch. 'D–don't think I know you, pal. Sorry.'

He stands up, moves to get past, but the guy gives him that fucking awful smile again, and turns to nod at the man walking towards them. 'No, we've never actually met. But you know my friend here. And he's *really* looking forward to seeing you again.'

23

Divisional HQ
Inverness

There's a buzz in the air when Mahler gets back to the MIT room; enough of a shift in the team's energy to tell him something's happened, even before he sees the looks of satisfaction on Dave Christie's and Fergie's faces.

'You've got something for us?' he asks Christie. 'From the clothing, or the belt?'

The scene examiner grins. 'Just call me crafty Christie. Still waiting for a couple of things to come back, but the belt buckle gave us some very faint prints – not sure how much use they'll turn out to be, but they're definitely there. That's not all we found, though. Wrapped round the prong of the buckle were not one, not two, but *three* human hairs.'

'They survived immersion in seawater?'

A near-identical grin on both faces now. 'Certainly did,' Christie tells him. 'And only one of them is a match for our victim. We've not turned up anything for the other two, but still . . . bit of a result, eh?'

No wonder they're smiling. Mahler looks round at the team. The heightened energy he'd picked up on earlier makes sense now; Dave Christie's information has given them a new focus, something concrete to build an investigation around, and they're itching to get on with it.

'Okay, this is looking good. Thanks to the expertise of Dave and his team – yes, take a bow, Dave, you've earned it – we've got prints *and* a potential DNA comparison source once we identify persons of interest to the enquiry. What I need now—'

No. He catches himself, scrubs the rest of what he'd planned to say. This is Fergie's show from now on; time to stand aside and let him take the lead. As soon as Mahler's explained exactly what they're dealing with.

'You're aware that our victim's been confirmed as Alex Fleming, a retired officer with the Met,' he tells them. 'What some of you won't know is that I have a personal connection to this case – Alex was my first DI at Charing Cross, which means that Fergie will be running the lines of enquiry. He'll be liaising with Orkney and the Met, with informational input from myself.'

A frown from Fergie at the catch-all phrase, but it can't be helped; there are times when Chae Hunt's managerial style has its advantages.

'This enquiry won't be straightforward,' Mahler warns. 'He lived almost entirely off-grid on Orkney, under an assumed name, so basically we've been playing catch-up from day one. And—'

'Maybe he was a prepper,' Gary offers. 'You know, those Yanks with the big beards and the checked shirts – they turn their backs on civilisation and live out in the wilderness. I was watching the Discovery Channel—'

'Thought that was just those pals of yours on the Black Isle,' Naz grins at Gary. 'I've seen what those Culbokie folk do to scarecrows.' Her smile fades when she turns to Mahler. 'It sounds like he was scared. Like he knew someone was out to get him.'

'Connected to one of his old cases, maybe.' Fergie nods. 'Makes sense. Would have to be a hell of a big case, though – he didn't work with the serious and organised crime guys, did he?'

Mahler shakes his head. 'Not that I'm aware of. But putting Gary's . . . unique input to one side for the moment, I want every aspect of Alex's life under the microscope from now on – this enquiry hasn't had the best start, so let's focus on getting it back on track.'

He leaves Fergie reorganising the sub-teams, and heads back upstairs to see if he can claw back some resources from Operation Absinthe. Harkness isn't going to like it, but Harkness doesn't have a developing murder enquiry on his hands.

Mahler refreshes his emails. No replies to his attempts to track down Jack Gillan, and no one's got back to him about Alex Fleming either. Which doesn't make sense; yes, some of his old contacts will have left, changed jobs, moved elsewhere. But he's starting to think Fergie's right.

His mobile lights up on the desk. The number's coming up as 'withheld', so he assumes it's his Special Ops contact getting back to him. But the voice on the other end is one he hasn't heard since his days in Charing Cross CID.

'Lukas?' Matt Shawcross's cheerful Welsh voice booms out at him. 'Got a call from Bea Colgan saying you'd been in touch with her. Been a while, eh? Last I heard, you'd headed back up north because your mam wasn't doing too good. You thinking of moving on again, then? Always looking for good DIs down here.'

'Settled here for the moment, thanks. No, I needed a word with Jack Gillan.'

'Ah.' The cheerfulness drops from Matt's voice. 'Ah, you haven't heard about old Jack then. Big C got him, must be a year ago now. Hell of a thing, it was. Mind, I suppose when it's your time . . . What did you want him for? Anything I can help with?'

'Maybe. Yes.' Like himself, Matt Shawcross had been a relative newcomer to Alex Fleming's squad. But with Jack gone, Matt's the only member of the original team left. Mahler tells him about the discovery of Fleming's body, and the alias he'd used. When Mahler's finished, there's silence at the other end.

'Not the best news to start your day with. I'm sorry.'

A dry bark of laughter. 'Christ, you can say that again. I can't get my head round this, Lukas. Not any of it.'

'You didn't keep in touch with Alex, then?'

'Tried for a while, but you know what it's like, once someone leaves . . . The Job was the thing you had in common, see? Once that's gone . . .' A sigh at the other end of the line. 'You'd moved on by the time he retired, hadn't you? Thing is, Alex wasn't in great shape by then.'

'His drinking, you mean?'

'Not just that. He'd been SIO on a run of bad cases – three on the trot, real bastards – and something like that, it stays with you. Messes with your head. But Christ, to do what he's done . . . If I was going to top myself, I'd pick the booze and pills route, not that.'

'That's not how it happened, Matt. What we've found – we're pretty sure he was murdered.'

A longer silence. Filled with an anger Mahler can almost touch.

'No.' Flat, disbelieving. 'No, that can't be right. How could that happen?'

'I have no idea – no witnesses, no leads, no nothing. Right now, we're scrabbling around in the dark. So if there's anything you can tell me, any sort of connection that might help—'

'Mate, it's been ages since I saw him. Just how far back do you think this connection goes?'

'Right now, I'm not ruling anything out.' Mahler offers Fergie's undercover theory. And listens to Shawcross's gentle incredulity filling up the silence once he's finished.

'Lukas—'

'I know, I know. But our Orkney enquiries are going nowhere. Alex lived like a hermit, miles from his nearest neighbour – we're struggling to find anyone up there who knew him. And there's this bloody name change. Alex goes long-term sick, retires in 2012 and goes off the radar – *completely* off the radar, as far as I can tell. Then he pops up again to buy Sandisquoy in 2013. Only this time he's calling himself William Spencer. Ring any bells?'

'Spencer?' Confusion in Shawcross's voice on the other end of the line. 'I don't . . . Hang on, there was a scene photographer guy, wasn't there? Looked a lot like him, I seem to remember. But he died in a car crash or something a few years back. Why would Alex nick his . . . Christ, that's why, isn't it? Because they looked so alike.'

'That part makes sense. The rest of it . . . Why do retired coppers suddenly need new IDs? That's the bit I can't get my head around.'

Silence. Followed by a long, slow exhale. 'You think he was on a job, don't you? Something that went tits-up all of a sudden, and he had to bugger off sharpish.'

'I don't know. But he wasn't some random victim, Matt. What happened to him was planned, and it was personal. *Very* personal. It's got to be connected to his past.'

'Yeah, maybe.' A sigh at the other end. 'Christ, I dunno. This is mad, mate. All the bad guys Alex put away over the years, and this happens . . . Look, I've a briefing in fifteen, and the guv's on my case already. Let me get my head straight and I'll get back to you before I go on leave tomorrow.'

More alerts flashing up on Mahler's screen as he ends the call with Shawcross: a voicemail from Anna, and a reminder that the Chief's expecting a detailed update from him in exactly five minutes. To complete the set, Harkness wants an urgent debrief about Gerrity.

He glances at Anna's number in his contacts list, lets his finger hover for a second and shakes his head. The news of James Gordon's appeal had come as they were taking the first tentative steps towards a real relationship, and it's thrown them off course; he needs to clear the air with Anna, but not by phone. This evening, Mahler promises himself. This evening he'll drive to Dornoch, and they'll talk.

He picks up a folder from his desk and heads upstairs to see Chae Hunt.

24

Sandisquoy
Six Weeks Before the End

The days have shortened; imperceptibly at first, the light ebbing by degrees, so that he's barely aware of it until the morning view from his top-floor window begins to change. Even here, in the brilliant white of his studio, the brightness feels faded, as though he's seeing it through some sort of filter. Though to be fair, that isn't far from the truth.

He'd been on the cusp of alcoholism before coming here, he knows that, but for a while this place had felt like it might be the answer. An answer, anyway. The chance of a second life; the chance to kick over the traces of the old one, at least. To rebuild.

Then the storm had come, and he'd found the underground room, or chamber, or whatever the hell it is. And what he'd seen there had sent him running to his old friend, the bottle. To his . . . what was the word? He frowns with the effort of remembering. His sanctuary, that's right. From some old film he'd part-watched once, back in his channel-surfing, too-wired-to-sleep days in the Met. Crap film, but the word had stuck in his mind somehow. Wasn't that what he'd thought this place would be, once upon a time?

Looking back, the booze had been gaining the upper hand for a while. He'd been losing his edge, starting to make mistakes; only small ones, at first, but enough for him to join the dots about his eventual destination if he didn't make some changes. The doc's warning at his last medical had been the wake-up call he'd needed, and finding Sandisquoy had seemed . . . well, timely.

For a while, moving here had seemed to work. He didn't miss the noise, the crowds, and he sure as hell didn't miss the Job. He'd even started painting again; lifeless, poorly-executed landscapes that made him grind his teeth in frustration because he knew he could do better. Had *done* better. Still, it had been a distraction. Living here had been a distraction, for a while. But now . . .

He looks down at his left hand lying on top of the covers, sees the faint but noticeable tremor there. And realises for the first time in months, something in his life has changed. There's a choice to be made. Action to be taken. He can't remember how long it's been since he had something to get up for, something to motivate him other than the physical needs of his body. How had he let himself become this . . . this *purposeless*?

He pushes the heap of blankets aside, gets to his feet. Slower than he should be, creakier than he should be. Out of shape, out of condition, his mistreated heart thumping dolefully in his chest as he contemplates what he needs to do next.

Clean himself up, for one thing. A shower, if the boiler can be made to work. Then breakfast. His stomach gives a quick, revolted twitch at the thought of eating; he's hungry all right, but it isn't for food. And he doesn't need that much, not this morning. Just a finger in the bottom of a glass, something to calm the pounding in his head and get him moving.

He looks around for his rucksack, picks it up. Frowns at its lightness. A twist of panic cramping his guts, he looks round for the whisky he knows he put in there last night. There was half a bottle left, for God's sake, he can't have drunk it all . . . But there's no sign of it. He gives up on the rucksack, chucks it on the floor in disgust. And hears the metal buckle on its strap hit something solid.

He bends down, moves his bedding out of the way; the bottle he'd been looking for is there, but there's barely an inch of liquid left inside.

He crouches down, stares at what he's found for a long, long moment.

You don't need this. Not right now.

Easy to say. Easier to tell himself that a little won't hurt. Just a finger in the bottom of a glass. After what he'd seen, what he'd found, who could blame him? But it wouldn't end at that. There's another bottle downstairs, one more in the van. And he would start, and then he'd carry on, he knows that perfectly well.

He kicks the bottle out of the way, reaches for the hoodie and tracksuit bottoms he'd dragged off sometime during the night. Feels a quick, bright flare of panic as his fingers find only emptiness in both pockets, before he remembers where he'd put the things he'd found. Safe, he tells himself. Bagged and tagged, that's what he'd done with them. No need to stress, right? Still, the thump of his heart takes several moments to return to normal.

He straightens carefully, waits for the pounding in his head to subside enough to let him make it downstairs. Food. Coffee. Then he needs to get out, get far enough away from the house to think things through. Make a plan if necessary.

Sanctuary. He had needed that for a time, and this place had given it to him. But now there's something else here, something he needs to follow to its end. Something that had been waiting for him, maybe.

And that means he needs to be ready for whatever it brings.

25

Divisional HQ
Inverness

Seven p.m. A low, river-borne mist hangs damply over the city, turning the queue of vehicles heading for Westhill and Smithton into a soft-focus ribbon of red and white lights.

Mahler checks through the briefing notes for tomorrow's press statement, makes a final amendment and closes down his laptop.

There's more admin he should be finishing off, of course there is; these days it spreads like a mutant virus in a sci-fi film if he leaves it unattended for any length of time. But the pain that had started at the base of his skull is burrowing behind his right eye, acid-bright and bitter, and the meds he's taken aren't coming close to touching it. If he doesn't want to spend the night stuck in his office and throwing up into the wastepaper basket, he needs to leave while he's still fit to drive.

He makes his way downstairs and heads for the exit, his footsteps echoing in the darkened foyer. Once the day shift's over, HQ all but empties; the difference between a working police station and what's basically an admin hub, Mahler supposes. But the building never seems—

A lone vehicle is sitting at the far end of the car park. Not the one at the side of the building, where he leaves his BMW;

the 4x4's been left by the trees, as far from the entrance as it's possible to get. As far from any of the well-lit areas and CCTV as it's possible to get.

Mahler runs through the list of people he knows are still in the building. Dismisses the ones he knows for certain don't drive 4x4s, let alone something as imposing as that dark Mercedes SUV. A visitor, maybe? But the Chief's not around—

Buzzing from his mobile. He pulls it out, glances down at another withheld number call. Takes a guess at it being Matt Shawcross this time, but gets it wrong again.

'Had a feeling you'd still be working.' Bea Colgan sounds amused, but there's a weary note in her voice he doesn't miss. 'You're a DCI now, aren't you? Need to pace yourself a bit, Lukas. The job doesn't own every bit of you.'

'*Acting* DCI. And I assume you're ringing on your work number, so—'

'Just crossing a few things off my to-do list. Did Matt give you the news about Jack?'

'He did. But it's Alex Fleming I wanted to find out about.'

He takes her through the Sandisquoy enquiry, summarises what they've got so far. When he finishes, there's a long silence at the other end.

'Using a false identity. Living as a virtual recluse.' Bea sighs. 'I can see why you thought of us.'

'That, and the length of time it took Met HR to send the files we asked for.'

'I can't answer for that, of course.' A hint of frost layering her voice. 'But if you're suggesting some sort of tampering's taken place—'

'If he had been working for you, I assume a few . . . amendments to his file might be necessary. Hypothetically speaking.'

Another silence. Followed by another sigh. 'Hypothetically speaking, that might be so. *If* he had been working for us. But in fact, the records are entirely correct. Alex suffered a minor heart attack in the spring of 2011, returned to work on the Whetstone Alley shootings, then requested early retirement on health grounds six months later. If you—'

Movement outside. The sound of a car door opening. Mahler looks up to see a segment of light appear and disappear as someone gets into the SUV.

He makes for his car, picking up his pace as the 4x4's engine starts up, but he's too late. By the time he's keyed in the door code, all he can see are the vehicle's receding tail-lights as it pulls out into the evening traffic.

'—Matt would know more about that. Lukas, are you still there?'

'Sorry. Noticed something that needed checking out.' He rewinds her last two sentences in his head, fills in the words he'd only half heard. 'You think I should talk to Matt Shawcross again? He said he hadn't been in contact with Alex for years.'

'Did he?' What sounds like genuine surprise in her voice. 'That's odd. I'm sure it was Matt who told me Alex had moved to Orkney.'

'Matt told you that? When?'

'Let me see, now . . . it must have been a year ago. At Jack Gillan's funeral.'

26

'Alex Fleming was a former police officer who retired to the Orkney mainland in the summer of 2013 to indulge his love of painting. A very private individual, he appears to have led a solitary lifestyle and had few close friends.'

Mahler looks up, catches the disgruntled expressions on the reporters' faces. Frankly, he doesn't blame them; lured to North Division HQ to hear a statement on the enquiry that's been making headlines all over the country, they're expecting to hear some sort of announcement – an arrest, maybe? News of a breakthrough, at least, to make up for the time they've been standing around in the chill of a dreich October morning.

Instead, they're listening to a weary DCI rehashing Tony Armstrong's press statement from a couple of days ago. With a small but significant tweak.

'We are keen to talk to anyone who knew Alex Fleming, or who may have had contact with him in the days leading up to his death. In particular, we are keen to talk to the owner or owners of a small, light-coloured vehicle seen parked on Sandisquoy headland the day before Mr Fleming's body was discovered. If you recognise this description or think you may have been in the area at that time, please get in touch with either—'

'Have you been able to trace Mr Fleming's relatives yet?'

'Do you know when the funeral's likely to be held? Where will it take place?'

'Can you comment on why Alex Fleming had been living on Orkney under a different name?'

No, he definitely *won't* be commenting on that. Mahler carefully doesn't meet the eyes of the rumpled-looking hat wearer in the front row who's just lobbed that little grenade at him. He exhales slowly, holds up a hand to halt the flow of questions before anyone else can pick up on the man's question.

He doesn't blame any of them for pushing him; he'd be doing it too, in their place. But the truth is, he's got nothing substantial to tell them. Today's statement is a placeholder, delivered because the Chief thinks it will keep the press on side, and the enquiry in the news. Frankly, Mahler would swap both those for some solid progress away from the public gaze.

He gives a couple of non-committal answers to the least challenging ones, fields the rest. And heads back inside, leaving Media Liaison to mop up as best they can.

When he gets back to the MIT room, Fergie's in the middle of the morning briefing. A couple of heads turn, but he nods at Fergie to carry on.

'Right, then, that's where we are so far. Kirkwall are following up this vehicle allegedly seen on the headland. It came in as an anonymous tip on the dedicated enquiry line, so make of that what you want. But it's all we've got right now, so—'

'We have a little more than that.' Mahler outlines his conversation with Bea Colgan. 'We know Matt Shawcross was in contact with Fleming as recently as one year ago.' He crosses to the whiteboard, adds a recent photograph of Shawcross and circles the date of Jack Gillan's funeral on the timeline. 'Why lie about it? What else isn't he telling us?'

Silence. Before Nazreen puts what they're all thinking into words.

'You think he could be involved? In his own boss's murder?'

'I think we need to talk to Shawcross. Urgently. I've spoken to his DCI, and he's on annual leave until Monday, somewhere in the wilds of Wales – inconvenient, but it gives us time to get our ducks in a row before we have that conversation.'

He nods at Shawcross's image. 'Let's take another look at ferry bookings and scheduled flights to and from Kirkwall – concentrate on males fitting his physical profile, travelling on their own.'

Fergie nods. 'He'd have needed transport to Sandisquoy. These reports of a vehicle out on the headland—'

'Could have been a hire car, yes. Liaise with Tony Armstrong in Kirkwall, get him to check it out. And we follow up anything that comes through on the enquiry line as a result of today's press briefing, no matter how daft it seems.'

'We had that psychic wifie from Conon on the other day, talking about a warning from beyond—'

'No matter how daft it seems, Gary, with the *exception* of the psychic wifie from Conon. Fergie, a catch-up after you've finished here – let's say fifteen minutes?'

Mahler leaves him with the daily allocations, heads back to his office. When Fergie appears in the doorway fifteen minutes later, he looks like someone steeling themselves for a particularly grim visit to the dentist. Possibly involving root canal work.

'You want me to interview this Shawcross guy, don't you? Aye, I know – you can hardly do it yourself.' He gives Mahler a hopeful look. 'Maybe we could manage by videolink, though? Much more, whatsit, efficient use of resources, eh? No need for me to trek all the way to London for it.'

'Nice try, but this needs to be face to face. And you're right, I can't be anywhere near it.'

'Aye, fine. Bloody EasyJet for me on Monday then, eh?' Fergie darts a glance at Mahler. 'You really think Shawcross is involved?'

'I spoke to him about a murder enquiry, and he lied to me. What the hell am I supposed to think?' Mahler sighs, shakes his head. 'Christ, I don't know. When those off-duties come in, go over them with a fine-tooth comb, see if there's any way he could physically have been on Orkney when Alex was killed – at least that'll give us a steer one way or the other. But let's not do anything to spook him until we've got some solid evidence to back us up.'

'Boss.' Fergie moves to leave, turns back. 'Sandisquoy's on the far side of Mainland, isn't it? Quite a way off the beaten track?'

'Quite a way from bloody anywhere. Why?'

'Wee bit of a coincidence that someone happens to spot a car out there, just around the time we're interested in. Not the sort of place you'd wind up by accident, is it?'

'Certainly not off-season. What are you saying?'

Fergie shrugs. 'The enquiry line's anonymous, isn't it? Just thinking it could be a bit convenient, like. If someone wanted to feed us a wee red herring or two.'

Not the kind of thought Mahler wants to have before he feeds back to Chae Hunt, but Fergie's got a point. 'We check and cross-check everything we get in – anything that sounds like a real outlier, we check it twice. And run it by Tony Armstrong.' He picks up his tablet to head upstairs, and a thought strikes him.

'CCTV. We're checking that too, right?'

'At Sandisquoy? I don't think—'

Mahler shakes his head. 'The airport. Let's see if we can spot anyone interesting coming or going for the period we're looking at. The ferry operators, too.'

He catches the look on Fergie's face, nods. 'I know, it's a long shot. But no one on Orkney knew who Alex Fleming was. And killing him like that . . . it took time, Fergie. Time and planning. By someone with a hell of a grudge.'

'Or someone with a lot to lose.'

Someone like Matt Shawcross. No need to say it out loud – his name's right there in the room between them. Mahler nods wearily. 'That too. So let's get that CCTV checked out.'

'Boss.' Fergie glances at the stills of Sandisquoy pinned to the whiteboard. Shakes his head. 'I still don't get it. Turning yourself into someone else, hiding away in the arse-end of no-where – Fleming *knew* someone was after him, boss. He must have done. But picking a house like that . . . Christ, it's like he *wanted* to be spooked.'

'Alex wouldn't have moved there without doing his home-work on the place. And he didn't spook easily.'

But as Mahler makes his way upstairs, he can't help remem-bering Sandisquoy's cheerless attic, filled with those strange, obsessive paintings. What did they say about his former boss's state of mind? Had the strain of hiding from something in his past begun to take a toll on his mental health – or does the truth about Alex Fleming's murder still lie within the walls of Sandisquoy itself?

27

Kirkwall
Orkney

The day shift is almost over when Tony Armstrong gets back to Kirkwall Police Station.

Strictly speaking, he could have allocated a junior officer to head over to the airport and have a word with the car hire firms; it's not an inspector-level job, he knows that well enough. And as expected, the trip had turned out to be a waste of time.

But despite what some folk might think, his team don't sit around on their arses drinking tea all day. They're working bloody hard, doing their best to service the community's day-to-day needs while dealing with the biggest murder enquiry in decades. Even before the whole Sandisquoy thing blew up, Tony hadn't had that many uniforms to play around with. And afterwards had been like a bomb going off in the middle of Broad Street.

For the first time in decades, murder had come to the islands. Murder of a stranger, true, a man who'd kept himself so much apart from everyone that afterwards, not a single soul had come forward to say they'd known him. A man shut away from everyone, living out his days with another man's name . . . and a head full of demons, judging by the paintings Tony had glimpsed in that cold white room at the top of Sandisquoy.

But still, a man who'd come to make a life here. And found only death. Now, as people try to come to terms with that, they need their local police inspector to be visible. They need to see him out there, doing . . . something. Anything.

Murdo Sangster's just coming out the back door as Tony gets out of his car. He looks like he's in a hurry, pulling on his jacket as he walks across the car park. Miles away, too; he doesn't register Tony's presence until they're within a couple of feet of each other.

'You off now?'

Murdo gives a startled nod. 'Didn't see you there. Aye, that's me done until Monday. Just as well – one more call from journos with pretendy local accents trying to get information out of me, and you'd have had to take me off the desk.'

'Rough day?' Stupid question, the grey, exhausted lines of his desk sergeant's face are telling him Murdo's had enough. 'Those calls shouldn't be coming through to you, though – just punt them off to Media Liaison as soon as they come in.'

Murdo gives a weary shrug. 'They're getting through somehow. Mind you, they're mostly wanting to know when Lukas Mahler's due back – to "take charge of the investigation", seeing we local cops apparently aren't up to it.'

'Ach well, he's a bit more photogenic than us old boys, Murdo. Can't really hold that against him.'

And Acting DCI Mahler isn't just keeping June Wallace's seat warm, that much is obvious; the man's on his way up the ranks, no doubt about it. Tony gets the feeling there's no love lost between Mahler and Chae Hunt, which also merits a couple of brownie points in Tony's book.

A tired grin from Murdo. 'There's that, I suppose. And the way Fleming died . . . what do you think really went on there, Tony? Been hearing all sorts of wild talk, about London gangs, drug-running, you name it.'

'Enquiries are continuing, as they say. Which as you well know, means no one's got a bloody scooby.' He glances at Murdo. 'What are you up to on Sunday, by the way? It's Karen's fortieth and we're having a wee do at the house—'

'Not this weekend, Tony. I can't.'

Armstrong frowns. Remembers what date it is, just before he makes an even bigger idiot of himself. 'God, of course not. Sorry.'

He glances at a non-existent message on his phone so he doesn't have to meet Murdo's eyes right away. 'How's Joyce doing these days? She still okay with where she is?'

'Ach.' Murdo zips up his jacket with unsteady fingers, tries for a smile. 'Ach, you know.'

Tony *does* know, that's the thing. At least his own father's dementia diagnosis had come late in life. But Joyce and Murdo had only just come back from the cruise they'd booked to celebrate his fiftieth before her early-onset Alzheimer's had started to take hold. Two years later, Murdo's living on his own in a one-bedroom flat, taking the Pentalina to the mainland to visit Joyce in a Thurso nursing home. And Tony's got a good idea every penny of the proceeds from the sale of their bungalow is going to help finance her care. And when the money runs out, what then?

'You could still put in for a transfer to the mainland, you know. If it would help.'

It's a conversation they have every so often, and he's expecting his desk sergeant to make his usual response. Instead, Murdo nods slowly.

'Been thinking about it, aye – things starting to catch up with me a bit, I suppose. I'm not sleeping that well, my joints hurt every bloody winter, and this Sandisquoy business . . .' He shakes his head. 'My gran used to tell stories about the place, you know. When I was a wee boy.'

'What sort of stories?'

Murdo shrugs. 'There was one about a spae wife – a sort of healer, you'd call her now. Lived in a cave down by the shore, sold charms to help with childbirth, that sort of thing. And one about evil selkies luring folk out to sea to drown – only bad folk, mind you. Only folk that deserved it.'

'Vigilante selkies, eh?' Tony glances at him, grins. 'Never heard that one before.' Though if the shapeshifting seal-folk actually existed and were in the business of sorting out evil-doers, Tony's got the names of a few politicians he wouldn't mind passing on to them. 'No winding up the journos with it, though, right? At the end of the day, the man died a bloody awful death within sight of his own house. That's evil enough for me.'

28

Sandisquoy

Halfway down the rutted track that leads to Sandisquoy House, Colin knows he's making a mistake.

He isn't a detective; not yet, anyway, just a baby copper, three months out of probation. But he knows Locard's principle of exchange, knows what happens when baby coppers blunder into crime scenes without protective suits. He shouldn't be here, doing what he's doing, but there's no way he can just let this go.

He picks his way down the track's grassy centre, doing his best to avoid anything that looks like a tyre mark. If he's right, if the thing that's just caught his eye means what he thinks it does, he won't risk contaminating the scene any further. He'll head back to the car, keep the place under surveillance from a safe distance and call for back-up.

And if he gets that right, if he does everything else by the book, maybe it won't look so weird that he came out here in the first place.

He glances at his phone, notes the time. *8.15 p.m.* By rights, he should still be in Kirkwall now, sitting in the Reel with Amy, listening to the jamming session the way they'd planned to. But Amy's cheating on him; if he wasn't sure before tonight, he is now.

Colin's not the sharpest tool in the box, as his da loves to point out, and he's seen the look on his Aunty Cath's face when he talks about taking his sergeant's exams in a year or so. Fine, so he's not DCI-level smart, like the English guy in the good suit and with the posh accent he'd met off the plane with Aunty Cath. But he's not completely daft either, and tonight had only confirmed what he'd suspected for some time.

Amy had been making excuses not to meet up with him, the way she did last summer when she was dating that archaeology student from the Ness of Brodgar dig. And he'd seen her going into Helgi's with Fraser Wilson an hour ago, looking great. Looking bloody fantastic, in fact, miraculously recovered from the stomach bug she'd told Colin about earlier.

His gut churning, he'd walked back to his car, intending to head home for a night in front of the telly with a takeaway and a few cans to drown his sorrows. But before he'd realised what he was doing, he'd left Finstown behind and was driving north-west; driving towards the place he'd dropped Aunty Cath and DCI Mahler before heading back to Kirkwall to file reports about vandalised sheds in Greenigoe.

The place where there's a decent-sized investigation happening right under his nose for the first time in ages. The place where an ambitious young officer bored with writing reports on vandalised sheds could maybe show a bit of initiative if he took a wee look round. Just to make sure everything was still secure, he'd told himself. Nothing more than that.

He'd pulled off the road and walked down the track, thanking the clear skies and full moon that let him observe the house without needing to use the torch function on his phone. Not that Sandisquoy made him nervous, of course not. Still, there had been something reassuring about the way that brightness could penetrate the darker shadows around the house as he approached it.

And as he gets closer, it's the tape that catches his eye; the blue and white incident tape across the front door, flapping lazily in the breeze that's sprung up while he's been walking. *Wind's caught it*, Colin tells himself at first. But there's something wrong with that picture, something that doesn't fit. It's only when he gets closer still that he sees a whole section of the tape is missing.

Not torn or ripped. Just missing.

Even then, he might have turned and walked away. Told himself to drive back to Kirkwall, get his boss out to take a look. Then he'd seen the door was standing part-way open. Caught a flicker of light in the darkness of the hall.

He reaches for his mobile, calls himself a daftie the next moment for even hoping to get a signal here. Takes the best snap he can of what's in front of him. And then he's standing on the doorstep. Nothing is moving inside, not that he can see; but there *had* been something, he's sure of it.

Colin pushes the door wide. It opens silently, easily, showing him an empty hall. And another door standing ajar at the far end, a faint grey outline in the gloom.

He calls out to identify himself as police. Waits to hear whoever's in there breathe, or move, to give away their presence, but there's only the silence of an empty house. Using his phone as a torch, he goes inside, peers into the rooms as he makes his way down the hall. Whoever he'd seen, he's pretty sure they've gone now. But where?

Kids, he thinks. *Kids on a dare, that's all.* He does a quick circuit of the remaining rooms, sweeping them with his phone the way he's seen US cops doing it on the TV. Heads for what's got to be the kitchen, right at the end. He pushes the door wide; nothing out of the ordinary, though the place is bloody freezing. Much colder than feels reasonable, given the house has only been unoccupied for week or so.

Nothing to see here either; the room looks like the rest of the ground floor, like it's hardly been used. Like it belongs in a museum. No point hanging around, then. There's no sign of anyone, and he can hardly feel his feet—

A muffled thud from somewhere inside the house. Then footsteps, light and fast-moving across a wooden floor. One of the bedrooms? Colin runs to the bottom of the stairs, calls up into the darkness.

'Police! We're investigating reports of a break-in at this property. Come downstairs – and keep your hands where I can see them!'

God, but that sounded crap. Like a bad *Line of Duty* episode. He clears his throat, calls out again. Waits there, in the chill air and the darkness, for a response that he knows isn't going to come. Where the hell could they have gone? *Where?*

He puts a tentative foot on the first tread. And shakes his head. This isn't working. Time to do what he should have done from the beginning: get back to the car and call it in. This whole Sandisquoy thing's been weird, right from the start, and he doesn't need—

The light from his phone cuts off without warning, leaving him in darkness. He fumbles for the button to switch it on again, but his fingers are shaking so much that the phone slips out of his hand and lands on the tiled floor with a crack.

Fuck. Colin drops to his knees, pats the floor around the place where he thinks he heard it fall. Got to be here somewhere—

Behind him, a floorboard creaks. He starts to turn, and something smashes down on his neck and shoulders, something hard and heavy. Pain explodes inside his head, and he pitches forward.

Silence. A sense of movement behind him. Then footsteps, running footsteps, heading down the hall and out across the gravel. Colin reaches round, touches the back of his neck.

Looks at the dark stickiness coating his shaking fingers. *Bad,* he thinks. *Really bad.*

He has to get out of there, has to get help. But making it back to the car's out of the question; everything's weirdly out of focus, and his legs aren't working properly.

He sees his dropped mobile, reaches for it. No reception in the house, not with walls this thick, but if he can reach the garden, maybe there's a chance. *Maybe.*

Moving on his hands and knees, Colin makes it to the back door. He hauls himself upright, takes half a dozen trembling steps out into the garden. Trips over an abandoned rake that sends him sprawling in the grass.

Fuck. Fuck. Fuck . . . Still no reception when he holds up his mobile. *Further into the garden. Over by the statue.*

He's crawling now, the pain and the dizziness making him want to throw up. And the statue . . . God, the look on its face. Like one of those evil angel things from *Doctor Who* when he was little. But there's a bar showing on his mobile now, one single, pathetic bar, but if he can hold the phone a little higher . . .

Colin makes a grab for the base of the statue, uses it to haul himself upright. Hits 999 and gabbles out half a dozen words as everything drifts out of focus and the world begins to grey.

Need to throw up. Christ, I'm—

His hand slips from the stone and he pitches forward. Sees the grass rushing towards him . . . and disappearing as it gives way beneath his feet and he plunges into emptiness.

29

Divisional HQ
Inverness

'I wasn't sure if you'd been notified about Mina Williamson,' Fiona Lomax tells Mahler when he calls to arrange his mother's return to her flat. 'It's just that Grace was a little upset about it when I spoke to her today. She wasn't a relative, was she? Only—'

'No relation. They were friends, that's all.'

He listens as the care manager tells him Mina had suffered a massive stroke, the day before she was due to be released from hospital. Looks through his emails and finds an update about it from Burnett Road CID. How the hell had he missed that? *Easy,* he realises. *Not red-flagged. Not urgent.*

'Grace wanted to know what would happen to Mina now,' the care manager tells him. 'Where she would be . . . you know, *kept.* What would be done to her. I told Grace I didn't have those answers, but I'd find out for her.'

'I see. Well, there's likely to be a post-mortem, given how Mina was found. After that, a file will go to the Procurator Fiscal.'

'Right. Of course. And getting Mina released for burial? I don't suppose you'd know how long—'

'Depends on the results of the post-mortem, I'm afraid.'

When Mina had turned up on his mother's doorstep, bleeding and semi-conscious, it had looked like an assault, and that's how Burnett Road CID had treated it at first. But despite public appeals, no witnesses had come forward, and the only CCTV captures of Mina on her way up to Crown hadn't shown any kind of head injury.

'I suppose so. It's just that Grace has been worrying about the funeral.'

A warning spike of pain behind his right eye. He opens his desk drawer, finds his pills and swallows one with the remains of his lunchtime coffee. 'It'll be a local authority affair, I'd think, unless you've got a next of kin on file. Is that what upset her?'

An odd discomfort in the care manager's voice. 'It's a little more complicated than that. Mina had a prepaid funeral plan and a proper will lodged with a solicitor. It's all in her case notes, apparently. The thing is, she wanted your mother to take charge of organising her funeral. And your mother agreed.'

Mahler replays those last two sentences in his head. Tries and fails to rearrange the words to make some sort of sense. 'And no one queried this? *No one?* When did this happen?'

A rustling of papers at the other end. And a crackle of frost in the care manager's voice. 'It was brought up at Grace's last review meeting, actually. The one you couldn't attend. I can check to see when the minutes went out if you like—'

'That's not necessary. Thank you.' Curt. Defensive. Unfair. Because he remembers receiving them, remembers looking – no, *glancing* at them. And putting them aside for later. Which makes this mess ninety per cent his fault. 'I'm sorry, that wasn't a criticism. Look, I'll talk to her tomorrow, see how much of it I can take off her shoulders—'

'Yes. Actually that was discussed too.'

'Oh?'

'The thing is . . . the thing is, part of Grace's long-term

recovery is enabling her to make her own decisions, then supporting her through those decisions. And Grace has told us very clearly this is something she wants to do. It *was* minuted very carefully—'

'And the crisis she suffered while trying to organise my grandfather's funeral, the one that saw her admitted to New Craigs hospital? I assume that was minuted too?'

The sound of a page being turned. 'It was. But that was over three years ago, and Grace now feels more confident in her ability to deal with these stressors. You remember she'd ended her CCBT sessions and started EMDR instead? It stands for Eye Movement—'

'Desensitisation and Reprocessing. Yes.'

He clicks the link he's just googled, scans the first few lines. 'And these eye exercises are actually helping her deal with . . . with . . .' The screens slam down inside his head. Cutting off the words, but not the images, as the pain behind his eye begins to pulse.

The smell of blood and fear. His feet, slip-sliding on the stairs.

'EMDR doesn't work for everyone, of course. But there's evidence that it can rewire people's reactions to past traumatic events, decrease the emotional distress experienced.'

'Flashbacks, you mean.'

'That's part of it, yes.' The sound of another page flipping over. Then another. 'And in the case of events within a family, sometimes there are other members of that family who might also benefit—'

'I'm sure that's true. But we have no other family members.'

Mahler invents an urgent email needing his attention, ends the call before she offers to send him links to people he'll never contact. Services he'll never use.

He fires up his emails again, starts working through the red flags. Harkness, the Chief—

Movement in the darkness outside the window. Something slumped, something . . .*No. Not that. Not again. Push through it. Concentrate.*

Sweat sheening his forehead. Images rising faster than he can control them, a slideshow of horrors playing on the darkened glass in front of him.

He looks away, puts his hands on the desk. Watches the tremor spread through his fingers as the slideshow runs on an endless loop inside his head. His mobile is there, only a couple of inches away, and for a moment the urge to call Anna, to finally unburden himself to another human being, is close to unbearable. But if he let himself do that . . . He reaches out. Feels his fingers touch the phone. And push it away, over to the far side of the desk.

The images in his head are his to deal with. His, and no one else's. His legacy from the cowardice he'd shown, all those years ago. His penance.

Blood on the stairs.

His mother's screams.

And then the silence.

30

Inverness City Centre

When the bottle of Peroni hits her in the city centre pizza restaurant, Nazreen knows it's time to leave Donna's engagement party.

There's nothing malicious about what happens; Gary's story about the muck-spreader and the Brexit Party canvasser had been really funny. Right up until he'd begun waving his arms around and sent the open bottle flying.

Donna yells a warning and Fergie makes a grab for it, but he's too late. It hits Naz's forearm, tips over . . . and deposits the foaming contents into her lap before she can retrieve it.

'Oh!' Gary's mouth is a wide 'O' of shock as Naz leaps to her feet. 'Oh my God, are you okay? And you a Muslim too!' Twelve pairs of eyes swivel towards him in the sudden silence. And his face turns the kind of red Naz usually associates with London buses.

'Fuck, I didn't mean—'

'Shut up, Gary.' Donna delves in her bag, hands Naz a pack of tissues. 'Folk with clean napkins, pass 'em over, quick!'

Naz grabs them, does her best to mop up the deluge. But the bottom half of her top's ruined, and the beer's soaked through to her jeans. Not exactly how she'd wanted her first real evening out with the team to go, looking as though she'd wet herself before they'd even ordered dessert.

'It's fine. Honestly.' She manages a smile for Donna, whose death stare at Gary is turning him redder by the minute. 'I need to go home and change, though. Sorry.'

Offers of jackets and cardigans from all round the table, but her top's sticking to her and her jeans feel damp and uncomfortable against her skin. She puts enough cash on the table to pay for her meal, says her goodbyes and turns to leave. But Fergie pulls on his jacket and gets to his feet.

'Where are you parked – the Eastgate? I'll get you back to your car.'

'What? No. Look, it's five minutes away.' And she's walked alone in worse places than Inverness on a Saturday night before now. Much worse. 'Ten at most. You don't have to—'

'Aye, well. I'll walk you back, just the same.' He chucks a couple of notes on the table, nods at Donna. 'I'll catch you up at Hoots. Don't let Gary drown anyone else in the meantime, eh?'

After the warmth of the restaurant, the cold hits Naz as soon as they get outside. It's a sharp, clear night, with a bite of frost in the air, and the wind as they cross the bridge plasters her still-damp top to her chilled skin.

'You sure you're okay?'

Naz glances at Fergie, sighs. 'It's not like vampires and holy water, you know. We don't *drink* alcohol, that's all – and believe me, I've had worse chucked over me on the beat in Maryhill. A lot worse.' She catches the look on his face, adds a smile. 'But thanks for walking me back, I appreciate the company.'

'Ach, well. I didn't want—' At the traffic lights he stops, holds his hand up. 'Did you hear something?'

'No. Maybe. What—'

Screaming, coming from somewhere close by. Her throat dries at the sound. Not just-messing-about screaming, not drunks-in-a-fight screaming; this is real screaming, the kind no police officer wants to hear.

'The river – down past Jimmy Chung's!'

When it comes again, they're both moving, running towards the sound. But Naz is younger and fitter; by the time Fergie catches up with her, she's already over the barrier and clambering down the steep bank towards the figure in the hi-vis jacket. And the slumped shape at her feet.

When she reaches the bottom, the figure turns. It's a young woman, hardly more than a girl, dressed in the navy and white of the Inverness Street Pastors. The hand she holds out to Naz is stained with something dark and sticky, and the man lying at her feet . . .

'Hi. Can you tell me what's happened here?' Keeping her voice calm as she moves closer. 'You look like you need some help. You and your friend.'

A hesitant nod. Good. 'Can you tell me your name? I'm Naz.'

'Sylvie.'

Panting behind her. And the unmistakable sound of an out-of-condition DI preparing to lower himself over the barrier. Naz calls over her shoulder to Fergie, asks him to stay where he is and call an ambulance. 'We're police officers, Sylvie. Is your friend—'

'He's not my friend.' The girl's shaking so much, she can hardly get the words out. 'I found him at the top of the slope there, sitting by the tree.' She nods at the place where Naz climbed over the barrier.

'I thought . . . I thought he was just sleeping, you know? Most of the folk we help, they've been out on the streets for a while, and they learn how to keep warm, but he only had a light jacket on. He didn't answer when I spoke to him and I was really worried about hypothermia, so I went to try and wake him up. But when I shook him, he . . . he just fell down the bank.' She holds up her hands again, stares at Naz. 'I went down after him, and then . . . then I saw he wasn't breathing. And his face ...'

'It's okay, Sylvie. You're doing really well.' Naz gives her a reassuring smile. 'Could you just wait over here a moment, while I take a look?'

She pulls on the nitrile gloves she always keeps in her pocket and crouches down by the slumped figure. His head's fallen forward, hiding most of his features, but there's something familiar about him.

She leans closer, lifts his hair out of his eyes. And feels her stomach give a sudden lurch as she sees exactly what's been done to him.

There must have been an ambulance nearby; as Naz gets to her feet and walks back to the Street Pastor girl, she can hear a wail of sirens. Moments later it's crossing the bridge, flashing lights reflected in the ink-dark river.

'Everything okay down there?'

Fergie's peering anxiously over the barrier at her. She swallows, nods. Waits until the ambulance has arrived, and the paramedics are taking care of the shivering girl, before taking Fergie to one side.

'What's the story, Naz? Was he a rough sleeper?'

Cold now, as the adrenaline starts to leave her system. Cold, and very, very tired. She turns up the collar of her jacket against the wind, gives Fergie an unhappy look.

'I don't think so. That guy the boss was trying to locate – the one Andy Black and DCI Harkness took into Burnett Road? I think that's him.'

'Are you sure?'

Naz gives a reluctant nod. 'He'd taken a massive beating, but yes, I think so. His face ....' She swallows down the sudden

135

flood of nausea as she recalls the sight that greeted her when she'd seen his features properly for the first time. 'His face was a mess, Fergie. His mouth was hanging open, and his tongue . . . It looked like someone had tried to cut it out.'

31

Divisional HQ
Inverness

8.30 a.m. The MIT room slowly filling up with yawning, caffeine-craving police officers, chewing on Harry Gow filled rolls or breakfast wraps from the canteen.

Talking about the latest Caley Thistle or Ross County matches. Talking about the decent weather at the weekend, rain-free and bright enough to get the last bits and pieces done in the garden before the frosts set in. Talking about *X-Factor* or *Strictly*. Talking about anything except the images of Liam Gerrity's brutalised face, staring down at them from the whiteboards.

Fergie takes them through the previous evening, briefs the team on what they know about Gerrity's movements.

'The last confirmed sighting we have of him is at the bus station café,' he tells the team. 'One of the staff remembers him and an old boy with a stick having a wee disagreement. This was a bit after he'd left Burnett Road where he'd talked to the boss and . . . DI Harkness, was it, boss?'

'DCI, I believe.' Though Mahler's got a suspicion Harkness's rank varies, depending on the company he's with. 'Gerrity's on CCTV as leaving Burnett Road at three-thirty and heading back into town. The bus station cameras pick him up outside the café, and there's a further sighting on Academy Street around four when he goes into McGregor's Bar. After that, nothing.'

'He went out the back. Nipped through the kitchens.'

Mahler nods at Donna. 'Makes sense. So was he avoiding someone? Did that someone track him to McGregor's and force him to leave with them? Who were they? We need to talk to anyone who was in the bar that afternoon. Most of all, we need to look at the CCTV outside Johnny Foxes and Jimmy Chung's, pinpoint the moment he was dumped by the river.'

'Pity we didn't keep an eye on him after he left Burnett Road.' Andy Black looks up from the pad he's been making notes on. 'It's obvious he knew more than he let slip to us. And whoever did that to him—' he nods at the whiteboard images, 'they weren't messing about. What about these guys that put the wind up him in Perth – are they still inside or should we be banging on their doors?'

'All good points. So we'll be concentrating our efforts on those two areas – Fergie, you manage the Inverness end. Andy, looks like you and DCI Harkness were on the right track. Take a look at Gerrity's prison acquaintances, see which doors you particularly fancy banging on.'

'Aye, no worries.' Andy looks as though he's relishing the prospect. 'But if I'm still seconded to Absinthe, won't Harkness want—'

'DCI Harkness has been recalled to Gartcosh at short notice. And the investigation into the Cazza MacKay/Styles brothers links is being mothballed for the time being. Apparently the initial intel's now being re-evaluated – so for now, looks like you're back with us.'

Andy makes an unimpressed noise. 'Intel was crap, in other words. Surprise, bloody surprise. But Gerrity's murder – come on, that's like putting out an advert saying, "killed because he knew something". Thought DCI Harkness would have been all over this.'

'He'll be receiving regular briefings from us, and we'll alert him to any Absinthe-related developments. But the murder happened on our patch, so we run the enquiry – which means we've a lot of work to do. Starting now.'

Murmuring, and the odd raised eyebrow at that; they're not entirely buying it, and Mahler doesn't blame them. Harkness's brief email had cited urgent developments in a separate Absinthe line of enquiry. Fine, as far as it goes; priorities shift rapidly on major operations in response to fresh intel, and personnel shift with them. This, though . . . Andy's right, something about it feels off. *Way* off. But right now, that doesn't matter. Finding Liam Gerrity's killer is what matters. The *only* thing that matters.

Mahler turns to the whiteboards. 'Two murders. Two brutal killings, both on our watch. Both horrific enough to get people's attention, even with the ongoing Brexit shenanigans – and trust me, our friends in the media are going to be all over what we're doing from now on.'

Groans from the back of the room. Mahler holds his hand up for quiet. 'I know, I know, but let's keep them on side if we can. Fergie, I've given Media Liaison a holding statement, but we'll need an appeal to go out today. Andy, talk to HMP Perth and draw up a hit-list of visits you and Gary can action.'

'Hey, a road trip!' Gary adopts a terrible American accent, grins at Andy Black. 'Bagsie I pick the snacks, eh?'

Silence as ten heads turn to look at him. 'What?' Gary spreads his hands, glances round the room. 'Just trying to lighten the mood, guys. Come on, I'm not—'

Mahler contemplates an eye-roll, decides against it. With great reluctance. 'Gary?'

'Boss?'

'Shut up.'

'Yes, boss.'

★

Mahler's on the stairs heading for his office when his phone vibrates.

Lukas, check your messages. I need to talk to you.
A

Anna's voicemail, the one he could have – *should have* – listened to earlier. He scans the rest of the alerts filling his screen: a review appointment with his mother's care manager, an email from the Chief, cancelling their scheduled briefing that afternoon. And one from a sender he doesn't recognise, headed 'Intriguing Images'.

Intriguing. *Aye, right*, as Fergie would say. Mahler's about to delete the email and listen to Anna's message when Dave Christie appears in the doorway. And this time, the scene examiner's expression tells Mahler he won't like what he's about to hear.

'Sent you on a report we've just got in from Orkney,' Christie tells him. 'Serious assault last night on an off-duty cop. Should be landing with you about now.'

'Orkney?' Mahler refreshes his screen, finds the scene examiner's email. He scans the first couple of sentences. Reads them again as the first twist of foreboding curls across his shoulders. 'Sandisquoy again. What is it about that place? And Colin McAvoy – that's the Fiscal's nephew, isn't it? What was he doing out there?'

Christie shakes his head. 'Won't know that until he regains consciousness – it was a miracle he managed to make that emergency call before passing out. He's being treated at the Balfour hospital in Kirkwall at the moment, but if he doesn't wake up soon, they'll transfer him to Aberdeen.'

'Bloody hell.'

'Aye. And that's not all. When a team went out from Kirkwall to take a look at the scene, they got a wee bit more than they bargained for. We don't have the images yet, but looks like your old boss had a bit of company at Sandisquoy. When they found Colin, he was lying in a sort of underground store room in the walled garden. Next to a pit full of human remains.'

32

Sandisquoy

More police tape guarding the entrance to Sandisquoy. More uniforms standing in the bitter wind, stamping their feet and trying not to look half frozen; the sun is brilliant against the clear blue sky, but it's a chill, crystalline sort of brilliance, the sort of hard but bright winter weather that still takes Mahler by surprise, four years after leaving the Met. Against it, the darkness surrounding the house is more marked than ever, as though the place is sucking in the daylight, absorbing all the brightness into its gaunt grey walls.

A breath of unease touches the back of Mahler's neck. Buildings are things of bricks and mortar, nothing more; violent crimes can't taint their fabric, can't lock memories of suffering within their stonework. But this house . . . Even from a distance, this house seems designed to repel, not invite company. What does that say about Alex Fleming's state of mind when he bought the place?

Mahler leaves his hire car at the side of the road and walks down the track to meet Tony Armstrong. Up close, the Kirkwall-based inspector looks as though he's had a hard night and a harder morning; there's a faint stubble on his cheeks, and his features have a grey, unhealthy cast.

'No spare DIs in Inverness, then?' Armstrong nods at the

uniform officer on the door to sign Mahler in. 'Wasn't expecting you to come yourself.'

'Both tied up on another case. And better to keep continuity – I've been with this case from the start.'

An argument that would normally have cut zero ice with Chae Hunt. But the Chief had been getting ready to leave for a reception at Bute House when Mahler had spoken to him, and the thought of meeting the First Minister had put Hunt in an unusually accommodating mood. 'Is that Dave Christie's van?'

'Got here on the early ferry, aye,' Armstrong confirms. 'Looks like at least two sets of remains, maybe more.'

He takes Mahler down the side of the house and into the walled garden. Christie's forensic tent has been set up beside one of the lichen-covered statues, its sides flapping back and forth in the rising wind. Christie's standing in the doorway, talking to a pale young man with a blond beard and an anxious expression.

'Can't be helped. We'll just need to—' He catches sight of Mahler, raises a hand. 'Lukas, just the man. This is Graham from the council's archaeology department. We were discussing how to preserve the site, given—'

'Archaeology? I thought we were dealing with recent remains.'

'So did we, at first. The problem is . . .' Christie shakes his head. 'Best if I show you. Come and take a look.'

Mahler pulls on a pair of protective overshoes, follows Christie into the tent.

Based on the scene examiner's brief description of where young Colin McAvoy was found, he's expecting to see a newly exposed open pit beside the statue's base. Instead, a narrow set of steps leads down to what looks like some sort of underground enclosure. The walls are rough slabs of stone, coated in a sheen of moisture, and there's a dank, oppressive feel to the air.

'Aye.' Christie nods at his look of surprise. 'Bit unexpected, eh? Watch your footing on those damn steps, they're slippery as blazes.'

'Noted.'

Mahler follows the scene examiner cautiously down into the central space. He's not normally claustrophobic, but the low ceiling and the walls' slight inward curve are making him more conscious than he wants to be of the weight of stone and earth directly above their heads.

'We searched the house and garden when Alex's body was discovered. How the hell did we miss this?'

'The entrance is right next to that creepy-looking statue,' Christie points out. 'I reckon you'd never spot it unless you knew it was there. Now, whether our boy fell through the gap himself, or someone threw him down here,' the scene examiner shrugs, 'hopefully he'll be able to tell us more when he wakes up. In the meantime, we've got plenty to keep us busy until the guy from CAHID gets here on the next ferry.' His expression darkens. 'The remains are . . . well, see for yourself.'

CAHID, the world-renowned Centre for Anatomy and Human Identification at Dundee; their expertise in complex forensic cases is legendary, but Dave Christie's no slouch himself. If the scene examiner needs CAHID's input, it's a safe bet this is going to be one of those cases.

Mahler walks to the edge of the pit, looks down. And sees a skeletal blonde horror reaching up for him.

'Bloody hell!' He steps back, almost losing his footing before Christie grabs his elbow. 'Is that . . . Has she been mummified?'

'Partly. But I don't think it was deliberate,' the scene examiner tells him. 'You've heard of those bodies that turn up in peat bogs, right? And Ötzi the Iceman? I think that's what we're looking at here – some weird mix of environmental factors coming together to preserve the poor lassie's remains.'

'Weird is right.' Mahler swallows, bends to take a closer look. Surrounded by what he assumes are the other remains Christie mentioned, the corpse is lying on its back, arms fully extended. The remaining skin has turned the colour of old leather and shrunk into a series of desiccated folds around its bones, and the face . . . Mahler suspects that face may have booked itself a place in his nightmares for some time to come. The eyes are closed, sunk back into their sockets, the mouth gaping open in an endless, silent scream, and a single earring dangles from one leathery, crumpled earlobe.

Mahler drags his eyes from the skull with its corona of bright blonde hair, looks down at the still recognisable T-shirt and jeans wrapped around the corpse's withered torso. Glances across at Dave Christie to see his own discomfort reflected on the scene examiner's face.

'A young lassie, aye. No more than twenty-five or so, I'm guessing.' Christie looks round, shudders. 'Bloody miserable place to breathe your last, eh?'

'No argument there. Any thoughts on how long . . .' Mahler takes a closer look at the girl's T-shirt, glances at Christie. 'You've seen this?'

'The Runrig shirt, you mean? Aye, hell of a shame, but terrible taste in music isn't—'

'It's not just a Runrig shirt.' Mahler points at the faint but still visible logo on the faded cotton. 'This logo's from their *Long Distance* album, released in '96, the year before Donnie Munro left the band. I know, because—'

'Because you've got one too.' Christie rolls his eyes. 'Of course you have. She might not have bought it at the time, mind you, but if she did, that's bloody useful, Lukas.'

'I do my best. No opinion on cause of death, I assume?'

'You assume right – I'm good, but I'm not bloody psychic.

As for the other remains, I'm not even going to hazard a guess at how old they are—'

'Oh, some of them are very old. Ancient, in fact. I suspect what we're looking at here is a late-era Viking cist grave. With, er, more modern additions.'

Mahler turns to see the council archaeologist coming down the steps towards them; he looks a little better than when Mahler had met him outside, but not by much.

'I thought ship funerals were more their style. Or burial mounds with cairns.'

The archaeologist nods. 'True. But as Christianity took hold and so-called pagan influence waned, it wasn't uncommon for people to repurpose some of the cairn stones for projects like . . . well, the walled garden connected to this house, for example.'

A tomb enclosing a tomb. Perhaps that's what Mahler can feel pressing down on him as he stands in front of the burial pit; a concentration of death, he thinks. He doesn't believe in curses, doesn't believe in places that hoard misery inside their boundaries like buried treasure. But if he did . . . He shakes his head, cuts off that train of thought before it can take hold, and turns to go.

'I need to head back into Kirkwall, so I'll leave you both to it,' he tells them. 'Dave, we'll catch up with Tony and the CAHID team before my flight tomorrow.'

At the top of the steps, he turns, looks back at the council archaeologist. 'You said this is probably a – what did you call it, a cist grave? Would you expect to find any sort of . . . inscribed items with the remains? Carved bone, something like that?'

The man purses his lips, frowns. 'That's complicated. Grave goods depend on so many variables – the deceased's social standing and profession, for example. I've seen farming implements, dismembered animals – don't ask me why, it seems to have been a thing – items of jewellery, weapons . . . Is there anything in particular you're interested in?'

'Runes.' A tumble of carved white bones, clattering over a steel mortuary table. Spilling from a dead man's pockets. 'I'm interested in runes.'

At four in the afternoon, it's already full dark by the time Mahler heads back into Kirkwall. The CAHID team won't arrive until the following morning on the ferry from Aberdeen, and Mahler had planned to catch the early flight to Inverness, but he needs an urgent face-to-face with them and Cath McAvoy, the Fiscal, before he leaves.

Signed into a comfortable B&B on the outskirts of Kirkwall, Mahler emails updates to Fergie and Chae Hunt, and a brief outline to the media liaison team. He isn't a fan of issuing holding statements so soon, but Mahler hadn't missed the interested looks his return had attracted. It won't be long before news of the latest discovery at Sandisquoy starts to leak out; better to take charge of releasing information from the outset. Because this case is about to explode, he can feel it. And the longer he stays part of it, the harder it's going to be to step away.

His mobile lights up with a call from Tony Armstrong. By the time he's halfway through his first sentence, Mahler's pulling on his jacket and heading out the door.

33

Kirkwall

There's a brand new hospital planned for Kirkwall, a sleek, curved construction being built on the south-west edge of town. But Colin McAvoy's being treated at the old site, a cluster of low 1930s buildings nearby.

When Mahler gets there, Armstrong's waiting for him in reception.

'How is he? Does he remember anything about what happened?'

Armstrong scrubs a weary hand over his face. 'He's awake and talking – Cath's with him at the moment. More than that . . . well, you'd better hear it from him yourself. His room's down this way.'

'Lukas.' Cath McAvoy manages a smile as Mahler enters, but it's clearly a struggle; the Fiscal looks shattered, the lines of strain taut around her eyes. 'Thanks for coming. I'll get the nurse to bring another chair—'

Armstrong raises a hand. 'Cath, we need to have a word with Colin on our own first. Maybe go and get a coffee until we're done?'

She frowns, looks across at the wan figure in the hospital bed. 'Col, are you up to this? If not—'

'It's fine, Aunty Cath. I'm fine.' Out of uniform, Colin

McAvoy looks barely old enough to shave, let alone be a police officer. But there's a hint of steel in his voice, enough for the Fiscal to nod after a moment and leave them to it.

When the door's closed behind her, he gives Mahler and Armstrong an apologetic glance. 'She's worried about my parents – my da, really. He's a lot older than my ma, and not in the best of health. This . . . this was a shock for him.'

Mahler nods. 'Of course. Inspector Armstrong said you're starting to remember what happened.'

'A bit. Maybe. But it's all mixed up. And the bit that isn't . . .' he swallows, looks away. 'It was my off-duty. I was due to see my girlfriend, but she . . . she cancelled on me.'

He tells them about driving out to Sandisquoy, seeing the severed incident tape and the door standing open. 'I would have called it in, but then I saw someone moving around.'

'Inside the house?'

McAvoy nods. 'It was dark, but there was a faint light of some sort – a torch, maybe.'

'So you went in.'

Another nod. 'Thought it might be kids on a dare at first. But it's not like there's a bus or something, so how could they get out there? It didn't sound like kids anyway.' He reaches for the water by his bed, takes a sip. 'It sounded . . . I don't know. Stealthy.'

Armstrong sighs. 'And you still didn't call it in. God's sake, Colin.'

'I know it was stupid. But if I'd waited for back-up, they'd have been gone, wouldn't they? Phone reception's rubbish out there anyway. I only managed the 999 call because I remembered you said it worked in the garden.'

Ah, the 'poor mobile coverage' plea in mitigation; Mahler's been known to use it himself on occasion, so he can hardly blame the boy for giving it a try. 'What happened when you got inside?'

'I called out to identify myself.' When McAvoy reaches for his water again, there's a faint unsteadiness in his hand. 'Tried to switch on the hall light, but the power was off. Then I saw there was someone in the hallway, for a moment. And then . . .' He looks up at Mahler. 'And then there wasn't.'

Mahler frowns. 'So you were mistaken? You hadn't actually seen anything?'

McAvoy shakes his head. 'There *was* someone there. I heard them moving around, I saw their . . . their shape in the darkness. Then they just disappeared – and yes, I know how that sounds. But they were there, sir. They were!'

His voice has risen to a near-shout, and he's breathing too quickly. Armstrong exchanges a glance with Mahler, raises a placatory hand.

'Calm down, son, no one's disbelieving you. All I'm saying is, you took a good knock to your head—'

'You think I was seeing things? I wasn't! I'm telling you, I *saw* him disappear—'

'Is everything okay, Col?' The Fiscal appears in the doorway, shoots Mahler an angry look. 'His BP's far too high, and he's on hourly obs. Can't this wait till he's more settled?'

Armstrong starts to say something, but Mahler nods. Colin's becoming too agitated, and Mahler suspects there's not much more he can tell them anyway. He thanks the boy for talking to them and tells him to get some rest.

In the car park, Armstrong turns to Mahler. 'An intruder that vanishes into thin air, and pops up again to bash him over the head. As though we didn't have enough to cope with right now.'

An undercurrent of something there. At Mahler's raised eyebrow, Armstrong gives a weary sigh. 'Aye, I know how that sounded. But Colin – look, he tries hard, I'll give the boy that. Keen as mustard, too, but he's not the sharpest tool in the box.

And Sandisquoy – it's that sort of locus, isn't it?'

'Meaning?'

A half-embarrassed shrug. 'You know as well as I do there are crime scenes you can't wait to get out of. Scenes that have you looking over your shoulder in the middle of the day, imagining all sorts. I've seen a couple, and I'm guessing you've seen a damn sight more.'

'Maybe. But Colin didn't imagine being hit over the head. And he didn't do it himself.'

'True enough.' Armstrong scrubs a hand over his face. 'I'm needed back at the station for a while, then I'm heading out to Sandisquoy. Are you coming?'

Mahler checks the time on his phone, glances at the scroll of mails and messages filling the screen. And shakes his head. 'I'm needed back at HQ. My flight's at eleven, so I'll have to Skype you and the CAHID team this afternoon instead. In the meantime—'

Footsteps hurrying across the car park towards them. Cath looks a little less strained than earlier, but her exhaustion's still evident in every line of her face.

'He's asleep, so I'm going back to the office for a couple of hours,' she tells them. 'As soon as your scene examiner guy gets something, I want to know, okay? Colin should never have— what is it? What's happened?'

The hospital car park's no place for a briefing, but Mahler gives her a quick update. And watches her face lose its last remaining trace of colour.

'Jesus, that poor girl. How come she wasn't missed? How did no one know—'

Mahler holds up his hand. 'CAHID's out there now, we need to let them do their stuff.' He turns to Armstrong. 'In the meantime, I need you to run an urgent MISPER check on her – Cath's right, someone has to know who she is.'

Armstrong nods. 'Already on it. I'll talk to my desk sergeant too. Murdo's Orkney born and bred – if she was a local girl, he'll know about it. Or know someone who does.'

'Good. And get a full team out to Sandisquoy – keep them out of CAHID's way, but I want every inch of it searched again.' Mahler scrubs his hand over his forehead. 'I think we messed up first time round, Tony. I think there's something in that house, something so incriminating that Colin's attacker couldn't risk us getting hold of it.'

Armstrong bristles. 'We might not be big city cops, but we don't have heather growing out our ears. If you're trying to say we don't know how to conduct a search—'

'I'm not saying that. I'm saying we all missed something. *All* of us. And we need to find out what. Because what we have at Sandisquoy . . . I've a feeling we've only scratched the surface of what happened at that house.'

He watches their faces change, sees their slow realisation of just how big the enquiry's likely to become. And just how complex.

Cath exhales slowly. Nods. And turns to Mahler. 'Aye, I reckon that's true enough. The thing is, this Alex Fleming – you're looking into him, right? Checking there's nothing . . . untoward in his past to connect him with that house. Because I don't see how—'

'There's nothing. Trust me.' Harsher than he'd intended, harsh enough for Armstrong to glance sharply at him. Mahler sighs, holds up a hand. 'I know, I know. But we're picking through every detail of Alex's life, and so far we haven't found anything to connect him to Orkney.'

'So far.' An odd, flat note in Cath's voice. 'But you'll keep him under the microscope, right?'

'Of course we will. Look, Alex was my first DI when I joined the Met – my mentor, I suppose. And I wouldn't be doing justice to his memory if I didn't pull out all the stops on this enquiry. So believe me, right now absolutely everything and everyone connected with that damn house is under the bloody microscope.'

34

Sandisquoy
Four Weeks Before the End

He's being watched. If he hadn't been sure of it before, he is now.

The first time it had happened, he'd been walking the shoreline in search of driftwood. An almost monochrome day, it had seemed, like so many of the days he's known here, the sea and sky blurring into ever-darkening shades of greys and blacks until he could barely make out where each one ended. There had been a haar coming in then too, one of the rolling sea fogs that creep in over the coast and blanket the land in chill dank shrouds.

Perhaps that's why he hadn't noticed the figure standing on the headland at first. The mist had started to come in faster than he'd expected, and though he's lived here long enough to be confident about finding his way back to the house in most weathers, something about the speed of its movement, the intensity of the cold it enveloped him in, had made him turn round well before he'd planned to and head back to the house.

Perhaps. Only that's another lie, isn't it? The cold and the damp and the damn sea fog had nothing to do with the bout of shivering that made him change his mind. The truth is . . . the truth is, he'd felt suddenly exposed out on the deserted shore. Ridiculous to think the figure on the headland had anything to do with that weird store room underneath the walled garden – how could it? Still, once the thought had crept inside his head, somehow he couldn't shake it.

Because the truth is — the real truth is — his recollection of what happened after he went down those stone steps is pretty hazy. And not just that; he doesn't remember going back to the house afterwards, doesn't remember much about the rest of that day, frankly. Or quite a few of the days that followed.

It's as though his memory is . . . not failing, exactly. But changing. Making him forget things he used to take for granted, like keeping the Aga going and the food cupboards well stocked. Still, there are some things you don't forget; some things you rely on even when your brain's so whisky-fogged the memories are leaking out of it.

Things like instinct.

It was instinct that had made him take note of the figure watching his progress as he made his way back along the shore. Instinct that told him not to relax, even when the sea fog had thinned enough for him to look back at the headland and see the figure had gone. Instinct that had told him what he'd seen wasn't just an off-the-beaten-track tourist exploring his bleak corner of the island.

Maybe he hadn't quite believed it, not completely. But he'd gone back to the house a damn sight faster than he'd set out, all the same. And checked and double-checked the locks on every door and window once he got there.

Three days later, with his supply of whisky running low, he'd made himself get the van out and head into Kirkwall. Thanks to a puncture, he'd got back later than he'd intended, as the day was fading to a grey half-light. He'd stopped at the top of the track to open the access gate, opened the door of the van . . . and seen a figure down by the jetty.

Not coincidence, not this time. Not a bloody tourist either; the 'Keep Off' signs are large and freshly painted, he makes sure of that. And there was something about the figure, an odd purposefulness about the way it was standing there, that sent sudden bursts of adrenaline spiking through his bloodstream.

He'd jumped out of the van and hared down the track to confront them; half looking forward to it, truth be told, once the shock of seeing someone trespassing on his property had worn off. But he's been putting on the beef lately thanks to the booze, and he's badly out of condition; halfway there, he'd been wheezing like an old man with a forty-a-day fag habit. He'd had to stop and catch his breath, let the tightness in his chest begin to ease.

When he'd looked again, the figure had gone.

35

Raigmore Hospital
Inverness

Another post-mortem. Another morning spent in Raigmore Mortuary's viewing gallery, watching a green-gowned figure do things Fergie doesn't want to think about. It's cold, it's uncomfortable, parts of what he has to observe are downright disgusting, and usually, Fergie's just fine with that.

As far as he's concerned, the living shouldn't feel anything but bloody grateful to still have a pulse in the presence of violent death. The day any of it stops bothering him is the day he hangs up his warrant card and looks at running that wee B&B in France, the way Zofia's always hinting at.

But today Marco McVinish is on sick leave, struck down by the same late autumn flu that's currently got half of HQ snuffling and sneezing through their shifts and praying for a quiet couple of days in the run-up to Halloween. His stand-in, Beth MacKintosh from Aberdeen, is a legend: fast, thorough, brilliant. And completely bloody terrifying.

Fergie's attended two of her post-mortems, and each time he's felt sorrier for her luckless assistants than the poor sod lying on the mortuary table. Her nickname, predictably, is Mack the Knife. But it's not because she knows her way around a scalpel. By the time Fergie escapes, there's a line of cold sweat inching down his back and he can feel a nervous twitch developing under his left eye.

When he gets back to HQ, the MIT room is half empty. Gary and Andy should have been back from Perth by now, but a jack-knifed lorry has closed the A9 in both directions at Dalwhinnie, and the boss has texted to say his Kirkwall flight has been delayed. So there's only Naz and Pete at their desks when Fergie gets upstairs, working their way through the witness statements and whatever's come in from last night's media appeal. And one look at their faces is enough to tell him how well *that's* going.

'No luck? Nothing at all? What about the CCTV footage from Johnny Foxes?'

'On the blink since bloody Thursday night.' Pete glares at the display on his screen. 'We've called in the feed from the Mercure, but it's a long shot. And the weather was crap, too, which means anything we do get might not be up to much.'

'Aye, I know. But keep at it – someone must have seen something.' Fergie pulls out a chair, slumps into it. He's got a hell of a headache building at the back of his neck, as though his brain's doing its best to push its way out of his skull. 'Gerrity's girlfriend – anyone done a follow-up with her?'

'Mel Paterson? Got one booked in for Wednesday,' Naz tells him. 'But she told Donna she'd moved on from "that wee bawbag" ages ago, to quote her exact words. So not sure there's much to get from her.'

Naz is probably right. By all accounts, the relationship had ended shortly before the attack on Gerrity in Perth Prison; just around the time Mel Paterson had finished working at Cazza MacKay's club down the Longman, in fact. And neither of these facts may mean anything, of course. On the other hand, they might.

'It's a long shot, right enough, but we've got bugger all else.'

The forensics are in the system now, samples from the body on their way to the lab. But without potential suspects to link them to, they're useless. 'Keep plugging away, Naz, you're doing grand.'

Christ, he sounds fed up. Enough for Naz to exchange a glance with Pete, and get to her feet, pushing her chair back.

'Time for a brew.' She waves her 'Staggies' mug at him. 'Get you anything? There's still a bit of cake left from Donna's birthday, if you fancy that.'

Fergie's eyes stray downwards to the gap between the fifth and sixth buttons of his shirt; his tie hides most of his belly's bulge, but not all. Monday, he promises himself. He'll start going to HQ's posh on-site gym on Monday. 'Ach, what the heck. Just a wee piece, then.'

Zofia would kill him if she knew, but after a morning with the Knife, Fergie reckons he's earned it. And maybe the sugar hit will give his brain the jump-start it needs today.

He powers up his laptop, looks at his emails. Looks at them for as long as he can stand before closing them down again and reaching for a file on his desk.

This paperless office notion is a fine thing, in theory. Smarter working, twenty-first century policing and all that; trouble is, his brain prefers the twentieth-century version, the one that likes to phone folk up and talk to them, not fill in bloody evaluation forms and spreadsheets.

And yes, sometimes he needs to have printed pages in front of him, actual pages that won't time out on him, pages he can look back at if he suddenly—

'Got something.'

Pete does something involving a lot of rapid typing on his laptop, peers at the screen and grins. 'Naz, take a look at this. What do you see?'

'A hen party coming out of Jimmy Chung's.' She leans

closer, pulls a face. 'Yuk, the one with the pink wig's throwing up at the traffic lights – aye, that's classy, doll. *Really* classy. They're heading round to Johnny Foxes now, and . . . wait, what's that?'

Fergie comes over, watches as three male figures come into view at the very edge of the footage Pete's running. They're gone the next moment, but there's something about them—

'The one in the middle. It's like they're holding him up.'

'I think that's exactly what they're doing.' Pete hits another key, zooms in on the image. 'I can't enhance it any more than this, but that looks like a logo on the big one's fleece.'

'Street pastors. Look, you can see half of a "T" there, and an "R" below it.' Fergie turns to Pete. 'Can you pick them up again?'

Pete shakes his head. 'Not on that feed, no. But take a look at this. It's from the camera up by the Town House.'

They watch the new footage in silence. It's only picked up two figures at first; they move *away* from the camera towards what looks like a vehicle and out of shot. When they reappear, a third, slumped figure is sandwiched between them as they walk down Bridge Street towards the river.

'Drugged.' A dawning horror in Naz's voice. 'But he's still semi-conscious, or he couldn't have walked to where they dumped him. Pete, can't we get a better look at their faces?'

'No, we bloody can't. They're not amateurs, Naz – see how they're careful not to get their heads in shot? They knew exactly what they were doing.'

Fergie stares at the screen. *Dying,* he thinks. We're watching a man dying in front of us. 'We need to pull in more witness statements. Someone must have seen them, noticed something—'

'I doubt it.' Pete takes off his glasses, rubs the red mark they've left on his nose. 'Think about it – anyone wearing a uniform, it's like they're basically invisible. Folk *see* them, but they just look through them. And if they were walking along with someone, someone who's weaving about a bit—'

'They're wearing Street Pastor fleeces and caps. It would look like he'd had a skinful and they were looking after him.' Naz nods. 'Okay, but they were taking a massive risk, surely. What about the cameras outside Johnny Foxes? They're walking straight into range.'

'They didn't care.'

Fergie tears his eyes from the dying man on the screen, turns to her. 'Those cameras didn't bother them, Naz. Not at all. They already knew the bloody things were down.'

36

Mahler had hoped to make it back to HQ before Chae Hunt, but his delayed flight from Kirkwall has put paid to that. Before he's even halfway up the stairs, he's summoned by text to the Chief's office.

A coffee aroma drifts down to Mahler as he climbs – impressively good stuff, the kind he limits himself to a couple of times a week – but the tone of Hunt's message suggests the Chief's not feeling particularly hospitable. Hardly surprising, Mahler supposes, if Hunt's read the update email he'd sent from Kirkwall Airport.

When Mahler knocks and enters, Hunt is stirring sugar into an espresso. He grunts an acknowledgement, waves Mahler over to the chair opposite his desk. And flips his iPad round so Mahler can see the list of TV and newspaper articles about Sandisquoy fill the screen.

'Trending on Twitter too – **#MurderManse**, apparently. And every nutter in the country is posting on our Facebook page about how useless we are.' Hunt pushes the iPad to one side. 'How long before we get a definite ID for the girl in the cellar?'

'Dave Christie and CAHID are still assessing, but I've got Jas in Media Liaison prepping an appeal with images of the victim's clothing – with luck, that T-shirt's distinctive enough to jog someone's memory while we wait for their reports.'

Hunt raises a disgruntled eyebrow. 'After twenty years? Bloody long shot there, even if she was a local girl. What about Fleming – he'd still have been a young man then, wouldn't he?'

'We've dug into his past very thoroughly, sir. No family connections with Orkney, nothing to suggest any sort of link to the area before he bought Sandisquoy.'

'As far as we know.' Mahler starts to speak, but Hunt holds up his hand. 'Take a look at the facts, man. Fleming retires from the Met. Disappears. Pops up again using a dead man's identity to buy a house with a sodding murder room in the back garden. If you can't see a link—'

'That's not the bloody link!' Swearing at a superior officer. *Not* how Mahler had planned to start his afternoon. 'Sir, the Job was Alex's whole life. The last case I worked on with him was . . .'

The summer of 2008. Birdsong in a neat suburban garden. Charred flesh and shattered bones.

Mahler swallows, shakes his head. 'It was a big one, and it took its toll on him. On all of us.'

'You looked up to him. Thought he was just a couple of steps lower than God, eh? Aye, of course you did.'

Hunt gives him a weary look. Sighs. Takes a second espresso cup from his desk drawer, fills it from his machine and passes it to him. 'Luckily for you, I had a very pleasant evening at the First Minister's reception yesterday evening, which means I'm feeling unusually mellow today. Which means you don't get your arse handed to you for that wee tantrum just now.'

'Sir.'

'Aye. It also means you get one more simple directive from me about the Orkney situation – your job is to oversee the enquiry. Given your particular connection to the case, you facilitate liaison with the Met, and you provide background intel as necessary. You do not – repeat, *not*, take an active part in the investigation.' Hunt sits back, folds his arms. 'Clear enough for you?'

Enough of a reproof in there to ensure Hunt's covered himself should things go pear-shaped, but non-specific enough to be open to interpretation. In spite of himself, Mahler's impressed.

'Perfectly, sir.'

'Fine. In the meantime, I've had confirmation through from DCI Harkness that the Absinthe mop-ups are winding down, so Andy Black's back with us permanently.'

'And the Gerrity enquiry?'

'Any Absinthe connections you red-flag over to Harkness, otherwise it stays with us.' He glances at Mahler. Sighs. 'Not sitting right with you, is it? Join the club. But Harkness's lot have their own priorities – trust me, you don't want their attention on you for longer than absolutely necessary.'

Harkness's lot, not Gartcosh. Interesting. Mahler nods. 'No argument there. And having Andy back will take some of the pressure off Fergie.'

'Only if you set it up properly. And then step back.' Hunt raises an eyebrow at his look of surprise. 'Andy's got his faults, but you point him at something, he'll go at it like a bloody terrier. He'll get there too, if you steer him in the right direction – that piece of advice is echoed by a mutual friend, by the way.'

'Sir?'

'I went to see June Wallace a couple of days ago. She was asking after you.'

June. The last time Mahler had seen his former boss, she'd been just about to start her cancer treatment. 'How was she?'

'Tired.' Hunt picks up the espresso cup, looks down at its contents. Puts it down again. 'No, she was bloody shattered.

And that was on her week *off* chemo.' He looks up at Mahler.

'Look, I get that this isn't an easy situation for you. Moving up to a DCI role takes quite a shift in mindset from being a DI. And if you've got your chance because of someone else's bad luck . . .' He shakes his head. 'Well, there we are. You were June's recommendation for Acting DCI. And on balance, I reckon she called it right. But we've got two brutal murders on our books right now, and we're making no headway with either – if that doesn't change soon, there's a serious amount of hassle going to be landing on my head from our bosses. And I don't need to tell you where it'll hit next.'

The CCTV footage Pete's located isn't the only piece of news waiting for Mahler when he goes downstairs; Andy Black's visit to one of Gerrity's former cellmates had thrown up a couple of potential names to look at, both with links to the Highlands. And one of them, Eddie Ross, has a connection no one had been expecting.

'Been all over the place, our boy Eddie,' Andy tells the MIT room. 'Born in Wick, worked in clubs in Manchester and Glasgow – aye, I thought you'd like that wee tie-in to Phil McMonagle and the Manchester twins. And guess who he used to go out with? Mel Paterson, Gerrity's ex, that's who. Oh, and he's done a few shifts recently at Johnny Foxes.' Andy leans back in his chair, grins. 'Things starting to come together a wee bit, eh?'

'Certainly looks like it,' Mahler agrees. 'Okay, Naz and Gary, talk to Mel Paterson again. Make our interest in Eddie Ross's whereabouts very clear, warn her about withholding information.'

Surprise on Andy's face – he'd expected to follow it up himself, but Mahler has something else in mind for him. He turns to Pete.

'We need to find that van. What if we work back from the time Naz found Gerrity's body, look for it driving off?'

'A light-coloured van?' Pete gives Mahler a reproachful look. 'That's all we've got to work with here, boss. Not even a partial plate – and no, I can't enhance it, this isn't an episode of bloody *CSI*. Look, we don't even know which way it went! Up Castle Street, down Ness Walk, over the bridge—'

Mahler holds up his hand. 'I know what I'm asking. But if anyone can pick up its trail, it's you. Fergie, what about Gerrity's post-mortem – anything for us to work with there?'

Turns out there's very little; even more non-committal than Marco McVinish. All Mack the Knife would confirm is that Gerrity's death had been a prolonged and painful one.

'Beaten, burned with cigarettes. And he had marks on his legs, too – animal bites, she thought.' Fergie swallows, looks down at the desk for a moment. 'Oh, and his tongue. That was "very carefully carried out", apparently. Only one artery severed so he wouldn't bleed to death.'

Silence. Thick, appalled, disbelieving. Mahler looks round at the team, sees the horror of the picture Fergie's painted marking every face. He can't afford to let that happen; can't let what they've heard get in the way of the job they've got to do.

He crosses to the whiteboard, adds a single word to the list of bullet points under Gerrity's name. Underlines it twice.

FEAR

'Liam Gerrity was in fear of his life when he came to us,' he tells them. 'Fearful what he knew would get him killed.'

'Aye, and he was right.'

Mahler glances at Gary, nods. 'If Gerrity had trusted us, we could have helped him. As it is, we failed Gerrity,' he tells the team. 'Failed him in the worst possible way. People are going to be scared, and getting them to talk to us won't be easy. But we've got a couple of decent leads here, and that's what we need to focus on – that's what Gerrity deserves from us right now.'

He ends the meeting, calls Fergie and Andy over as the team files out. He brings them up to speed with the developments on Orkney, updates them on his conversation with Hunt.

Andy glances up at the whiteboard and back at Mahler. 'You seriously think anyone's going to talk to us after this bloody fiasco? If Phil McMonagle's boys are mixed up in it—'

'We need to find that out,' Mahler tells him. 'You've worked with DCI Harkness on Absinthe, you'll know where to start looking. And make finding Eddie Ross a priority. That was a good job today, by the way – you and Gary make a decent team.'

'Aye. Well.' Andy gives him a wary look, straightens his shoulders. 'Better get to it, eh? I'll grab a coffee and a smoke, check he's on top of this visit to Gerrity's ex.'

When Andy's gone, Fergie turns to Mahler. 'Gerrity was a fantasist, boss – a wee pretendy hard man. Whatever he thought he knew, I'll lay odds it was all talk.'

Mahler looks up at Liam Gerrity's image on the whiteboard. The man had been terrified during his interview at Burnett Road; terrified, but willing to cooperate. Yet Harkness had mishandled him so badly, Gerrity had got up and walked out. Right into his killers' hands. *Operational reasons,* Mahler thinks. And feels a twitch of wrongness creep between his shoulder blades.

'Someone thought otherwise,' he tells Fergie. 'Someone very definitely took him at his word. We just need to find out who.'

37

Inverness

Mel Paterson, Liam Gerrity's one-time girlfriend, has a flat on the outskirts of the city, overlooking Culduthel Woods. It's only a short drive from Inshes HQ, which means Naz only has to put up with Gary's attempts at conversation for something like fifteen minutes. But by the time they pull up outside the white-harled apartment block's communal entrance, she's heard more than she ever wants to about the lads' weekend he's organising for a mate's fortieth.

'Sounds like you've got it all covered.' Naz gets out, looks round. Points at the third building on the left. 'Come on, that's the block we want.'

The door to the communal entrance is wedged open, so they make their way up to the top-floor flat. There's no answer to their first few rings, but after a minute or so, Gary's determined thumping on the door pays off and it's yanked open.

'Not you lot again.' Mel Paterson's wrapped in a white dressing gown, as though she's not long out of bed, but not a strand of her honey and caramel hair is out of place. She looks them up and down. Curls her lip over the most perfect veneers Naz has ever seen, and folds her arms.

'I told you, Liam and me finished ages ago – I signed a bloody statement for you, didn't I? What the fuck do you want now?'

'Just to clear up a couple of things. Mind if we come in? I mean, we can do it here if you like, but—'

Voices in the stairwell – teenagers, a mixed group, Naz reckons, the boys doing their best to out-cool each other, the girls alternately mocking and egging them on. Mel hesitates for a moment, sighs. 'Ten minutes. Come on, get in.'

She closes the door behind them, puts the chain on. Leads them through to an open-plan living area that wouldn't look out of place in a city penthouse and nods at a pristine cream leather sofa. She perches on the edge of a teal velour armchair and glares at Gary, who leans back on the sofa and knocks a scatter of carefully coordinated cushions to the floor.

'Can't take him anywhere.' Naz gives an apologetic smile as Gary bends to retrieve them. 'So, Mel – is it okay if I call you Mel? – I'm sorry if this is hard for you. I know you'd finished with Liam, but even so, it must have been a real shock.'

'Aye. It was.' Mel shifts in her seat, picks at a speck of fluff on its arm. 'Fair did my head in when I heard.'

'You'd split up with him a while ago, you said?'

She nods at Naz. 'Before he went to Huntly. And aye, I know I called him a wee bawbag – doesn't mean I wanted something like that to happen to him. Christ, no one deserves that!'

Gary leans forward. 'And you'd no idea he was back in Inverness?'

'None. I always thought he hated the place.'

'Must have come back for a reason, though. Maybe he thought there was a chance to get back with you?'

'Never going to happen.' Mel glances out of the window, gets to her feet. 'Look, not being funny, but I've got a hen party booking I need to get to. If there's nothing else—'

'We know you visited him in Huntly, Mel. Two weeks after you said you'd split up.'

Shock painted across her face. And something else, something close to panic. Naz offers a sympathetic smile.

'Hard to cut someone out of your life like that, isn't it? Even if you know it's the right thing to do. But you need to be honest with us, Mel – did you know Liam was back in Inverness?'

'No!' Mel sits down heavily. Sighs. 'Okay, I went to see him in Huntly. Felt sorry for him, I suppose – he was a right wee chancer, but he was cute too, you know? But when I saw him . . . Christ almighty, his face!' She shudders. 'I couldn't deal with it. Couldn't even look at him. And he knew it.'

'Good-looking bad boys, huh?' Naz smiles. 'I get it, Mel. I really do. And you'd moved on by then, hadn't you? To Eddie Ross.'

'Eddie and I were over ages ago.'

Gary shakes his head. 'Not what we heard. Thing is, we need to talk to Eddie about what happened to Liam. So if you know where he is—'

'I told you, we're not together.' A glance at her phone, and her eyes flicker to the window again. 'Now like I said, I'm going out, so—'

'You want to get ready. Got it.' Naz gets to her feet. Gives Gary the *time to go* look, and follows with a little gentle pressure of her heel against his instep when he doesn't move.

'Thanks for talking to us, Mel. I'll leave you my card, will I? In case you remember something after we've gone.'

Naz puts it on the side table by Mel's phone, nods at Gary again. By the time they've left the flat and reached the foot of the stairs, he's stopped limping. More or less.

'What was that for? It's not like I didn't catch on—'

'Keep walking.' Naz takes his arm, steers him briskly back to the car and gets in. 'I want her to see us leaving.'

'Because—?'

'Because that flat's got high-end chic written all over it,' she tells him. 'There's no way Mel can afford that by doing a few beauty treatments. And didn't you see the way she kept looking out of the window? She's either expecting a visit, or someone's coming to pick her up. Someone she didn't want us to see.'

'She was a bit twitchy, right enough. So—'

'So let's not spoil her plans. Drive towards the exit, then pull in over there, in that first row of parking spaces.'

'She'll see us.'

Naz points at the yellow council vehicle making its way along the street. 'Not with that bin lorry in the way – come on, hurry up!'

As the bin lorry rumbles past, Gary moves the car. Partially screened by a muddy white transit van, they've got a reasonable view of the entrance to the flats. But as the minutes tick by and no one goes in or out, Gary shakes his head.

'Nothing happening here, Naz. Maybe she *was* going out, but she changed her mind? That's the rain on now. And—'

A car turning in. Driving slowly past and stopping further on, the engine idling. The BMW's mud-spattered number plate is only partly legible, but Naz takes out her phone, snatches a couple of shots. Moment later, Mel Paterson comes out of the entrance and gets in.

The car immediately turns around, heads back towards the main road as Gary starts to pull out . . . and the bin lorry lumbers past, cutting off their view, just as a Royal Mail van turns in and stops at the pillar box on the other side.

By the time Gary's managed to manoeuvre past both vehicles, the car carrying Mel Paterson has disappeared.

'Now what?'

Naz's shoulders slump. 'Back to HQ, I guess. I've sent the shots to Pete, so if he can enhance the plate, maybe—'

'There.' Gary points at a car making a cautious turn out of the driveway of a large B&B on the corner. 'That's them, isn't it – the blue BMW, heading for Culduthel Road? What do you reckon – waiting until we'd gone?'

'Yes!' Naz punches his arm in delight. 'Come on, then, get moving – let's see if Mel's really off to do makeovers on a hen party.'

Gary gives her an uneasy look. 'I don't know, Naz. We're talking surveillance here—'

'Of course we aren't. That would need to be authorised, wouldn't it? We're just . . . heading back to HQ. Maybe stopping off to get cakes at Harry Gow on the way, and – hey, what's going on there?'

The little white Clio in front of the BMW has stalled; a new-ish learner, Naz's guessing from the L-plates. As the lights turn green and it doesn't move, the Beamer sounds an impatient horn. When nothing happens, the driver leans out, bellows a volley of insults. Finishes with an unmistakable gesture. Turns to speak to his passenger—

'Bloody hell, it's him!' Gary starts up the engine as the learner finally manages to get moving. 'Naz, get the boss on the phone – tell him we've found Eddie Ross!'

38

Naz is still trying to raise Mahler or Fergie when the Clio finally moves off. It's bunny-hopping along at twenty-five miles an hour, heading for the Slackbuie roundabout, and the Beamer is sitting impatiently on its tail as the rain starts to come down in earnest.

'If we get to the roundabout, that's it,' Gary tells her. He hangs back, waits to let a little red Fiat reverse out of a driveway ahead of them. 'We can't follow them, Naz, even if—'

'It's a clone!' Naz reads off the message Pete's just sent her. 'That plate's off a taxi in Doncaster. He's driving around in a dodgy motor—'

'Fuck!'

Naz looks up. Feels her stomach pull into a tight, hard ball as she sees the Clio lurch to a sudden halt in the now near-horizontal rain. Gary swears again, pulls over onto the grass verge by West Heather Road. Reaches for the radio as the Beamer slams into the learner's car, shunts it towards the roundabout. And the Fiat—

Brakes squealing, uselessly. Metal grinding, twisting. The scorch of rubber in a surreal, slow motion world. Then silence.

Naz leaves Gary calling it in. She gets out of the car and races to the scene as the Clio's doors open and two dazed figures stumble out. She checks they can walk, guides them to safety. Looks back to see Gary wrench the Fiat's passenger door open, lean in. And turn away, talking rapidly into his Airwave.

Injured. How badly? Naz starts to run towards the Fiat, but Gary holds up a hand and gestures at something behind her. She turns at the sound of a car door opening. And sees Mel Paterson fall out of the BMW onto the road.

Mel scrambles to her feet, half runs, half staggers towards her as the driver's door swings open and Eddie Ross gets out.

He's bleeding heavily from a head wound, and he looks unsteady on his feet. But what he's holding . . . Naz looks at the gun in his hand, and her heart does a series of ragged little double-beats.

More sirens. *Louder. Closer.* She can hear Gary behind her, radioing updates as Mel begins to scream. Ross looks as though he's having trouble remembering what day it is, but if he fires at this range—

'Police!' Naz steps in front of Mel, blocking Ross's sightline. 'Put the gun down. Come on, Eddie, don't be daft.'

Maintaining eye contact. Fighting to kill the tremble in her voice. Tuning out the sirens, tuning out Gary's shouts and Mel's screams. Tuning out everything but the man standing in front of her.

'Dangerous driving, possession of a firearm with intent to endanger.' Naz shakes her head. 'I won't lie to you, Eddie, that's not good. And Armed Response are coming for your arse – if I were you, I'd put the gun down now. If not—'

A smile. Or maybe a grimace of pain, she can't tell. He takes a step towards her. Stops. Stumbles, but manages to right himself. Raises the gun . . . and buckles at the knees, pitching forward onto the asphalt as the noise of the approaching sirens grows to fill the world.

★

'Eddie's got concussion,' Fergie tells Mahler when he arrives at the hospital. 'Double vision, throwing up, the lot. Couldn't happen to a nicer chap, eh?'

'And the occupants of the other vehicles?'

Fergie's face clouds over. 'Whiplash and bruising for the couple in the Clio. But the young lassie in the Fiat's still unconscious, and her friend has multiple fractures.' He shakes his head. 'Man, what a mess. Is the Chief—'

'Heading back up the A9 the minute his meeting finishes.' Giving Mahler less than three hours to find out what the hell's happened, get a report together for Hunt and give Media Liaison a statement to feed the gathering of journos he'd spotted on the way over. 'If Nazreen's okay, I need to talk to her right away.'

'Through here.' Fergie takes him down a corridor to A&E. 'She's a bit shaken up, but . . .' He darts a glance at Mahler. 'You're going to kick her arse? After what she did?'

'Two people are seriously injured, and she almost got herself killed – damn right I'm going to kick her arse. What?'

'If she hadn't stopped Eddie Ross, Mel Paterson would be dead.' Fergie shows his ID at reception, waits while Mahler does the same. 'You'd have done the same, boss.'

'Not an argument the Chief is going to buy. And Gary's not off the hook either. What—'

'Which one of you is in charge?' A harried-looking nurse sticks his head out of a cubicle, gives them an irritated look. 'If you're done shouting the odds, there's someone here wanting a word with you.'

'That would be me.'

Mahler pushes back the curtain, enters the cubicle with Fergie following. He's expecting to see Naz, but the woman sitting wrapped in a blanket, her hands gripping it tightly closed, is Mel Paterson.

Her jaw is swollen on one side, her cheekbone is badly bruised, but in place of the shock he'd expected to see, there's a steady burn of anger in her eyes. The kind of anger that tells of scores to settle.

She looks him up and down, frowns. 'You the big cheese? The real high heid yin, I mean?'

'I'm DCI Mahler. And my boss is . . . elsewhere right now, so I'm the biggest cheese available. What can I do for you, Mel?'

Her mouth twists in a bitter smile. She reaches for the water glass beside her, takes a careful sip. Winces. 'Bastard hit me,' she tells Mahler. 'My fault for letting my guard down, I suppose, but I thought Eddie was one of the good guys. Thought we were . . . well, just goes to show, eh?'

'Where was he taking you?'

'He said he had a job for me. I wasn't keen at first, but the money was too good to pass up.'

'You worked for him?'

A shrug. 'He put work my way sometimes. There were parties me and some other girls would go to, the kind you need a special invitation for. And sometimes there were wee . . . errands his bosses needed running. That's what I thought today was about. Until I saw the gun.'

She takes another sip of water, puts the glass down with an unsteady hand. 'I mean, what the fuck was that about, man? A bloody *gun*!'

'Aye, well, if you hang around with folk like Eddie Ross . . .' Fergie lets the sentence hang. 'You were lucky today, Mel. Lucky our guys were nearby.'

'He'll be charged, though, right? He won't get bail or anything?'

'Bail's unlikely,' Mahler tells her. 'But the people who gave Ross his orders are still out there, aren't they? And to them, you're just a loose end they need to tidy up.'

He leans forward. 'How do you feel about that, Mel? How do you feel about being an inconvenience someone wants to make go away?'

'Trying to scare me now?' Her mouth twists in a bitter smile. 'Trust me, I'm way ahead of you – why do you think I wanted to see you? I just . . . I need to know I'll be safe. I need you to promise they won't find me.'

'Help us, and I'll do everything I can. I promise.'

Silence. Then she swallows, nods. 'Fine. It . . . it's not much, okay? But get me somewhere safe, then I'll tell you what I know. About Eddie. About his bosses. And a pal of his called Frankie Mason.'

39

Divisional HQ
Inverness

Perhaps it's the prospect of his forthcoming autumn break, or perhaps the afterglow from the First Minister's reception hasn't completely faded. But although Chae Hunt winces at the budget implications of moving Mel Paterson to a secure location, he signs off on it more easily than Mahler had anticipated after reading through her initial statements.

There's also better news from the hospital. Both occupants of the Fiat are recovering well, and Eddie Ross's concussion turns out to be less serious than first thought, meaning he should soon be fit for interview. Mel's still being cagey about the details of her association with Ross, but she's given Mahler a list of names to look at in the meantime. They include local businessmen and a couple of well-heeled second-home owners, but not, as he points out in an update email to Harkness, a certain Carl 'Cazza' MacKay.

At his daily briefing with Fergie and Andy Black, Mahler tasks Andy with following up on the names.

'Softly-softly at the moment, Andy,' Mahler warns. 'I think Mel's got a lot more to tell us, but let's not ruffle too many feathers yet. When we get to question Ross, I want him to think we're holding all the cards. Same with his flat when the search warrant comes in – thorough but low key. Leave the big boots at home for now, okay?'

'You sure about this, boss?' Fergie asks once Black's left. 'Softly-softly isn't really Andy's thing. Whoever Eddie was working for, they know all about what's happened by now. If we start nosing about in the wrong places—'

'It could blow up in our faces. Agreed. Which is why we start poking around the edges first – I want whoever was running Eddie to see us going after what looks like local small fry. They'll smell a rat if we don't do anything, but I want them to think that's all he's given us – and I certainly *don't* want them taking a closer interest in Mel's whereabouts.'

Fergie nods. 'Aye, true enough. But once we start turning over Eddie's place—'

'Things could get interesting. Yes. Which is why we need Mel to open up to us – who's with her now, Donna? Get Naz to take over the next shift. Mel knows her, and Naz has a knack of drawing people out.'

'And she's keen to get back in your good books after yesterday's arse-kicking. Okay, I'll get it sorted.'

'Yesterday's . . .?' Mahler shakes his head. 'That wouldn't even have counted as a mild talking-to from June Wallace, and you know it.'

'Ach, I know. But the lassie thinks a lot of you, and . . .' Fergie shrugs. 'You know she's talking about trying for a promotion board? Maybe a wee word of encouragement wouldn't go amiss. If you think she's got a chance, like.'

'Already? Bloody hell.' Mahler's got no doubts about Naz's competence, but with no prospect of a sergeant's vacancy on the MIT for the foreseeable future, it's hard to imagine her staying with the team if she's successful. Still, he can't fault her ambition.

'I think we both know she'd walk it,' he tells Fergie. 'Tell her to go for it with my blessing. I'll talk to her as soon as I get a chance.'

'Fair enough. I'll tell Naz about Mel, then – and tell her to get practising those test papers, eh?'

He nods, gets up to go. Frowns at the email window Mahler's left open on his tablet.

'You getting those phishing emails now, boss? Gary had one on his phone the other day.'

Mahler glances at the screen. Sighs. 'I had one yesterday, too. No idea how they're getting through the firewall.'

He touches the screen, ready to send it to deleted email hell. And three words leap out at him. Three words he's willing to bet were in the previous email, the one he'd dumped without a second thought.

Three words that might offer vital clues to finding Alex Fleming's murderer.

40

'You thought it was spam.'

Disbelief warring with a near-arctic chill in Anna's voice when she answers Mahler's call. 'An email from someone I spoke to on your behalf – asked them to help you out as a favour to me – and you didn't even look at it. Christ, Lukas, I even left you a message about it! Didn't you even think to check the source?'

'Clearly not. I'm sorry.' He's already apologised once, but he suspects it might be a good idea to do it again. Particularly as he'd only listened to her voicemail ten minutes before calling her.

'Then let me help you out. The email's from my colleague, Gudrun. Gudrun Jónassdóttir, from the Institute for Northern Studies in Kirkwall? She's visiting from Reykjavik University, researching symbol and gender in Norse mythology – and she's very knowledgeable about early runic scripts, which is why I asked her to take a look at the images you sent me.'

Mahler opens the email, rereads the scant couple of sentences. 'She said they were intriguing and unusual. And left a mobile number, which she doesn't seem to answer.'

'She was up to her ears in conference preparation! And she still took time out of her busy schedule to help you out. When you didn't get back to her, she obviously assumed you were no longer interested.'

'I was. I am – I need to talk to her. Urgently.'

A sigh at the other end. 'And this is about the Orkney murder you're working on? The ex-policeman?'

'He wasn't just an ex-policeman. He was my first boss when I joined the Met. And a friend, I suppose.'

'You suppose.' A muttered something on the end of that, something that sounded like a curse. 'Was he a good friend?'

Alex, who'd watched out for him since his first day at Charing Cross nick. Who'd seen something in the young misfit he'd been, and given him the chance to carve out a place in the Met's best CID team.

'Yes.' Mahler swallows, pushes away the image of the bloated grey thing he'd seen lashed to the jetty at Sandisquoy. 'Yes, he was a good friend.'

Silence. A long silence, during which he feels the temperature between them drop to levels he suspects aren't scientifically measurable.

'Anna—'

'So one of your good friends was brutally murdered, and you didn't feel the need to tell me. No, of course you didn't – not like we're, I don't know, close or anything, is it? Bloody hell, Lukas!'

'I'm sorry.' The lash of anger in her voice is no more than he deserves. 'I'm not . . . not very good at close.'

'No, I'm starting to realise that.'

'Again, I'm sorry. Truly. Look, there have been developments – significant developments – in the enquiry, and I really need to talk to your colleague. But her phone goes to voicemail and she's got an out-of-office on her work emails.'

'That would be because she's travelling. Maybe if you hadn't waited three days to try and contact her . . .' Another sigh.

'Fine. Gudrun's staying at mine tonight before she flies to Cologne. I'm picking her up at the airport in an hour – if you want to talk to her, we can grab a coffee there.'

Mahler had expected to get to Dalcross before Anna, but he'd forgotten she was working in Inverness for a couple of days. By the time he gets to the airport, Anna's texted him to say she's in the café with her colleague.

Gudrun Jónasdóttir is a short, cheerful-looking woman with electric blue hair and a crackle of restless energy around her. She brushes off Mahler's apologies over the email misunderstanding with a shout of laughter.

'It's the first time I was accused of sending porn, for sure! My bad for being so cryptic in my response to you. But I was in a rush, and . . .' she shrugs. 'These writings were found on Orkney, you say?'

'A place called Sandisquoy, yes. So it *is* some form of runic writing, then? Have you seen this sort of thing before?'

Gudrun rips open the pack of tablet she's bought, drops a chunk into her coffee and stirs it round. 'Love this stuff. Terrible for me, but I tried it last year and now I'm addicted.'

She takes a sip of coffee, gives a small, satisfied sigh. Smiles at Mahler. 'Aah, that's so good. Yes, I have seen . . . not these, but something similar. My brother Einar was working at University College, Dublin – the School of Archaeology – and there were some remains found during a development of a new shopping centre.'

'Viking?'

Gudrun nods. 'Three warriors. All three had hand-axes – but only one was male. The other two carried bows. And pouches of small, carved stones inscribed with runic derivations like these.'

She rummages in her travel bag, pulls out an iPad and opens

up a folder with the images Mahler sent her, set side by side with what are clearly stills from an archaeological dig. Even to his untrained eye, the similarities are obvious.

'I say derivations because these writings are of a special sort,' Gudrun explains. 'The younger Futhark, the runic script of the Vikings, consisted of sixteen characters.'

She picks up a fresh coffee stirrer, uses it to tap the Sandisquoy images. 'But these three – these are something quite different. They're composites, formed by combining individual runes together to produce a new meaning.'

'They're bind-runes? Fascinating.' Anna leans forward for a closer look. 'Einar talked about their use at the Reykjavik conference last year, didn't he?'

'So the *Brennivin* drinking session afterwards didn't burn out all your brain cells – I thought your hangover wasn't so bad. Einar was worried, though.' She gives Mahler a grin. 'My brother, he was very protective of Anna.'

A sudden flush on Anna's cheeks. Connected, apparently, to the mention of Gudrun's brother and a conference she had attended with him. Mahler files the Icelander's name away – for research purposes, he tells himself – and turns to Gudrun.

'These bind-runes were . . . what, a new type of alphabet?'

'Not exactly.' She glances at Anna. 'You probably know as much about this as I do, *vinkona*. You read Anneliese's paper on the *Galdrar* of Jón Guðmundsson, didn't you?'

'I didn't know he used bind-runes, though.' Anna turns to Mahler. 'Guðmundsson was an Icelandic poet and alleged sorcerer. According to some theories, bind-runes could be used to predict the future. Or in the practice of *galdrar* – casting of spells.'

'Spells. As in witchcraft?'

The word drying on his tongue. Pointing him towards something dark. Something unthinkable. *The summer of 2008. A neat suburban garden in North London. Planted with a vision of hell.*

'Witchcraft would be one use, certainly.' She gives him an odd look. 'My email was—'

She glances at her phone as the display lights up. And mutters what can only be a selection of Icelandic swear words. 'Sorry, I need to take this.'

She mouths a name at Anna, moves off towards the café entrance.

'Her daughter,' Anna explains. 'Freyja's applied to study at Glasgow, and . . .' She glances at him, abandons the rest of her sentence. 'Lukas, are you okay?'

He swallows, nods. 'I hadn't expected . . . Gudrun's email said the bones may have been tools?'

'She meant tools of the practitioner's trade, I think – like a clairvoyant's crystal ball. Or tarot cards.'

Tarot cards. A ritual knife. And a pentagram, scratched into scorched and blackened grass. Is that where this is leading, to one of the worst murder cases he's ever worked on? The case that had almost broken Alex?

'Sorry.' Gudrun's smiling as she comes back over and slides into her seat. 'Freyja has been ill, and worry is not good for her. But she has an acceptance! We can all relax at last.' She glances at Anna. 'And you have had a talk now too?'

'I was telling Lukas how the bones would probably have been used.'

'Ah.' An odd look of disappointment on her face. 'Ah, well. So, the seal bones . . . On Orkney, that would be a very powerful symbol indeed, given the selkie myths. It's where the islands take their name from, of course – *Orkneyjar* means "seal island" in old Norwegian.'

'Selkies?' Mahler rakes his memory for the precise definition. 'Like mermaids, right? Seals in the water, people on land.'

'Exactly,' Anna tells him. 'According to legend, they

shape-shifted by shedding their sealskins. The way to capture a selkie wife was to steal her skin and hide it. If she ever found it again, she'd transform back into a seal and gain her freedom – a pretty convenient explanation for missing spouses, I've always thought. "She turned into a seal and swam away". Yeah, right.'

Gudrun taps one of the images again.

'This one . . . this is fascinating, actually. It's a little more worn than the others, but I think it's a combination of *Thurisaz*, representing danger, and *Tiwaz*, standing for victory. Though of course, there's speculation over the validity—'

'And this?' Mahler points to another of the carved symbols. 'It seems to recur a number of times. What does it represent?'

'Interesting that you should see that one so clearly. But yes, you're right.' Gudrun looks at the image, and back at him. 'It stands for *wyrd*, or fate, you see. Destiny working itself out, no matter how we try to run from it.'

41

Mahler watches the team file into the MIT room, sees a range of expressions on their faces as they take their seats for the briefing: weariness, confusion, unease. Given what he's set out on the whiteboards, all three are understandable.

He runs an eye over the boards, revises a date. And turns back to face the room.

'To the media, they were the Witchfinder Killings,' he tells them. 'Alex Fleming was the SIO, and he hated the term. But before long, we were all using it. Even Alex.'

He adds the final image, watches the shiver of recognition ripple through his team.

'Three women murdered in the London area in the summer of 2008. Three women, all either strangled and then burned or drowned. In each case, an item associated with some form of occult practice was found on their bodies, or placed near to it — tarot cards for Liz Clarke. A ritual knife, called an *athame*, for Alison Balfour. And Ruth Osborne—'

'A pentagram.' Nazreen flushes as everyone turns to look at her. 'Burned into the grass next to where they found her body. I remember seeing it on *Crimewatch*.'

Pete stares at her. 'Bloody hell, Naz. What were you doing

watching something like that back then? You must have been about ten.'

'I was thirteen, if you must know. And my whole family watched it because Alison Balfour lived three doors down from my auntie and went to the same school as her daughter.' Nazreen swallows, looks at Mahler. 'I think I met her once, actually. She was nice to us kids, I remember. Kind.'

Mahler nods. 'The door-to-doors for all three women all said the same thing.'

Not always to be taken at face value, of course. But the Witchfinder's victims had been genuinely well liked by everyone they'd encountered, making their horrific murders even more disturbing.

'He was never caught, was he?' Gary asks. 'The Witchfinder guy?'

Mahler shakes his head. 'No one wanted to use the phrase "serial killer", but it's what everyone was thinking. But there were no leads, no reliable forensics – and after Ruth Osborne, the killings simply stopped.'

'This was back in 2008, though.' A creak of leather jacket as Andy leans back in his seat. 'You surely don't think the same guy's running around Orkney bumping off ex-cops, eight years later?'

'Unlikely, but we can't dismiss it out of hand.' Mahler draws three connecting lines between the images on the whiteboard. 'Links and similarities. One, Alex was SIO in charge of the Witchfinder enquiry. Two, the items found with Alex and the Witchfinder bodies share a common theme. Three, Matt Shaw-cross, Fleming's DS at the time. Fergie, where are we with locating his off-duties for the week of Alex's murder?'

'Chased it again this morning, but there's some sort of stomach bug going around the admin staff down there so they're up to their eyeballs,' Fergie tells him. 'And this annual leave

Shawcross is on turns out to be some sort of adventure thing in the middle of Wales, with zero phone reception and no means of getting in touch.'

Some shuffling in seats at that; Mahler looks round at the team, sees them struggling with the thought no one wants to articulate. In the end, it's Pete who speaks up first.

'Shawcross would have been looked into at the time, though, wouldn't he? I mean, his DNA would have been checked and eliminated. If, like, there was any hint—'

'No bloody forensics found, man. Pay attention.' Andy's eyes travel down the images on the board. 'And I'm guessing the off-duties weren't checked either, right?'

Mahler shakes his head. Never a line of enquiry they'd considered; and yes, with the benefit of hindsight, he knows exactly how that sounds.

'Witnesses?'

'None. All the door-to-door enquiries, appeals for information, all the hours spent viewing CCTV footage. None of it came to anything. Which left the team . . . not in a good place.'

Shattered. Dispirited. Alex Fleming walking around as though he had the weight of the world on his shoulders. Three families whose lives had been torn apart; ripped into pieces and scattered by a killer Alex's team never even came close to catching.

'What happened to the team?' Nazreen asks. 'After Ruth Osborne, I mean. When did you know—'

'That there wouldn't be another Witchfinder killing? We didn't, not for a long time. There had been weeks between Liz Clarke and Alison Balfour. Then Ruth Osborne was discovered, only two days after Alison. The same positioning of the body, same type of occult object left nearby. With one crucial difference.'

'She was pregnant, wasn't she?'

Mahler nods. 'Found by her husband, who'd been on a

business trip. She'd been unwell, so when he couldn't find her in the house, he was worried right away. He was phoning round her friends when he noticed the patio doors were slightly open. He went out into the garden, and he found her.'

A pentagram, scratched into the scorched and blackened earth. And at its centre . . .

'It was a big house, with a large, secluded garden. So the killer had plenty of time to set the scene. And get out of there afterwards.'

Silence. Not a disbelieving silence because they're all cops. But there are pictures, unwelcome ones, settling into their minds.

Fergie clears his throat. 'What about the girl in the cellar? If she's been there for nearly twenty years, how does she fit in to any of this?'

'Until we get her forensics back, your guess is as good as mine. Fergie, can you chase those? And it goes without saying, we need to trace whoever lived in that house back then – Pete and Naz, I'll pass that to you. Any MISPER reports look promising?'

'Not so far.' Pete gives his tablet a morose tap. 'I've allowed as broad an age range as I can, but even then, there just aren't that many. Plus, we don't even know if she was a local—'

'Not for sure, but it's highly likely. Think about it – temporary visitors have lives to get back to, jobs and families waiting for them. When that doesn't happen, people notice.'

Nazreen frowns. 'Maybe she was a seasonal worker in one of the hotels? Or a student?'

'Maybe. But again, why did no one miss her? Twenty years ago, travel to the islands wasn't as fast or easy as it is now, and the population would have been more static – someone out there knows who she is, knows what happened to her. We need to find them. As for the apparent Witchfinder connection to Alex

Fleming's death . . .' He shakes his head. 'Until we have more intel, we keep the occult angle out of the public domain – it's a weird case from start to finish, but let's not muddy the waters more than necessary.'

As the team files out, Fergie comes over. 'Am I still off to London on Monday, boss? It's just that we'll be a bit thin on the ground here, what with Gerrity and the new Orkney victim—'

Mahler shakes his head. 'Orkney's turning into a bigger can of worms than we thought, and you're needed here. I can liaise with Tony Armstrong and Cath McAvoy, but you'll have to handle Matt Shawcross's interview by videolink.'

Assuming Shawcross *is* back at work when he's supposed to be. Assuming the can of worms isn't going to get even bigger than it's looking at the moment.

'Aye, right enough,' Fergie agrees. 'So, this Witchfinder stuff. I get why we're not going public with it – but if it *is* the same guy, why's he switched his MO? And what's set him off again, after eight years? Most serial killers either escalate or give up, you know that.'

'Or they get banged up for something else. Have an enforced hiatus and then go back to work as soon as they're released. Taking out Alex could be some sort of signal from our killer that he's out and ready to start playing again.' Mahler isn't buying that, not really. But Fergie nods slowly.

'Could be. But maybe not the way you think.'

'Meaning?'

Fergie sighs. 'Your old boss managed a pretty good disappearing act after Witchfinder. But someone tracked him down, all the way to bloody Orkney – either they held a hell of a grudge for eight years or something changed.'

'About Witchfinder?'

Fergie nods. 'He found out something – remembered something, maybe – that made him a threat to the killer. But he doesn't want to get involved with us, not officially. Who would he talk to?'

'Matt.' Now Fergie's pointed it out, Mahler can't believe he'd overlooked something so obvious. 'Alex would have told Matt Shawcross.'

42

Sandisquoy
Two Weeks Before the End

He wakes a little after three, with the taste of blood and whisky in his mouth.

He turns his head, spits into the basin he keeps beside the couch up here. The bottle of Highland Park has rolled under the stool next to the canvas he's been working on, but it's not a problem. He sits up, pulls his rucksack towards him and takes out his trusty standby; it's a cheapo blend from Lidl and tastes like peaty drain-cleaner, but it'll do what he needs it to right now. He takes a slug, lies down again. Shudders as the burn arrives in his guts. And tries not to think about what might have awoken him.

Of course he's not afraid of the dark. Not afraid of the sounds he sometimes hears in the quiet hours of the night. Old houses make noises; they're made of noises, sometimes, joists and floorboards settling as the warmth of the day subsides. And this is an old house, the oldest he's ever lived in.

It had been a manse, according to the details on the website, built in the days when churches were like corner shops or Chinese takeaways, two or three to take your pick from everywhere you looked. Isolated, perched on the very last bit of habitable land before the shoreline begins, it was run-down enough for the guy to look embarrassed when showing him round, in spite of the guff he'd spouted about walled gardens and original features. But back then, run-down and isolated suited him just fine.

Yes, there had been a heaviness in the air, the kind of stale, damp-scented atmosphere that hangs around old houses if they haven't been lived in for a while. That's all it had felt like then; not enough to put him off, that's for sure. Why would it? He'd found the place by sheer dumb luck; turned on the TV out of boredom and caught the end of one of those 'Celeb has-been goes to find their roots' shows.

The programme had been rubbish, but the Orkney footage had blown his mind. And with the money from the sale of his London flat, it had been easy to find the kind of property he was looking for. Somewhere to live a new kind of life. Somewhere remote, sparsely populated. Sanctuary. *Sandisquoy had been all that, and more.*

In the beginning.

Hard to say when things began to change. Over the course of the winters he'd spent there, maybe; that first one had been like nothing he'd ever known. Six hours of bleak, unconvincing daylight. Rain battering against the windows, winds threatening to rip the van door out of his hands when he ventured into Kirkwall or Stromness for supplies. He'd never been much of a whisky drinker, though he'd always liked his booze. But by God, he'd started to get the taste for it that first winter.

At first, the painting had helped. He'd knocked down the cheap partition that divided the attic in two, cleared it out and whitewashed all the walls. Let the light in, started a couple of canvasses. Even thought about renovating one of the outbuildings, turning it into a gallery. New place, new life. Why not?

Then he'd found the room. And everything it held. Had it all been waiting for him, mute and patient in the long, long darkness? The last rational part of him insists it couldn't have happened like that. But he's not sure how much longer that part of him will survive in this house. Or what will happen once it's gone.

He shakes his head, reaches for the whisky again. There are some things you can't paint over, he understands that now. Some noises you can't make go away, no matter how loud you play your music through your headphones. Some things you can't un-see, even if there's no way – no way – what you've seen and heard, what you've half glimpsed crouching by the stairwell, can be real.

No, he's not afraid of the dark. Of course not.

Just what it might contain.

43

'Just say you'll come to Cologne, Anna. You know you want to.'

A clinking of glass and a muttered *Danke* as a waiter dips in and out of Gudrun's FaceTime image from the swish riverside hotel where the conference is being held. She holds her phone close to the iPad camera so Anna can see the list of flights she's called up.

'See, you could get here on Thursday – the plenary session will have wound up by three, and we can have the whole weekend with Heike and Ulla. They said they'd love to see you.'

'You've asked them already? Gudrun, honestly—'

'You need a break, Anna.' Gudrun's smile fades to a look of concern. 'You're too young to look so tired, *vinkona*. And maybe if you come over this weekend, we will talk some more about this crazy thing you're going to do.'

So that's what this is about: the letter Jamie Gordon's father had handed her, with the visiting order made out in her name. 'I haven't made up my mind—'

'So we will definitely talk about it. What did Lukas say?' When Anna doesn't answer, Gudrun sighs. 'You didn't tell him because he would agree with me, yes? Listen, this Jamie

Gordon, this . . . this *Andskotans ógeðið* who murdered your sister? You owe this piece of shit nothing.'

'I wouldn't be doing it for him.'

'Then why? Ach!' Gudrun reaches for her replenished wine glass, holds it up to the camera. '*Skàl*. We'll talk about this again, I'm sure. So, this strange story of *galdrar* runes your Lukas brings me – I have spoken to Einar, you know. He was very interested to see the pictures.'

'Does he think they're genuine?' Anna leans forward. 'Maybe if the murdered man had found an undiscovered cache of Viking artefacts—'

'It could be a thriller story, you think? Killed for Viking treasure?' Gudrun shakes her head, smiling. 'They're treasure, certainly, but only to historians. And maybe, if they were passed from mother to daughter . . . but this is your area of study, not mine, *vinkona*. Why not look into the stories of these Orkney women, see what you can find?'

She means the infamous Orkney witch trials. Anna frowns. 'I'm shifting to a more European focus for next year's modules,' she tells Gudrun. 'Will you thank Einar for me, please? I'll pass his thoughts on to Lukas. But I think that's probably where my input ends.'

Gudrun gives her a doubtful look. 'If you say so. Well, enough of that – so, are you coming this weekend? Come on, you know I'll keep nagging until you give in.'

She drains half of her wine, puts the glass down and holds up the iPad so Anna can see the view from where she's sitting. 'Beautiful, isn't it? I love the Rhine. And that's the cathedral, over there . . . I could live here, you know,' she tells Anna. 'There would be a job if I wanted it, I think.'

Anna stares at her. 'You said you were settled in Orkney. And now Freyja's applied to Glasgow Uni—'

'She's applied here too. And after what happened in

September, I think this might be a better place to be.'

It takes Anna a moment to work out what she means. 'You mean, because of Brexit? You're Icelandic, though. Surely you aren't worried?'

Gudrun picks up her glass, twists it in her hands before replying. 'Worried? No. But sad. Very sad. Because I think soon every foreigner will be looked at a little differently – oh, maybe not right away. But it's going to change, Anna. The question is how long it's going to take.'

She drains the rest of her wine, puts the glass down. 'You could move on too, you know. If things got really bad.'

Anna shakes her head. 'Things will settle, after a while. And I couldn't leave again so soon.'

'Your mother? Or your beautiful Lukas?'

'Lukas isn't . . .' She shrugs, abandons the rest of that sentence. Mainly because she has no idea how she and Lukas Mahler currently fit together. 'I like being home, and I like my work. For now. But whatever I decide to do in the future, Lukas's life is here.'

'Maybe. Who knows where his *wyrd* will take him?' Gudrun glances at her phone, sighs. 'Now I have an informal session to attend, which will go on too long and will put everyone to sleep. Please come, Anna. The break will be a good thing for you, yes? If not to Cologne, at least visit me in Orkney when I get back.'

Anna promises to think about it, holds her smile until Gudrun's call disconnects.

She opens her desk drawer, takes out the letter from Jamie Gordon. As soon as his father had gone, she'd chucked it in the bin unopened. Fished it out again. Shoved it in the drawer, right at the back, and left it there for days. When she'd finally steeled herself to open it, the few scrawled lines had asked her – *pleaded* with her – to visit 'so we can really talk about what happened'.

No apology, no acknowledgement of the thing he'd done, the devastation he'd wrought on her family. She'd grabbed the letter and the visiting order, marched over to the shredder . . . and stopped, her finger hovering over the button.

The thought of coming face to face with Jamie Gordon again makes her want to vomit; she'd fought off Morven's murderer when he'd tried to kill her too, but those terrifying moments on the cliffs at Badbea still have the power to wake her, sweat-drenched and shaking, from her nightmares. Two years ago, and the memories are just as vivid; and the worst of them all, the one that slams into her when she's least expecting it, is the knowledge of her awful, shaming terror on the day she'd faced her own death.

She'd never seen herself as a fearful person, that's what hit her hardest; fight or flight, she'd always assumed she'd be someone who stood her ground, no matter what. And in the end, that's what she'd done. But she wonders if that day had damaged her, somehow; used up all of her courage in the space of a few hours. Because here she is, on the verge of throwing up at the very thought of coming face to face with Jamie Gordon again.

And yet . . . and yet. This could be her only chance to find out what's going on inside his head. Why is he going ahead with this appeal? He's got to believe he can win. But why? How?

She has to find out what's behind it all. *Has to.* Because if she closes her eyes to this, if she buries her head in the sand and he somehow manages to get his sentence reduced, how will she be able to live with herself then?

Gordon had put her family through hell two years ago. Whatever it takes, she can't let him do it a second time.

44

'Can't fucking believe this, mate. What were you thinking, Lukas?'

The videolink technology is having an off day, and Matt Shawcross's voice is weirdly distorted. But there's no mistaking the disbelief on his face as he glares up at Mahler through the camera. His boss leans across to say something, but Shawcross shakes his head.

'I know it's a bloody informal – didn't stop him asking for my bloody shift records, did it? What the hell's going on in your head, man?'

Mahler holds up a hand. 'Matt, this isn't something I should be involved in.' He pushes his chair back, starts to get up. 'Iain here is my DI, and he's leading on the investigation—'

'No way. This is your gig, mate.' Shawcross folds his arms, leans back. 'Go on, then, let's hear it. Where's this pile of crap come from?'

'Fine.' Mahler sits down again. Nods at Fergie, who passes him a folder. 'Let's start with your shift records, shall we? Which show three days' annual leave from the 16th to the 18th – the period immediately prior to the discovery of Alex's body.'

'For my niece's wedding. In the bloody Lake District. You

want to see the photos? Got them on my phone somewhere.' He glares at his boss. 'Even showed you a couple – don't you remember?'

Shawcross reaches for his phone, but Mahler holds his hand up. 'We've seen the photos, Matt. We know you were at the wedding. It was on the morning of the 16th, and you drove up on the 15th.'

'Because I had an early that day, yes. So?'

'So your next shift wasn't until the 20th, and you were only booked into the hotel for two nights, the 15th and 16th. Where were you for the rest of the time? Why did you book those extra days off?'

Shawcross shrugs. 'Had myself a bit of a holiday, didn't I? Had my camping gear in the back, so went up into the hills, grabbed a bit of peace and quiet. It's what I do when I need a break.'

'By yourself?'

'Bloody hard to get peace and quiet otherwise. And no, I don't have anyone who can vouch for me.' He glares at Mahler. 'Didn't know I'd need someone, did I?'

Lying. Matt's too good a copper to let the usual 'tells' give him away; there are no nervous swallows, no sideways glances towards the exit and away from his interrogators. But there's something in the set of his shoulders, the tension around his jawline . . . Mahler glances at Fergie, who picks up his cue.

'Wee bit of a problem, that. No way to know if you're being straight with us, is there? We *do* know you're telling porkies about something, though. We know you lied about your last contact with Alex Fleming.'

'I didn't—'

'You told Bea Colgan he'd moved to Orkney. But you told my boss here you hadn't heard from Fleming in years.'

'Oh, Christ.' Shawcross passes a hand over his forehead. 'Jack

201

Gillan's funeral, wasn't it? It slipped my mind, I swear. And I said he'd *talked* about it. Alex talked about a lot of things when he'd had a drink.'

Some undercurrent there. Some old, half-buried bitterness. Fergie leans forward. 'Occupational hazard in the job, isn't it? The booze, I mean. That why you fell out with him?'

'I didn't . . .' Shawcross sighs, nods. 'Okay, yeah. We fell out – it happens, doesn't it? He went on the sick, I got made up to DI, moved on. After that, we lost touch. Just like I said.'

'What was it about?'

'Something and nothing, probably. How most things start, isn't it?'

And there it is: so quick, Mahler almost misses the way Shawcross's eyes flicker towards the meeting room door. It only lasts for a moment, but it's all Mahler needs.

'We don't have time for this.' He holds up his hand as Shawcross starts to say something. 'Alex's killer knew who he was. They knew he'd worked on Witchfinder. They knew every single thing about it, right down to the placing of the ritual objects. How did they know all that?'

'It was all over the media, that's how. You know that.'

'Not all of it.' Mahler opens the folder, turns to a bookmarked page. 'Whoever killed Alex dressed the scene, Matt – they stuffed his pockets with some occult junk, got him high and then they left him there to rot. Do you think that was a good way to die? Because I'm damn sure I don't.'

He flips the folder round, holds it up to the screen before Shawcross can look away. 'This is what was left of Alex Fleming by the time I got there. Want to see more?' He turns a page. 'How about this one? Or this?'

'No.' Shawcross jerks away from the screen. 'I don't—'

'Don't want them in your head? Fine. Stop bloody lying to me. Or I'll show you every single—'

'You threw up, didn't you?' Anger in Shawcross's face as he turns back to look at Mahler. 'That day at Ruth Osborne's, you took one look at what we found and emptied your guts all over the roses. And you've got the nerve, the bloody *nerve* to show me Alex looking like . . . like that.'

'You want an apology? Earn it. Start telling us the truth, Matt. Or this is going to get very formal, very quickly.'

Silence. Getting heavier as the seconds tick by. Then Shawcross nods abruptly. Sighs.

'Witchfinder broke him.' He scrubs his hand over his eyes. 'That's the bloody truth of it, Lukas. Then Billy Spencer got killed in that bloody car crash, and everything seemed to be going even more tits up. And Alex was getting sloppy. Making mistakes. Drinking more than usual. But he was the boss, you know? One of the best. So I looked out for him, kept an eye on things. Too much, maybe.'

'What happened?'

'There was a sister. Ruth Osborne's, I think, or maybe it was one of the others, I can't remember now.' Shawcross tells him. 'Young. Pretty. Nervous. She and Alex . . . I don't know how far it went, but I saw them once, and . . .' He shakes his head. 'We had words, and he put a stop to it. But that was when I knew it was time for me to move on. Because I found out later, she wasn't the first.'

'Alex would never have done that.'

The words are out before Mahler can stop them. Bloody unprofessional. Fergie shoots him a look of disbelief and starts to say something, but Shawcross gives a cynical bark of laughter.

'Forgot how much you hero-worshipped him, back in the day. Thought the sun bloody shone out of him, didn't you?'

'And you didn't?'

A sudden weariness on Shawcross's face. 'Maybe. He was the boss, wasn't he? And when he was on form . . . All I'm saying is, he wasn't a bloody saint. And when the pressure started getting to him, he made some bad decisions.'

'You could have talked to someone about it. Got him some help.'

'Yeah, I could have. If I wanted to get known as the guy who grassed on Alex Fleming.' Shawcross runs a hand across his forehead. 'Anyway, he carried on in the job for a while, but everyone knew he couldn't hack it. I heard he'd retired, and I thought it was for the best. Then he got back in touch.' He clears his throat. 'He was talking about Orkney. A whole new start, putting everything behind him. Including Witchfinder.'

'By using Billy Spencer's name? Why would he do that, Matt? Use a dead man's name?'

'He didn't tell me that. But he and Billy looked a lot alike, didn't they? So if he needed new ID . . .' Shawcross shrugs. 'All I know is, he sounded better when he told me about Orkney, more like the old Alex. But the next time we spoke, he'd changed.'

'When did you last speak to him?'

'I rang to let him know about Jack Gillan's funeral,' Shawcross tells him. 'Had the right to know about it, hadn't he? But he was . . . different. *Strange* different. Talked about seeing things down on the shore, things that didn't look right. Even said he heard things, sometimes. In his house.'

'What sort of things?'

'Christ, I don't know – truth is, he sounded like he was coming apart and I knew I couldn't hack it, not again. So I told him to get out more and cut out the booze. And then I . . . I cut all contact. Changed my number, blocked his calls, the works.' He gives Mahler a despairing look. 'Maybe if I hadn't—'

'Not your fault,' Fergie cuts in. 'What happened to Fleming wasn't down to you. Making us spend time on this when we could have been doing other things? *That's* your fault. *That's* down to you, Matt. So if there's anything you can tell us now, anything at all—'

'Why do you think I went climbing at the weekend? When I heard about Alex, I needed to get away from everything. Then I heard that news report about the occult stuff – and I was back there, Lukas. Back in that bloody garden in Finchley. Back watching Alex fall to pieces because of it.'

He scrubs at his eyes, looks right at Mahler. 'You want to know why I lied? The truth? Because I couldn't hack letting all that shit inside my head again.'

Silence after the call ends. Mahler pushes his chair back, swears in what Fergie's pretty sure is a mix of at least two languages, and hits the button on the posh coffee machine he inherited from June Wallace with enough force to make it squeak in electronic alarm.

'Could still be Shawcross, boss.' Fergie rubs the tightness at the back of his neck, loosens his tie. 'If he drove up, went on the ferry as a foot passenger—'

'Check it out, Fergie. Check it all out, every single detail – starting with this sister Alex's supposed to have been involved with.'

Denial stamped across the tight lines of Mahler's face. Denial, and disgust, mixed with a flicker of something dark and bleak. Too close to this, Fergie tells himself. *Didn't I tell you, boss? We haven't got time for this.*

He starts to say so, but Mahler holds up his hand. 'I know. I was out of line in there – out of line and unprofessional. It won't happen again.'

'Aye, well. It can't, boss, that's the thing.' *Christ, but this is awkward.* 'Look, screw-ups can happen when the pressure starts to pile on – you've got enough high-profile investigations under your belt to know that. It's knowing when you're doing it that counts.'

Silence. Then the boss gives a weary nod. 'Noted, Fergie. Noted. Anything else leap out at you?'

'Shawcross thinks Fleming was losing it,' Fergie points out. 'He thinks he's the only one Fleming kept in touch with, but we don't *know* that, do we? What if there was someone else, someone who couldn't risk Fleming going mental in case some stuff came out—'

He shuts his mouth about thirty seconds too late as the coffee machine beeps and the boss looks at him. And carries on looking until Fergie feels his face turn from faint flush to shoot-me-now.

'Boss, I didn't mean . . . I know your mam—'

Mahler shuts off the machine, holds up his hand. 'Understood. But to use your phrase, if Fleming was going "mental" and needed to be silenced, why not just knock him over the head and into the water? Why all the Witchfinder hints?'

'Window-dressing? Chucking all the occult stuff around's a good way to get us chasing our tails, isn't it? What if Fleming found the girl in the cellar and started making his own enquiries?'

Mahler frowns. 'Alex was ex-Job, he'd have gone straight to Tony Armstrong. Made it official.'

Fergie looks at Mahler's grey, exhausted face. Wonders if he should say it. And goes for it anyway.

'The man you knew back then? Aye, maybe. The man who drank himself out of the Met and took a dead man's name? Seems to me, we don't know anything about that man, boss. Not a damn thing.'

45

Fergie heads back to the MIT room by way of the canteen. It's on the ground floor, so the extra steps will get him a wee bit closer to the magical 10,000 daily target his blasted fitness band keeps nagging him about. Not that he's ever hit the target, but if he can make it halfway there for once, maybe Zofia will ease up on the little motivational videos she keeps sending him.

She worries about him, he gets that. And most of him is grateful there's someone in his life who cares enough to try to keep him on the straight and narrow, health-wise. But watching clips of former fat bastards showing off their London Marathon medals with smug grins on their faces, or laughing at the massive trousers they used to wear is not the inspiration Zo thinks it is.

Anyway, after an interview like the one he's just done with Matt Shawcross, his brain needs a wee fix of carbs and cholesterol to get it working again. And as far as Fergie's concerned, a morning roll with Lorne sausage and coffee fits the bill nicely.

He gets his order, makes his way to his usual table in the corner. And tries to work out why this enquiry's got him so rattled.

He's been a cop for a long time, and one rule he learned early on was never to let the job come home with him; if you don't leave the darkness at work, if you give it space inside your head during your down time, then pretty soon you'll find it's made itself a home there. So why is he finding it so hard to keep this bloody Sandisquoy thing in a box?

Maybe it's the sheer brutality of Alex Fleming's death he can't get his head round; a man broken so badly by the job and the booze, he'd turned his back on everything he'd known to try to make a new start. Maybe it's the shock of seeing Mahler struggling for the first time, trying to run two complicated enquiries while trying to play down his grief over his friend; because he *is* struggling, no question there. Fergie's seen the boss stretch the limits of his liaison and oversight role so far it's a miracle Chae Hunt hasn't pulled him back in line yet. And with the discovery of the latest remains at Sandisquoy, the damn enquiry's widening all the time.

Fleming had no links with Orkney, at least none Naz and Pete have been able to discover, and the estate agent who'd sold the house said Fleming's only viewing had lasted all of fifteen minutes. Why? Had he been so desperate to leave his old life behind he didn't care what he bought? Or is there something in his past that connects him to the house, something they haven't been able to discover because they've been looking in the wrong places?

The girl in the cellar.

God knows, that's not a thought Fergie wants to have about an ex-cop. But now that it's there, it's shouting to be heard; Fleming had let the darkness in, no doubt about that. The question is, how much of it had he brought with him – and how much had been waiting there to welcome him home?

Fergie taps out a laborious note on his phone, a reminder to revisit everything they've gathered on Fleming. He finishes the last of his roll, picks up his mobile again to stuff it in his pocket. And sees Naz's number flash up on the screen.

'Fergie, is the boss still around?'

The phone signal out at the safe house is notoriously patchy, and she's breaking up a little, but there's no mistaking the excitement in her voice. 'Mel's been opening up to me, and she's ready to talk to us – according to her, the people Eddie worked for do a regular drugs run every month, operating from a farm outbuilding out in the sticks. Regular, as in regular like clockwork, Fergie. First Friday of every month. And today's—'

'Friday the third.' Fergie pushes back his chair, gets to his feet. 'Keep talking.'

'Frankie Mason goes up there to drop off the goods. Then Eddie or one of the other couriers pick up the packages and distribute them to their outlets round the city.'

'Aye, we guessed that's how it would work. But unless Mel knows where it is—'

'She does! She's pretty sure, anyway – Eddie was taking her and another girl to, er, entertain at a weekend do at some posh house party. He was in a tearing hurry and desperate not to be late – but then he stopped the car in the middle of nowhere. He blindfolded both girls, told them not to move a muscle, but Mel sneaked a look. She saw him go into this barn, and reappear with a couple of packages, so . . . Fergie, are you *running*? I'm not sure you should be doing that. I can hear wheezing—'

'I am *not* wheezing.' He's a wee bit out of breath as he pelts up the stairs, true enough, but this is something the boss needs to hear right away. 'Thing is, Eddie's not told us a bloody thing so far. But these folk don't know that – if they'd heard Eddie's been lifted, they'd have stripped the place bare and moved on—'

'They won't, though. Because Mel says Eddie got blind drunk one night and started boasting about how they're a sort of brotherhood. He talked about Frankie Mason like he was family, like he was proud that Mason had taken him under his wing. And these guys only deal with people they trust, people who've signed up to their rules – like not talking to us, no matter what. Because if you do, word is that you end up like Liam Gerrity.'

46

Twenty years since it became a city, Inverness is like an adolescent on a growth spurt; every few months, it seems to Mahler, it expands a little further, overwriting fields and farmlands with a sprawl of new-builds. But there are still places where the developers' advance has faltered – places like this, where the road finds a narrow, twisting route into the hills, and derelict farm buildings sit abandoned in the gorse and heather landscape.

Abandoned. But not by everyone, it seems.

'That's it.' Mahler points to the rutted track Mel Paterson had described. 'Get us as far off the road as you can – quietly, if this heap can manage that.'

Fergie gives him a wounded look. He thumps the gearstick, wrestling with the steering wheel until the ancient Audi finally lumbers into position. From here, they've got a decent line of sight to the tumbledown building Mel had told them about, but they're reasonably well concealed themselves. It ought to be reassuring, but there's a kick of anxiety in Mahler's gut that refuses to go away.

Fergie unclips his seatbelt, glances at the text that's flashed up on his mobile. 'Andy's at Ross's lock-up with Gary. Going in now.' He looks out at the empty stretch of moorland. Shakes his head. 'I'm not liking this, boss. Not liking the feel of it at all. If Mel's stringing us along—'

'What would be the point?' Mel hadn't volunteered the information about Ross's drug-dealing partners or the mysterious Brotherhood right away; it had taken all Naz's patience and people skills to win the traumatised girl's trust; and she *had* been genuinely traumatised, Mahler's convinced of that. But if he's wrong—

A nondescript dark Kuga pulls in behind them. Fergie glances at the text on his phone, turns to Mahler. 'Amir's lot are ready to go.'

'Tell them to get in position.'

A twist of unease deep in Mahler's gut. Too quick, all of this, he knows that; a plan that should have taken days to work on had been cobbled together in a matter of hours, bodies drafted in at the last minute to make up the numbers. At first, Chae Hunt had been reluctant to give him the go-ahead to proceed without Harkness's agreement. But all attempts to contact Harkness directly had failed, and he hadn't responded to Mahler's email. If they want to get their hands on Frankie Mason, they have to move now. *Have to.*

Mahler looks out of the window, gauges the fading daylight; not much time left for someone to show up. If he's got this wrong, if Mel's playing them for some reason . . .

'Something coming up the brae. Lights on dip.'

He follows the line of Fergie's pointing finger. A Land Rover: old, mud-spattered. Farmer making a last-minute check on something before dark? Heading down the track, coming straight towards them . . . At the last minute, it leaves the main track and veers left.

'Not slowing down . . . Yeah, he's going straight there.' Fergie reads off another text. Exhales. Looks at Mahler. 'One guy only, looks like. Getting out, going inside . . . We're doing this, aye?'

Mahler takes out his phone. Types, hits *send*. 'We're doing it. Let's go.'

He gets out, sets off down the track with Fergie following. The countdown's running in his head, adrenaline twists like ice-picks in his gut. *If this goes wrong—*

Shouting. Lights. Boots running. More lights. He picks up his pace, narrowly misses falling on his face thanks to the chunk of fallen lintel half buried by the entrance . . . and gets his first good look at the massive figure glowering in one corner, flanked by two of Amir's biggest OCCT officers.

Liam Gerrity hadn't been exaggerating when he'd described 'Frankie' Mason as a monster; at least six foot six in height and well over twenty stone, his features have an unfinished look, as though one of the Easter Island statues had enjoyed an illicit coupling with a vat of lumpy porridge. But it's the suitcase on the makeshift table next to him that gets Mahler's attention. And accounts for the grin of satisfaction on Amir's face.

'This is Mr No Comment,' the OCCT officer tells him. 'We found him packing his bag over there for . . . What would it be, a wee trip, do you think?'

Mahler runs an eye over the suitcase's contents, makes a half-hearted attempt to estimate their street value. Gives up after the fourth package. 'Something like that. What—'

'Bloody hell.' Fergie wheezes his way over to take a look. 'That'll keep you boys busy for a while, eh? Meanwhile, we need to have a chat with him down the cop-shop. About a pal of his called Liam Gerrity.'

Amir's smile fades. 'This is supposed to be a joint operation, guys. OCCT—'

'Want the kudos for all this crap you've got your paws on.

Aye, I know – don't worry, you can have him when we're done with him. But I've just got a call from Andy, who's been having a wee look round Eddie's flat.' Fergie turns to grin at Mahler. 'And you're not going to believe what he's found.'

47

As joint operations go, it's been a slick affair; well put-together, well executed. Fast. Even so, news is already breaking on social media and there's a BBC Scotland van pulling into the visitors' car park when Mahler and Fergie get back to HQ.

'There's another one.' Fergie nods at the ancient Citroën limping into the car park behind a local radio car. 'Bloody hell, it's Columbo again – thought I saw him outside HQ the other day. Would trample your granny for a story, that one. Or a photo he could flog to the nationals.'

'Tough. All anyone's getting tonight is a holding statement – we'll fill in some of the blanks for them tomorrow.'

Quite a few of the blanks, in fact, if tomorrow's interviews go according to plan. The arrests they've made are going to generate the usual mountain of paperwork, but by tomorrow morning Fergie and Andy will be going in to interview Mason with a file full of texts unequivocally linking him and Eddie Ross to the killing of Liam Gerrity. And images of a Street Pastor cap found in the rubbish bin outside Eddie's flat.

Apart from demanding to speak to their lawyers, Ross and Mason had remained silent. But an inspection of Mason's vehicle had revealed extensive bloodstaining to several surfaces. With Dave Christie's team going over it centimetre by painstaking centimetre, Mahler suspects it won't be long before there's forensic evidence to place at least one of them unequivocally at the scene of Gerrity's murder.

He sends Fergie home and heads upstairs to work on the statement. Media Liaison will fine-tune the draft he sends them, but it's down to him to balance the public's right to be informed with the enquiry's operational needs. Right now, that means offering maximum reassurance and minimum detail. Which, it turns out, reads very much like the update he sends Chae Hunt.

He roughs out an interview strategy for tomorrow, thinks about calling it a day. But there are red 'urgent' flags all over his inbox, and there's only one way to get rid of them. He's working his way through Fergie's unique take on overtime cost projections when Anna's number flashes up on his mobile. It's only when he answers that he realises why she's ringing. And where he's supposed to be right now.

'It's the photography exhibition's official opening tonight, isn't it? Hell!' He grabs his jacket, goes to close down his emails. 'Anna, I'm so sorry. Tell Mum I'm on my way—'

'It finished an hour ago, Lukas.' There's no reproach in her voice, which somehow makes it worse. 'Don't worry, Grace was okay about it – disappointed, but okay. I told her you'd rung to say you'd been caught up in something at the last minute.'

'I genuinely was, but thank you. How did it go?'

'Her pictures were definitely the most popular ones. The reporter from the *Courier* said—'

'It's going to be in the papers?'

'I think so, yes. The local STV reporter filmed part of it, so Grace might even pop up on the early evening news. Why?'

'Did she agree to that? Because if not—'

'I doubt they'd have done it otherwise,' Anna points out. 'And she seemed absolutely fine with it. Maybe Grace is starting to move into a new phase of her recovery? I know how ill she's been, but—'

'Believe me, you don't.'

An intake of breath at the other end of the line. His words, his tone hanging in the silence. Gathering weight.

'Anna, I'm sorry. That wasn't—'

'No, you're right. Of course I don't understand. It's just when I met her that first time, she seemed so sad, Lukas. So . . . so lost.'

'I know. That's how she felt, I think.'

Two years ago, his mother had been standing bewildered and uncertain outside her flat, in one of her deeply troubled phases. Anna had come upon her by pure chance, had seen her distress and stepped in to help.

'The trouble is, recovery from the sort of trauma she suffered . . . Let's just say there have been a few bumps along the road. Things lie dormant, and then . . .' he looks down at the fingers of his right hand, forces the tell-tale tremble to subside. 'And then they don't. I've learned not to have expectations about where we'll get to, long term.'

'I'm sorry.' Something that might have been a sigh at the other end of the line. 'Lukas, I'm not pressing you. But some of the things you've let slip about Grace . . . I know something bad happened when you were young, something to do with your father. You do know you can always talk things through with me, right? It's part of that whole getting-closer-to-someone deal.'

'I think we decided my aptitude in that area was limited.' As soon as the words are out, he wants to bang his head on the desk at their utter stupidity. Idiot. *Idiot*. Why say that to her? *Why?*

'I'm sorry, that came out incredibly badly. I didn't mean—'

'It's okay.' But the strained note in her voice suggests it isn't, not really. 'It's just . . . look, Grace talked about going back to study, maybe doing something with her photography online. Even if it doesn't come to anything, looking ahead like that has got to be a positive, surely?'

'Perhaps. I'd have to discuss it with her care manager, get her input.'

'So Grace doesn't get a say in her own future?'

'That's not . . .' Not how it is, he'd been going to say. But the chill in Anna's voice is telling him how it looks to her. How it sounds. 'It's best to be cautious, that's all. But I'm glad you were there with her. Thank you.'

'No thanks required, I enjoyed it. By the way – those runes you asked Gudrun about? I thought the place name you mentioned sounded familiar, so I did some archive searches. I've sent you a couple of excerpts from the articles I found.'

Mahler opens his emails again, glances at his inbox. 'They've just come in, thanks. So there are historical records about Sandisquoy?'

'Mainly about a former occupant. Eliza Rattray.'

For a moment, the name doesn't mean anything to him. Then he remembers seeing it in the file Pete had pulled together about Fleming's purchase of the house. 'Elderly and unmarried, yes. She spent her final eighteen months in a nursing home, I believe. Is there something I should know about her?'

'I'm not sure. Maybe. She was an eccentric, I suppose you'd call her. Published a weird little book of folk tales back in the forties, and she definitely had a thing for selkies. Mightn't mean anything, but kind of interesting, isn't it? After everything Gudrun said.'

'It certainly is. Thank you – and thanks again for standing in for me tonight.'

'Always glad to help if I can. You should know that by now.'

'I should, yes.' And he should try to repair some of the

damage he's done. 'Anna, if you're around tomorrow evening, I was wondering—'

'There's a paper I really need to finish. Sorry.' The hint of returning warmth in her voice fades. 'Look, tell Grace I'll be in touch. And thank her again for inviting me.'

Silence after the call ends. Mahler stares down at his mobile, thinks of all the ways that conversation could have gone. *Should* have gone, perhaps. But with James Gordon's appeal date coming closer, Anna's got her own monsters to deal with; he can't introduce her to the one inside his head.

The smell of blood and fear. His mother's screams . . . Twenty years later, he can still taste the memory of the last time he'd set eyes on Jochen Mahler. Twenty years, in which his mother had clawed her way back to something like recovery after his final, brutal assault. Twenty years of keeping her head down, living as much under the radar as humanly possible. In case the psychopath she'd married found out he hadn't wrecked her life as completely as he'd thought.

After all this time, it would be easy to believe the danger's over. Jochen had vanished without trace on the night of the attack, vanished so quickly and seamlessly, Mahler's convinced his father had an escape route planned in advance. Since then, no one's seen or heard from him for twenty years.

He could be half a world away by now, living a different life. Hell, after so long he could be seriously ill, or dead; as long as it involved intense pain and loss of dignity, Mahler's got no problem with either scenario. He just can't make himself believe in them. After twenty years, he's learned to live with most of the memories of that night. Except for one.

Blood on his hands. His mother's screams. His feet, slip-sliding on the stairs as he ran for the door. He'd wrenched the door open, turning at the last minute to look back as Jochen appeared on the landing, blood spattered across his white shirt. Mahler's fourteen-year-old self had frozen in place, unable to move, unable to speak as the man at the top of the stairs took a step towards him. Stopped. And waved him away, like a small, bothersome insect.

Run, his father's face had said. *Don't get in my way, and maybe you'll be safe. For a while. But I'll be watching you, Lukas.*

I'll always be watching you.

48

HMP Perth

Like most Invernessians, Anna has only a vague idea of where the city's Porterfield prison is located; tucked away somewhere in Crown, she thinks, if she thinks of it at all. Close enough to the castle to allow swift transportation of prisoners when the court's in session, but not close enough to unsettle the tourists taking selfies in front of Flora MacDonald's statue.

By contrast, HMP Perth is situated in the middle of a busy industrial estate. Grey and dour, the early Victorian building sits uncompromisingly in its grounds, not pretending to be anything other than it is: a place of locks and walls and hopelessness. But isn't that exactly what her sister's killer deserves?

Inside the main entrance, Anna shows her ID, puts her bag and phone in one of the lockers. Submits to the indignity of being searched, her mouth and shoes inspected before being allowed through to the visitors' waiting area. It's only when she sits down that she sees how much her hands are shaking. She'd psyched herself up for this, studied the visitor guidelines so she'd know what to expect. But now she's actually here, the reality of what she's committed herself to is starting to sink in.

They are tired, most of the women in this impossibly hygienic-smelling room. Young-old faces tight with what they've just gone through, or the thought of what lies ahead. Talking, too fast or too loud or not talking at all. A lone baby crying. Children playing unenthusiastically in the corner with a box of dog-eared books and battered building blocks. And what the hell is she doing here, waiting with them? What on earth is she hoping to achieve? She'd almost called Lukas back last night, told him what she was going to do. But telling him would feel weirdly like asking for approval; that, or asking him to share responsibility for something that, in the end, has to be her choice.

She's still deciding whether she wants to go ahead when a door opens and a prison officer appears to take them through to the visiting hall. And she knows there's still time to call a halt to this, if she wants to. All she needs to do is ask to be let out of here, to somewhere that doesn't smell of bleach and Glade and desperation. But if she leaves, she leaves with all her questions unanswered; she won't have the guts to come again, she knows that.

Worse, he'd know she hadn't been able to face him. And there's no way she's giving Jamie Gordon that satisfaction. Anna gets up and walks over to the group of women making their way to the visiting hall. She'd assumed he would be there already, but they're told to take seats and wait.

After a moment, a door at the far end of the room opens and the prisoners file in. Anna's leaning forward, trying to pick Jamie out of the crowd, when a heavily built man appears in grey jogging bottoms and top. He walks over to her table and sits down.

'I didn't think you'd come.'

'Neither did I.'

'You look good. Very . . .' His hand describes a circle in the air. 'I don't know. Polished. Is that your new job? It suits you anyway.'

'I didn't come to talk about my work.' Sitting up straight,

meeting his gaze squarely. Trying not to show her shock at the change in his appearance.

He's put on weight, for one thing, his stomach rounding the front of his prison-issue sweatshirt, and she can see the first touches of grey along his hairline. But it's the scar on his cheek she can't take her eyes away from; obviously still healing, the purpled skin looks *gouged* in places.

'What happened?'

'This?' He gestures to the scar. Shrugs. 'Someone objected to the way I looked at them. In here, that's all it takes.'

She starts to say she's sorry, then catches herself. The truth is, she isn't. Why shouldn't his exterior reflect what he really is? 'Learning to co-exist in this environment must be difficult.'

'You have no fucking clue what difficult is, Anna. None at all.'

His tone is light, conversational, so it takes her a moment to realise what he's said.

'How. Dare. You.' She starts to rise, but Jamie holds up a hand, as though in apology.

'Anna, that wasn't . . . Look, thank you for coming. I never thought you would.'

'You said that already.'

'So why did you? Some sort of "closure", is that it?'

Air quotes round the word. She shakes her head. 'You don't get to question me, Jamie. Just tell me why you're going ahead with this bloody appeal. There's no way you're going to win, you must know that.'

'Must I?' He leans forward. Smiles, as though he's about to share a joke with her. 'How do you think it feels to be locked up with people like these? Keeping your head down, trying not to catch anyone's eye? And every day stretches out before you, day after day after day – what do you think you'd do, in my place?'

'I have no idea. But then, I haven't killed three people.'

He flinches, jerks his head back. 'Janis fell from that balcony. I don't expect you to believe it, but it's true. Then Morven found out I was there that night, and threatened to expose me . . . That was my *life*, Anna. My whole fucking life your sister was planning to destroy. I just . . .' He spreads his hands. 'I don't know what happened, I swear I don't.'

He looks straight at her. 'We were friends, weren't we? At uni?'

'I thought so at the time. But—'

He nods. 'We were on the same wavelength, you and I. Right from the start. You did feel that, didn't you? It wasn't just me?'

A flash of the old Jamie there – the shy, overweight boy she'd known back then. *Thought* she'd known, she corrects herself. 'I didn't come to talk about the past. I just want—'

'Of course you did.' His hand clamps around her wrist. 'You *know* me, Anna. You know I'd never do the things I've been accused of. It was like . . . like something took over my mind, made me do those things. I swear to you.'

Nausea rises to the back of her throat. The same lies he'd told at the trial, the same lies he'd put in the letter he'd written her. But what had she expected, that he'd suddenly develop a conscience once they were face to face again? She pulls her hand away, feels his ragged nails rake across her skin. 'I think we're done here.'

She stands, turns to go, but he calls after her.

'What about your fucking closure, Anna? If you walk away now, what happens to that?'

One of the prison officers is coming over. Anna raises her hand to show everything's okay, goes back to where she'd been sitting. Smiles down at her sister's killer.

'What happens is, I get to walk out of here. I get to go home,

go out with friends for a drink, or maybe a nice meal. And you?'
She looks him up and down. Makes it slow. Contemptuous.
Dismissive. 'You don't get to do any of that.'

'My appeal—'

'Your appeal will get laughed out of court. You'll be sent
back here for a bloody long time. And if you get a chance of
probation? I'll be doing everything I can to stop that happening.
You don't deserve to get out of here, Jamie.'

She lowers her voice, so that he has to lean forward to hear
her. Curves her mouth into a bright, malicious smile. 'You
don't even deserve to be *alive.*'

Then she's standing up and making herself walk, not run
away, as he gets to his feet and yells obscenities after her. Not
looking back. Not stopping. Passing through the various security points again, grabbing her belongings from the locker
and waiting to be buzzed out. Still walking, still not running,
until she's outside the prison walls. Then she's shaking all over,
barely able to make it to her car and unlock it before her legs
collapse from under her.

Not going to throw up. Not happening. She reaches for the water
bottle she keeps in the cup holder, guides it to her mouth with
both hands and takes slow, careful sips until the nausea subsides
and her heartbeat returns to something approaching normal.

The worst thing about what she's just put herself through
isn't his complete lack of remorse, his refusal to take any responsibility for his crimes. It hadn't even been the vileness he'd
screamed at her as she walked away.

The worst thing about it had been the look in his eyes. As
though she'd given him something he'd been waiting for.

49

Kirkwall

There's still a month or so to go before storm season hits, but this year's going to be a bad one, Tony Armstrong's sure of it.

Maybe it's global warming, maybe it's just the planet getting fed up of everyone making a godawful mess of things and deciding to give them a wee fright now and again, but it feels like every year the floods start that little bit earlier, and last that little bit longer.

By the time he gets out of the Emergency Co-ordination Group meeting, midday's yellow weather warning has turned amber, and the flood barriers are going up along the seafront. He glances uneasily at the darkening sky, hopes Karen had the sense to cancel the mobile library's scheduled run over to Rousay. Time to head home himself, make sure everything's—

'Sir! Sir!'

Colin McAvoy, tearing across the street towards him like an overexcited labrador.

Tony feels his acid indigestion bite him in the guts. Excited, maybe, but not in a good way; the boy's movements have an odd jerkiness to them that makes Tony think it's just as well he's not back on duty yet. Whatever Colin's got to tell him, Tony's damn sure he isn't going to like it.

'Need to talk to you, sir.' Close up, Colin looks even worse.

There's a clammy-looking sheen to his face, and he's breathing as though he's run a half-marathon. 'It . . . it's Sandisquoy. I went out there this morning, and—'

'What the hell for? You're still signed off sick, aren't you?'

He nods. 'But I . . . I had to do it. Had to try and work it out.'

Tony's acid indigestion bites a little deeper. 'Work what out?'

'The guy who attacked me – he came out of nowhere. I mean, *really* nowhere, like a bloody ghost!' Colin glances at him, nods. 'Aye, I know, it sounds mad. But that's what happened. And I just . . . I wanted to know *how*, because I couldn't get it out of my head.'

'So you went out there.'

Another nod. 'I talked to Graham, the archaeology guy, and he's like, aye, fine, go ahead. Because he wasn't looking at the house, was he? Just that peedie cellar place. So I worked my way round every inch of the ground floor. And I found this.'

Colin taps the screen of his mobile, holds it up to show him.

At first, all Tony can see is the hallway at Sandisquoy, dimly lit and still bearing the marks of the forensic team's examination. Then a thin line of light at floor level, roughly a metre in length, catches his eye; it's faint, almost undetectable, but it's there. Which means—

'It's some sort of opening, isn't it? That's how he got in without you noticing.'

'If it hadn't been for the archaeologists' lights shining through the gap this morning, I doubt I'd have spotted it,' Colin tells him. 'But once I'd seen them, I knew there had to be a door of some kind hidden behind the dresser. So I moved it out of the way. And I found the entrance.'

'Bloody hell.' The video shows a narrow opening in the wall, leading down a dark, timbered passage. 'It goes down to the chamber?'

Colin nods. 'There's more. Halfway down, I found this.' He taps the screen again, holds up a new image. 'Do you think there'll be DNA or something on it? Sir, are you – are you okay?'

Tony stares down at the phone. Starts to tell the boy no, not a chance. Not if the dull, dust-shrouded item half hidden on the earthen floor turns out to be what he thinks it is.

'You didn't touch it, didn't disturb it at all?'

'Of course not! And I told Graham to keep his boys well away until we'd got someone out there to protect the chain of evidence.'

'Good lad. Back to the shop to get things rolling, eh? If you're up to it, that is – you're still looking a bit rough, and I don't want your Aunty Cath on my case—'

'I'm fine.' The overexcited labrador look is back on Colin's face. 'We'll need forensics out again, won't we? Something for Media Liaison too, asking folk if they recognise it. And—'

'Aye, aye, we'll need to do all that. On you go, then, I'll meet you back over there.'

Tony manages a smile for the boy. Holds it until he's walked across the road and turned the corner, out of sight. Colin's not had the easiest time since joining the force, truth be told; the job's hard enough in a small place like this where everyone knows your business, but when your aunt's a high-flying procurator fiscal . . . well, that's quite a load to carry. Still, the boy's surprised him this time, no doubt about it.

Tony digs out the pack of chewable Gaviscon he keeps in his pocket, puts one in his mouth to try to quell the acid burning in his gut.

And sends Karen a text to say he'll be home a wee bit later than planned.

50

It's just before seven-thirty when Fergie pulls into the car park. He'd been aiming for seven, but there had been a sharp frost the previous night and the Audi had looked like a ghost of itself, its windows layered with whorls of ice. By the time he'd scraped enough of it off to drive, his shirt was sticking to him, and he could feel the sweat gathering on the back of his neck. Definitely going to get back to the gym, he tells himself. As soon as work eases up a bit. Definitely.

He collects a coffee from the machine and heads upstairs. There's no one else in yet, apart from the boss, but that suits Fergie fine; he's got overtime spreadsheets to sign off, which means fighting with bloody Excel again. He fires up the laptop, stares out of the window at the traffic building up at the Inshes roundabout. Tells himself he's not putting the paperwork off, just psyching himself up to get properly stuck in before the boss has to give him another bollocking.

Naz has done her best to teach him what to do, but Fergie's starting to think he's a lost cause; as soon as Naz starts talking about populating fields and formatting cells, his brain goes into automatic shutdown. If someone had told him when he joined

229

Northern Constabulary that he'd end up feeding figures into a wee computer—

'And here's me thinking I was hallucinating that rust bucket of yours in the car park.'

Dave Christie appears in the MIT room door, waves a paper bag in Fergie's direction. 'Bacon roll? Got two from Harry Gow's at Fairways, but Angie's not coming in until later, so I reckon hers is up for grabs.'

'I've had . . .' *breakfast,* Fergie's about to say. But what he'd eaten under Zofia's watchful gaze was a couple of spoons of yoghurt and granola with some fruit, and Fergie's not sure that qualifies as breakfast, not really. 'Aye, go on. Thanks.' He catches the bag Christie lobs towards him, opens it and inhales. 'Got any brown sauce?'

'Here you go. Right, then.' Christie sits on a desk, leans back. Grins at Fergie. 'Do you want the good news, or the *really* good news that's just come in about the Sandisquoy chamber remains?'

'Any sort of good is fine right now. What have you got?'

'I'll send over the full report later, but basically the young female is confirmed as being the only recent set of remains. Three others have been identified, both fully skeletonised, both way older, so looks like the council archaeologist guy was right about the Viking link.'

'Okay, that's a good start,' Fergie concedes. 'What about the young lassie – any more on her?'

'There is indeed. We reckon she's probably been there around twenty years or so – which fits in pretty neatly with our Runrig fan-boy's estimate.'

'Do we know how old she was? What about DNA?'

Christie takes a bite of his roll, chews. 'Again, it'll all be in the report. But the forensics indicate she was under twenty-five when she died, probably closer to twenty. Impressed?'

'Not bad, aye.' A little twitch of adrenaline, deep in Fergie's gut. Telling him they're finally on the track of *something*. 'You think the forensic artist guy at CAHID could do a facial reconstruction? If we could get that into a press conference, give folk something concrete to look at . . . what?'

Christie grins at him. 'Told you there was more. That off-duty cop who was attacked at the house? Apparently he remembered seeing something a bit weird just before someone cracked him over the head. It had been bugging him ever since, so as soon as he got out of hospital, he trotted over there again to take another look.'

More roll. More chewing. Fergie picks up a folder from his desk, hefts it in his hand and feints a throw at him. 'Will you get that roll down your neck and stop milking this?'

'Come on, Dave. Spill.' Mahler's standing in the doorway, looking . . . well, the boss doesn't usually do scruffy, but he's on nodding terms with it this morning, for sure. 'Trust me, we could do with the good news right now.'

'Fair enough.' Christie finishes his roll, chucks the empty bag into the waste bin. 'Sent you on a couple of pics from the locus.'

Fergie nods. 'Just come through. What am I looking at?'

Mahler comes over, frowns at the image filling the laptop screen. 'It's the entrance hall. But I don't remember that door being there, and I checked out the entire house.'

'It was behind that massive dresser, that's why.' Christie taps the screen. 'Not the fault of the Kirkwall guys, mind. I doubt anyone would ever have spotted it, if the boy hadn't remembered something weird about the way the light from his phone was falling when he dropped it.'

'It's — what, a passageway? Going down to where he was found?'

Christie nods at Fergie. 'All the way down. And that's not all. Scroll to the next two images.'

Fergie squints at the small, blackened object next to a marker flag. At first glance, all he can see is a few broken metal links from some sort of chain—

'A necklace?' Mahler peers at the screen, turns to Christie. 'No, a charm bracelet. My mother's got one.'

The scene examiner nods. 'Very popular back in the twentieth century, fell out of favour a bit since the millennium, I'm told. Just preliminary images, of course, but it was found close to the chamber end of the passage. Interesting, huh?'

'You think it could be the victim's?'

Christie shrugs. 'No way of knowing for sure. But it would fit with the timeline, wouldn't it? And take a look at this.' He leans in, taps the screen. 'Thought it was just a normal heart-shaped charm at first. Then I enlarged it – should be the next pic, Fergie.'

Fergie scrolls down, expands the image. Feels that twitch of adrenaline give a sudden jump as he works out what it is he's looking at.

'It's a name.' The boss sounds as though he's just bought a scratchcard and come up with enough numbers to keep him in sharp suits for the rest of his days. 'Bloody hell, Fergie, I think we've got a name for her.'

Tony Armstrong isn't a betting man, and twenty-five years of policing have taken the shine off his optimistic view of the human race. Still, he'd lay odds that none of his officers would have gone blabbing to the media about the latest Sandisquoy discoveries. But someone's done exactly that; by the time he gets back to the station from Sandisquoy, the alerts on his mobile are going crazy, and Murdo Sangster, surrounded by shrilling phones, looks like a man in the grip of the worst migraine of his life.

Murdo's not up to this, Tony thinks. Not anymore, not with poor Joyce away in that nursing home on the mainland. But how are any of them supposed to deal with what this Sandisquoy thing is turning into?

When he gets through to his office and signs into the video-link call with Inverness, he's bracing himself for Chae Hunt's reaction to the leak. But the Chief's halfway down the A9, it turns out, on his way to a partnership meeting, and when Tony broaches the subject, Lukas Mahler shakes his head.

'Stable door, horse. Leave that for later, and let's get a strategy together to deal with what we've got right now. Which is where I hand over to Dave.'

Tony listens as the scene examiner takes them through everything the on-site CAHID team have found so far. 'Because of the condition of the remains, DNA recovery might not be straightforward,' he warns. 'Luckily, there's a good chance we've got something even better. The bracelet I mentioned isn't in great condition, but we've managed to clean up a couple of the images enough for use in a press statement. Tony, not sure if you got the most recent email I sent—'

'Just got back to the station. Give me a minute.' He opens his inbox, finds Christie's email and watches the images download. Feels the acid pool in his stomach as the tarnished silver charms appear, one after the other.

'Not the best-quality silver,' Christie explains. 'A couple of the charms look like they've been bent, or twisted out of shape. But the name on the heart-shaped one—'

'Is Isla. Yes. Isla Stewart.'

Tony looks up, sees what they're thinking stamped across their faces. And shakes his head.

'I never knew her,' he tells them. 'But I know who gave Isla that bracelet. And I know where you can find her.'

233

51

Flora Stewart runs a boarding kennel outside Dingwall, barely a half hour's drive from Inverness. Armstrong's former girlfriend is a tall woman in an ancient Barbour jacket with faded blonde hair and a thin, anxious face. As Mahler and Fergie pull in, she's waiting at the foot of her drive.

'I can give you thirty minutes,' she tells them, to the sound of distant barking. 'After that, I've got people coming to pick up their dogs. If you leave your . . .' she hesitates, runs an incredulous eye over the Audi, 'your . . . vehicle . . . by the oil tank over there, I'll take you over to the office.'

Mahler glances at Fergie, shrugs. 'Of course. But wouldn't you be more comfortable—'

'I'm trying to get my tax return done in between sorting out last-minute cancellations by bloody thoughtless customers, so no, the office will be fine.'

While Fergie moves the car, she takes Mahler down a side path to a small wooden hut. The closer they get to the kennels, the more frantic the barking becomes.

'Not a dog person, are you?' She unlocks the door, ushers him in. 'Don't worry, I'm not going to shove a puppy in your face to try and convert you. Too many unwanted animals in the world already in my book.'

234

She picks a pile of paperwork off a chair, dumps it on a filing cabinet in the corner and nods at him to sit down.

'Your colleague can take the bean bag over there – from the look of his car, he won't mind roughing it a little. How's Tony, by the way? I assume he told you where to find me.' She catches the look on his face, sighs. 'You're shocked, aren't you? Trying to decide whether I just haven't taken in the news about Isla, or I'm really as hard-hearted as I sound?'

Fergie appears in the doorway. He sizes up the seating position and opts for standing. 'Takes folk in all sorts of different ways, something like this,' he tells her. 'You'd be surprised. If you need to have someone with you at any time—'

An irritable glance at her watch. Flora Stewart shakes her head, folds her arms. 'There's no one. Just ask me your questions and I'll answer as best I can. And no, you don't need to show me those photos again, that's definitely Isla's bracelet. She wore it all the time.'

'You're sure?'

A flicker of something in her eyes as she looks away. 'I bought that charm for her eighteenth, so yes. My friend's mam used to make them for a wee shop in Stromness. They were quite popular at the time.'

'So people who knew Isla would recognise that bracelet?'

'More than likely, yes,' she tells Mahler. 'Isla designed a couple of the charms herself, so they were quite distinctive – I always thought she could have gone to art school, actually. Though knowing Isla, she'd have got herself chucked out for arguing with the tutors. Not a fan of authority, my sister. Or hard work.'

'You didn't get on, then?'

An irritable glance. 'That's not what I said. Look, she was four years older than me, and a bit of a party animal. We just didn't have that much to do with each other.'

Mahler nods. 'I understand. But we're trying to put together a picture of Isla – who her friends were, what her life looked like. Do you remember any particular boyfriends, for example, people she'd hang out with regularly when you lived on Orkney?'

'Isla didn't do regular. She liked to think of herself as a free spirit – which meant she did what the hell she liked. As soon as she was old enough, she got the ferry to Aberdeen. Made a bit of money, came home for a few months and buggered off again. Over time, she came home less and less. When her visits stopped completely, it felt inevitable, I suppose.'

'What about your parents?' Fergie asks. 'How did they feel about that?'

A shrug. 'I doubt they noticed, frankly. Mam was in her own little world most of the time, and my dad . . . well, he spent enough nights wrapped around a bottle even before Mam got sick. Once she died, he stopped even trying to stay sober. So we were pretty much left to our own devices, growing up.'

Fergie gives an understanding nod. 'That must have been hard. Sometimes that sort of thing brings folk together, though. Were you close back then, you and Isla?'

'Close?' She gives a mirthless laugh. 'No, we were never—' A chorus of barking erupts outside. She sighs, holds up a hand and makes for the door. 'Need to see what that's about. Back in a moment.'

As she disappears down the path, Mahler's mobile bleeps with a couple of message alerts. He's about to open them when Flora Stewart returns. She's carrying a bag of dog kibble and her thin face is flushed with annoyance.

'That's the Pattersons here already, and their spaniels are hyperactive little sods.' She dumps the bag on her desk, picks up a clipboard and pen. 'It'll take ages to get them settled. So if we're done here—'

'I'm sure they'll be okay to wait a bit. In the circumstances.' Fergie checks his notebook. 'We know Isla was working at one of the bars in Kirkwall in the summer of '95.' Tony Armstrong doesn't remember which bar and he'd been pretty hazy about the dates, but right now it's all they've got. 'Can you remember the last time you saw or spoke to her after that?'

'I can't, no. And I'm sorry, but I really have to get on.' She crosses to the door, opens it in an unsubtle hint. 'Look, if I knew anything else, don't you think I'd say? I honestly don't know what else you think I can tell you.'

'No, *I'm* sorry.' Enough anger in Mahler's voice to stop her in her tracks, and make Fergie turn to look at him. 'I'm sorry we need to convince you to help us find your sister's killer. Sorry you don't think that's important enough to tell us everything you know.' She starts to protest, but he holds up his hand. 'You want to know what else we need from you? Something a bit more useful than "I don't know" or "we weren't close" would be good – in fact, it would be excellent. Because she was a young woman who died alone and lay forgotten in a bloody unmarked grave for over twenty years. So I'll ask you again, what can you tell us, Flora?'

Fergie's expression is telegraphing *too much, boss*, and there's no colour left in Flora Stewart's face, none at all. Then she gives an abrupt nod.

'Okay, then. I can tell you I was afraid of her. That when she stopped coming home, I . . . I was glad.' Her mouth curls in a weary half-smile. 'Weren't expecting that, were you? But it's true.'

'Afraid?'

Another nod. 'Isla was always different. Moody, a bit disconnected, I suppose. Like the rest of the world didn't exist for her. And when she hit her teens, it got worse. A lot worse.'

'You said she was a party animal,' Mahler points out. Flora Stewart gives a weary sigh.

'I did, didn't I? But I think maybe that was just a mask she sometimes liked to wear.'

'Meaning?'

She shrugs. 'Isla was about fifteen when things got really bad. I assumed she was on something, at first. The way she acted, the way she looked. The things she said. But now I think she had some kind of mental illness.'

'What makes you say that?'

'She was so . . . so *weird,* like she was two people. Sometimes she'd stay out all night, come home so drunk she could hardly see straight. Other times she'd lock herself away in her room, reading for hours, or take off down to the shore and listen out for those bloody seals.'

For a moment, Mahler thinks he's misheard her. 'Seals?'

She nods. 'Isla was obsessed,' she tells him. 'All those old folk tales of shape-shifters, selkie folk, nonsense like that? She *believed* it. But that wasn't the worst of it. Have you heard that calling noise they make?' She shudders. 'Straight out of a bloody Stephen King novel. But Isla thought she could talk to them. That's what those charms were for.'

'The ones she designed herself?'

Another nod. 'Bindings, she called them. Said folk had forgotten where they came from. And why they were made.'

'What did she mean by that?'

Flora Stewart stares at him. 'How should I know? My sister was off her head, Inspector. Nothing she said made any sense. Nothing. Now if you've got what you came for—'

'For the moment. Thank you.' Mahler glances at Fergie, crosses to the door. Stops dead as something she said leaps out at him. Something his anger at her callousness had almost made him miss. 'You said Isla went down to the shore to talk to the seals. Where did she go, exactly? Can you remember?'

Flora shrugs. 'Anywhere the seals gathered, really. Anywhere she could walk or bike to. But Isla liked . . .' Her voice falters, as though she's only just realised the importance of what she's about to tell him. 'She liked to go to Sandisquoy.'

52

'Yes, I have your email with the photographs and the articles Anna found. I was going to look at them after my next tutorial.'

Something different in Gudrun's voice this time when Mahler calls her; not an unfriendly something, not exactly, but there's a distance that hadn't been there when he'd met her with Anna at the airport.

'You're busy, and I'm disturbing you. I'm sorry,' he tells her. 'But there's been a further development in the murder enquiry I'm investigating, and I'd appreciate your input.'

'Another body has been found – a young woman, yes? I heard . . . what is it you say, heard on the grapevine? And these charms were buried with it?'

'They were found nearby.' The news is out already, then. Inevitable, Mahler supposes, with so much police activity in such a small community, but it's the last thing the team needs right now. 'I need to know if they're like the ones found with Alex Fleming. And if they actually mean anything.'

A tapping of keys on the other end of the line. An intake of breath. And then a silence.

'So, they are definitely bind-runes. Not the same maker, I think. But yes, the same.'

'I see. Is there a particular meaning to them?'

'Of course. The first one is a simple protection *galdrar*, a spell to keep the wearer safe. The second . . . I don't know how to explain, but it ties knowledge to bravery and danger. Quite an unhappy combination, actually. For an academic.'

Trying to make light of it, perhaps. But that odd, strained note is still in her voice, and the twist of instinct at the back of Mahler's neck pulls a little tighter. 'Gudrun, if there's something else about this, something that's worrying you—'

'It isn't . . .' A sigh on the other end of the line. 'These things are not taken seriously, you know? Not by any respected academics.'

'But?'

'The seal-bone runes, the ones found with your poor dead friend. Did you send me all the photographs you had?'

'Only the clearest ones,' he tells her. 'A couple of the bones were too damaged-looking to get decent images, so—'

'Please send them to me. *All* of them.' An odd sharpness in her voice. 'Your friend was a good man, yes? A kind man?'

'One of the best. Gudrun, if you're thinking he had anything to do with what happened—'

'I'm not thinking that. I don't know what I'm thinking, not yet. Bear with me, yes? I just need to do some research. Maybe talk to Anna, now that she's—'

Silence – a sudden, guilty kind of silence. The kind Mahler's used to hearing in interview rooms. From persons of interest, usually.

'Now that she's what, Gudrun?'

Another silence. A longer one, this time. Then a sigh. 'I thought she would have told you. I'm sorry. Lukas, I worry she has maybe done a stupid thing. And I couldn't find the words to stop her.'

He listens as Gudrun tells him about Anna's visit to James

Gordon. Listens, tries to turn what he's hearing into something that makes sense. And comes up with nothing.

'What did you say when she told you?'

'I said she should speak to you, of course. But I think she had already made her choice. Then when she came back . . . Lukas, you should talk to her.'

Fergie appears in the doorway of his office, the briefing folder under his arm. Mahler glances at his watch, nods.

'I'm not sure what that would achieve,' he tells Gudrun. 'As you say, she made her choice.'

What sounds like a sentence composed entirely of Icelandic swearing erupts in his ear. Followed by an exasperated sigh. 'You're too smart to be so stupid, Lukas. Swallow your anger, and talk to Anna, you hear me? Talk to her soon.'

Isla Stewart had lived and died pre-Facebook, pre-Instagram. So the photograph Mahler pins on the MIT room whiteboard is a grainy copy of the one her sister had pressed into his hand as he and Fergie were leaving.

She hadn't liked having her picture taken, that much is obvious; she's glaring at the camera, pale blonde hair falling over a strong, resentful face with clever, challenging eyes.

'This is the only photograph we have of her so far,' he tells the team. 'We know she left school in 1993, and the last time Flora Stewart remembers her being back on Orkney was two years later, but that's it. Which means we've a hell of a lot of blanks to fill in if we're going to find her killer.'

'Bonny girl.' Andy Black roots in his pocket for a mint, blows the fluff off it and puts it in his mouth. 'The sister said she was off her . . . eh, she had mental problems, aye? Any history of hospital admissions, run-ins with our pals in Kirkwall, maybe? Or social services?'

Fergie shakes his head. 'Nothing. She wasn't registered with a GP, and her school attendance was patchy, to say the least.'

'Dead mother, alcoholic father. Is it any wonder?' Naz shoots him an angry glance. 'And unless she presented with bruises or black eyes or started hearing voices, she'd just have fallen through the cracks, wouldn't she? Her *and* her sister.'

Something in Naz's voice, there. Something more than a copper's weary bitterness about those the safety nets don't catch. Mahler frowns, nods.

'Sadly true. So we focus on her contemporaries to start with. I've spoken with the Fiscal, and Tony Armstrong's putting out a holding statement at lunchtime, asking for anyone who knew Isla to get in touch.'

'Obviously, we're concentrating on Orkney, but her sister thinks she worked at various bars in Aberdeen, so we need to be liaising with our friends in Queen Street as well. Andy, you've got contacts there already, so now the Gerrity file's ready for the COPFS—'

'There's another wee trip to Furry Boots town on the cards for me and Gary?' Black nods. 'Aye, fair enough – we'll talk with the sister again, see if she's remembered any names to start us off.'

'Cause of death?' Fergie asks. 'Anything on that?'

'No single cause as yet. But according to Dave's initial report, she suffered multiple bone injuries at or near the time of death – leaving us with several unanswered questions.'

Mahler crosses to the whiteboard with the map of Sandisquoy, points to where the bones were discovered. 'One, was she killed at the scene or brought there post-mortem? Who knew about the underground chamber, and how were they able to access it without disturbing Eliza Rattray?'

'Family member. Or a close friend, someone she trusted. Maybe even a carer.'

Naz shakes her head at Fergie. 'No relatives we've been able to trace, no close friends who've come forward – the estate agent told us Rattray was a virtual recluse. And no carers until shortly before she went into the nursing home.'

'A housekeeper, then? Or a gardener? She couldn't have managed a property that size by herself,' Mahler points out. 'Or was Rattray herself involved somehow?'

A range of expressions on their faces. Gary speaks up first. 'Boss, sounds like the lassie was beaten to death. I've met some terrifying grannies in my time, but—'

'But it was Rattray's house. And we can't rule anything out at this stage. Particularly given some background information I've been made aware of.'

Mahler tells them what he'd learned from Anna and Gudrun, and crosses to his laptop. He hits a key, and an image projects onto the viewing screen.

'Two of the other charms from Isla's bracelet. According to Professor Jónassdóttir, they represent a particular kind of Viking symbol, sometimes used in the practice of magic – and yes, I know exactly how that sounds. Bear with me.'

He hits another key, pulls up two more images. 'These are close-ups of the carvings on the seal bones found with Alex Fleming's body. The actual charms are slightly distorted, but as you can see, the shapes themselves are identical.'

Silence. A couple of sideways glances. Then a snort of derision from Andy Black. 'You're having a laugh, right? Are you seriously telling us there's some sort of spooky crap going on here? And here's me thinking Halloween was last month.'

'I'm saying two brutal murders have happened at that bloody house, and that "spooky crap" is the only lead we've got right now.'

He scrolls to the next image, the excerpts from Anna's email. Watches the expressions on their faces cycle from amusement to disbelief and back again.

'A "servant girl from Sandisquoy, Agnes Seton. Turned out of the parish by reason of divers ill practices", whatever the hell that means.' Andy Black shakes his head, skims the rest of the screen image. 'Oh, here we go – "the making of charms and calling of selkies". You have *got* to be kidding. You expect us to take this guff seriously?'

'Of course not. But Flora Stewart told us Isla believed she could communicate with the seals, *and* she spent hours down by the shore. What if she met her killer there? A killer who knew about the house's history – and had access to the chamber?'

Fergie nods slowly. 'I'll buy that. So what about Fleming? Where does he come into this?'

'He found her.' Pete looks up from searching on his tablet. 'Dave said someone had looked at the area recently then sealed it up, but not made a great job of it. Come on, it was Fleming's house! Maybe he found the place by accident?'

An eye-roll from Andy Black. 'Aye, right. And he just covered it up again without telling anyone? He was ex-Job, for God's sake! He'd have been straight down the cop shop.' He folds his arms, looks at Mahler. 'Wouldn't he?'

The Alex Fleming Mahler had known in the Met? Without a doubt. The man who'd moved to Orkney and closed his door on everyone? 'Alex wouldn't have walked away,' Mahler agrees. 'But he wasn't always what you'd call a team player. If he thought something needed following up—'

'He'd have started nosing around himself? Fuck. So if he *did* find something—'

'We're potentially looking at a motive for his murder,' Mahler nods. 'One that makes a lot more sense than Viking runes and occult window-dressing.'

53

After the briefing, the team files out. Mahler's on his way to see Dave Christie about the initial report from CAHID when Nazreen comes over.

'Sir, Isla Stewart . . . I don't think talking to her contemporaries is going to be much help. She didn't attend school regularly, left as soon as she could and headed for Aberdeen. Who's going to remember her after all this time?'

Mahler frowns. 'She would have had friends, presumably. And her sister said she was a party animal. But after twenty years, I do appreciate—'

'You don't, though!' Her voice rising enough for a couple of interested looks in their direction. Naz flushes, shakes her head. 'Sorry. I just . . . You don't know what her life would have been like. You can't.'

And there it is: the dark, more-than-bitterness he'd heard in her voice during the briefing. Mahler glances across at Fergie, but Fergie's sorting out the daily actions, so he nods at the desk in the far corner of the room.

'Talk me through what you're thinking.' As they sit down, his mobile beeps with an alert. He puts it face down on the desk, pushes it to one side. 'Don't worry about that. In your own time, Nazreen.'

After a moment, she nods. 'You're assuming she could main-
tain friendships. Assuming she knew from one day to the next
whether she had clothes clean enough to go out in or if there
was food in the house. Her life . . . it wouldn't have been like
that. So any of the normal rules?' She shakes her head. 'Forget
them. They don't apply.'

'No. So her sister might have been confused about the extent
of Isla's social life?'

Choosing his words with the care of a man stepping through
a minefield; because this is personal to Nazreen, that much is
obvious.

'I don't know. "Party animal" would have been in her genes
– it's that or total abstinence for most alcoholics' children.' Naz
looks at Mahler, sighs. 'I'm a Muslim, yes. But that's not the
only reason I don't drink alcohol.'

'Ah. I see.' A cold sweat of embarrassment pooling in the
small of his back at the sheer pointlessness of his response. 'I'm
sorry, Nazreen.'

She shrugs. 'My father died five years ago. But something
like that . . . you look for ways to make sense of things, is what
I'm saying. For me, it's my religion. For Isla, maybe it was the
occult stuff?'

A whisper of something, there. Not the twist of copper's gut
he's felt before, not quite. But a push. A *nudge*. 'So how did
that happen?'

'Sir?'

'Where did she learn about Viking bind-runes, pre-internet,
pre-Google? Where's the one place Isla could have found out
everything she needed – a free source of easily accessible knowledge, and somewhere warm and comfortable to read it all?'

Naz stares at him. 'Her local library. And the sort of books
she'd borrow – they wouldn't still remember her after all this
time, would they? After twenty years?'

'Worth a try, don't you think?' Not a nudge; a definite push this time. 'Talk to Kirkwall Library. See if—'

Mahler's mobile beeps again. He turns it over, gives it an impatient glance. And reads the text from Anna reminding him *exactly* where he should be right now. Who he should be with right now.

He looks up to see Fergie trying to catch his eye, but there's no time to explain. He grabs his jacket and heads downstairs at a run. Knowing another couple of minutes probably won't make that much difference, but—

The short, stocky figure that barrels into Mahler as he rounds the corner of the building isn't paying attention, and neither is he. Mahler absorbs the impact, but the man's knocked backwards and lands on his backside, the smartphone flying out of his hand and landing on the concrete with an ominous crack.

'You okay?' Mahler offers.

He stretches out a hand, but the man bats it away. Mahler doesn't catch the comment that accompanies the gesture, but he's pretty sure it ends in *off*. Which in the circumstances, is absolutely fine by him. He watches the man get to his feet and dust off his raincoat, moving easily, no sign of discomfort. Good.

He retrieves the smartphone, hands it over. 'You dropped this. Sorry, I'm running late—'

'DCI Mahler?' Shrewd, assessing eyes in a craggy, fifty-something face. 'My lucky day, eh?' The crags splinter into a grin. 'Finlay Houston.' A grubby business card makes its way into Mahler's hand. 'Any chance of a wee word for the *Advertiser*? Seeing you malkied my phone, like.'

'Never heard of it. And press briefings go via Media Liaison.' Mahler glances at his watch, resists the urge to swear. 'Get the phone fixed and send me the bill, okay? I need to be somewhere else.' He turns away, heads for the BMW. Reaches it

248

to find Houston's only a pace or two behind him. 'I said, I'm running late—'

'Won't . . . take . . . a minute.' Houston's breathing like a bronchitic rhino and his sweat-shiny face is a disturbing purple colour. 'Jeez-oh, man – real Usain Bolt, aren't you?'

He delves into his pocket for a tissue, hawks up something green into it and stuffs the sodden paper up his sleeve.

'Isla Stewart. You didn't find her when that ex-cop's house was searched – what happened there? And—'

'As I said, talk to Media Liaison.' Mahler steps round him, opens his car door. And gets the smartphone thrust in his face. *Recording?* 'Move that. Now.'

'Come on. Just one quick question—'

'I said, shift it. Or *something*'s going to get seriously "mal-kied". Your choice.' Something rising in his voice, his face, then. Something dark enough to make Houston raise his hands and make a show of retreating.

'Cool your jets, son. Moving, see?' He does a quick side-step, then another. 'Not one to stand in the way of the boys in blue, me.'

'Good to hear.' Mahler gets in the car. Starts the engine and revs it more than strictly necessary. As he reverses out, Houston holds up the smartphone and gives him an ironic wave.

54

If he'd left even fifteen minutes earlier, Mahler would probably have made it to the crematorium to catch the end of Mina's funeral service. Probably. But he's reckoned without the lunchtime train to Glasgow; when he gets to the Raigmore roundabout, the level crossing is closed and the traffic is going nowhere.

By the time he gets across the city, he's already pushing it. And when he gets to Torvean, a leisurely group of Lycra-wrapped cyclists on the A82 wrecks any remaining hope he had of getting there on time.

When he pulls into the car park, Anna is sitting on a bench by one of the flower beds, a little way from the crematorium entrance. She's wearing her scarlet scarf, a flash of bright against her dark coat. And if he needed any confirmation of how much he's messed up, it's there in the rigid set of her shoulders and the tight line of her jaw.

He gets out, walks over. 'I couldn't help it. I'm sorry. Is my mother—'

'Gone for a walk. She wanted a few minutes by herself.'

'Is she okay? How did everything . . . how did it go?'

'How do you think?' Anna looks at him. Sighs. 'She'll be fine. She's done what Mina wanted, and I think it's helped her confidence. Which doesn't get you off the hook, by the way.'

'I'm aware of that.' He spreads his hands. 'Look, I'm sorry for letting her down. Sorry for leaving it up to you to take her here. It wasn't fair on you—'

'No, it wasn't fair on Grace. She's grieving, and she needed you to be here for her.'

'Grieving for Mina? Mina bloody *Williamson*?' He tries to keep the disbelieving anger from his voice. Tries, and fails. 'Mina, who got thrown out of every hostel she'd ever been in for drinking or fighting or both. Thieving, freeloading Mina, who knew how to spot a soft touch and battened onto my vulnerable mother like the heartless bloody leech—'

Footsteps on the gravel behind him. His brain registers Anna's shocked expression and relays it to his vocal cords. Too late. Far, far too late. He turns, spreads his hands.

'Mum, I'm sorry. I know I should have been here—'

'Yes, you should. She was my friend, Lukas.' A weary hurt in the look she gives him. 'I know you didn't like her, but you didn't have to. You just had to respect my choice.'

'Mina was—'

'I know what she was! And what she did. But she was kind and she liked to make me laugh. And now she's gone, I . . . I don't know what I'll do.'

She's crying, silently, because it's how she's trained herself to do it. Trained them both, back in the time when it was the only safe way to be. The only safe way to survive.

Blood on his hands. Blood on the stairs. And his mother . . .

He forces the image away. Locks it in the dusty, shuttered place inside his head he keeps the memories like these. 'I know. And I'm sorry. Look, perhaps we could get . . . I don't know, a commemorative rosebush or something for Mina? Then tea at the Floral Hall?'

'I've already picked a flowering cherry for her. And you

251

don't have time for tea, do you? I saw you looking at your watch.' She manages a smile for Anna. 'Thank you for coming with me. Are you going back to Dornoch now?'

'I have to, I'm afraid. But now Lukas is here, he can take you home—'

His mother shakes her head. 'I'm going to walk. The sun's out now, and I need a bit of thinking time. I'll call you, Lukas. In a wee while.'

She sets off down the path towards the exit. Mahler starts to go after her, but Anna catches his arm. 'I'll call her later and let you know how she's doing. Give her the space right now, okay? And I wanted to talk to you anyway.' She pulls at her scarf, winds it round her hands. 'I've been putting it off a little, but—'

He raises a dismissive hand. 'If this is confession time, you're too late. Gudrun told me about James Gordon.'

A wash of pink creeps across her cheeks. 'I'm sorry. I wanted to tell you—'

'But you chose not to. What were you thinking, Anna? Why would you risk letting that bastard inside your head again, for God's sake?'

'Because he's never bloody left, that's why! If you knew . . .' She shakes her head, draws in a ragged breath. 'I don't expect you to understand, but it was my decision to make. Mine alone.'

'Like hell it was!' His voice rising again, loud enough for the couple getting out of their car at the other end of the car park to offer disapproving looks. 'You told me I wasn't good at being close. Apparently I'm not the only one.'

'No.' A slow unfolding sadness in her face as she looks at him. And looks away. 'No, maybe not . . . which makes this conversation easier, in a way.'

'Meaning what, exactly?'

'Meaning I actually wanted to talk to you about a visiting

252

lectureship Gudrun told me about.' She looks down at the scarf in her hands, as though she's wondering how it got there. 'It . . . it's in Reykjavik.'

'Reykjavik.'

She nods. 'I need to get away for a while, Lukas. Now more than ever. Nothing might come of it, of course—'

'I'm sure Einar the Viking will put in a good word for you. Invite you to – what was it Gudrun said, share his *Brennivin* stash again on those cold Icelandic nights?'

His words gather weight. Fall into a chasm of silence as Anna stares at him. The couple from the car hurry past, skirting round him as though he's carrying some contagion. And now that it's too late, the understanding of what he's just said builds a slow and terrible rawness in his gut.

He stumbles out the start of an apology, but the frozen look on Anna's face stops him in his tracks.

'Didn't expect that from you, Goth Boy. I really didn't. So that's what you think my academic career's been based on? Not the books I've written, the list of journals I've been published in for more than ten *years*?' She exhales, a long, unsteady breath. 'Well done for outing yourself as a sexist git, Lukas. Amongst other things.'

'God, Anna, no! I'm sorry. That wasn't—'

He reaches out a hand. And gets the same response as Finlay Houston had offered, served up with a look of blistering contempt. All of which he deserves. And more.

He watches her walk over to her car, get in and drive away. It's only then he spots the virulent green Citroën parked behind her. *Houston.*

Mahler breaks into a run, but the Citroën's already moving off. Ignoring the *20* signs, Houston speeds towards the exit and disappears out onto the main road.

55

Fergie opens the file sitting on his desk, reads through the latest couple of pages he's added to it. And closes it again. What had he expected, that they would suddenly have changed to tell him a different story? The phone call he's just taken, from a retired DI in the Met, has provided the enquiry into Alex Fleming's death with important new information. But he has no idea how the boss is going to take it.

He'd planned to warn Mahler after the briefing, but he'd got caught up in answering one of Gary's bloody daft queries. And looked up just in time to see the boss run from the room like his arse was on fire; by the time Fergie had made it to the stairs, Mahler was heading for the exit.

Fergie had weighed up his chances of catching up, told himself not to be an eejit and pulled out his mobile to call, or text, or something. Then he'd seen the date, remembered where Mahler was supposed to be, and slipped his phone back into his pocket. It wasn't like the news he had to tell the boss couldn't wait. He'd gone back to his desk, made a couple more calls. And got a couple back.

And as though the day couldn't get any worse, Fergie's staring at the web page Pete's just forwarded to him when Mahler appears in the doorway. He's seen the boss look rough before. Seen him look exhausted. But Christ, this—

'Sorry I had to rush off.' Mahler starts to explain, but Fergie shakes his head. 'My bad, boss. I should have realised.'

No point asking how it went; one look at Mahler's face is enough to tell him that. 'Look, maybe you should have a wee break. Get a coffee from the canteen or something.'

'I'm tired, Fergie, not tired of life.' The boss pulls out a chair, slumps into it. 'What have I missed?'

Fergie pulls the file towards him. Clears his throat. 'You wanted me to check out Shawcross's story – I'd made a start before all the Mel Paterson stuff blew up, but there were a couple of folk I needed to hear back from, before . . .' He glances at Mahler. *Ah, Christ.* 'Before I passed on what I found out about Alex Fleming.'

'Go on.'

Fergie nods. Gives him the good stuff first: the ex-colleagues who'd talked about the way he'd always had their back, how he'd been out there with them, doing the grunt work. 'Made them into a team,' he tells Mahler. 'No reason to doubt any of that, boss, I'm not saying that.'

'But?'

But there had been slip-ups, too. Nothing major, not in the beginning; nothing that you couldn't put down to the sort of bone-numbing exhaustion that comes with working complex, high-profile cases. Nothing a supportive DS couldn't alert his boss to, maybe tidy up behind them a little on occasion. Fergie goes through the list he's compiled, watches Mahler's expression change.

'Burn-out, Fergie. Alex wasn't immune – God knows, none of us are. But—'

'Throughout his career, he had a series of relationships – affairs, whatever you want to call them – with relatives of murder victims. Seems to have been his thing. And that's not right, boss. You *know* it's not right.'

Silence. He sees the frozen look on Mahler's face. And realises too late the reason it's there. 'Not like you and Anna. I didn't mean—'

Buzzing from Mahler's mobile. He answers, listens. Turns to Fergie. 'Craig Falconer from CAHID. Hold on a second, Craig – DI Ferguson's with me, so I'm putting you on speaker. We worked together on the Culloden farmhouse, didn't we? What have you got for us?'

'That's me. I've been working on the material recovered from the Orkney site, and I wanted to give you a quick update before the full report goes out.'

'Go on.'

'Okay. Briefly, we've now been through everything connected to the site and recovered four distinct sets of remains.'

'*Four* sets?'

'Including Isla Stewart,' Falconer clarifies. 'At least, we're expecting DNA from the sister to confirm that. The other three sets are definitely historical – well over the seventy-year cut-off, which is good news, I guess. As far as you're concerned.'

'There's more, isn't there?'

'Oh, yeah.' Falconer sounds as though he can hardly believe what he's about to say. 'And all of it's . . . weird. We think the historical remains – the *human* historical remains – were wrapped in sealskin. It looked like there were more remains at first glance because the pit looks like it was a sort of burial pit for seals. Must have been more than a dozen in there in total.'

'I see. Four dead women. Three wrapped in sealskin. Surrounded by dead seals.' Mahler pulls out a bottle of water from his jacket. Looks at it as though he was hoping it was something stronger, and takes a long drink. 'That's certainly added a further dimension to our enquiry, Craig. Thank you.'

The call ends. Fergie looks at the boss, starts to say something, but Mahler holds up his hand.

'I know, I know. Maybe we should call ourselves the Weird Homicides Investigation Team.'

Fergie shakes his head. 'We'd be the WHIT. Too many jokes, boss. Trust me.'

'Good point.' Mahler presses the area at the base of his skull, as though he's got a headache building there. 'Right, we're way past the stage of trying to run this remotely. I need you in Kirkwall to head things up at that end.'

'Boss. The thing is, those Viking rune things that Icelandic professor wifie identified, and now all this seal business – we're not seriously thinking about an occult connection? I mean, I know there's a link with Fleming's murder, but we're keeping that under our hats for now, aren't we?'

'God, yes. There's no way we want any of it getting out—What?'

'Er. I'm thinking it might be a bit late for that.' Fergie fishes out his mobile, taps the screen a couple of times. 'Pete was checking up on feedback from Tony Armstrong's press statement, and he found this.' He passes the phone to Mahler. 'It's from the *Advertiser Online*. It's not their top story, mind, but—'

'*Cursed by a Viking Witch*.' Mahler stares at the photograph accompanying the clickbait headline. Reads a couple of sentences. And produces the most inventive string of curse words Fergie's heard in a long time.

'It's only online at the moment, boss. Plus a couple of wee retweets. It'll maybe not get coverage in the nationals—'

A message alert flashes on the screen of Mahler's mobile. He glances at the preview, looks up at Fergie. And shakes his head. 'I don't think the Chief agrees. If anyone needs me urgently, I'll be in his office. Probably for some time.'

56

Divisional HQ
Inverness

Chae Hunt leans back in his ergonomically designed leather chair, folds his arms. Frowns as much as his newly botoxed forehead will allow as he waves Mahler to what's universally known as the bollocking seat.

'First of all, the wee pat on the back,' he tells Mahler. 'Good solid police work, bringing the Gerrity enquiry to a successful conclusion. Our pals in OCCT are a bit put out they haven't bagged any bigger fish, but it's still a bloody good result. So be sure to pass on my appreciation to the team.'

'I'll do that, sir.'

'Fine.' Hunt taps the screen of his tablet and pushes it towards Mahler with a look that suggests he'd prefer to have thrown it. With some force. 'Credit where credit's due. Now tell me what the buggering hell *this* is.'

Mahler looks at the website Hunt's just pulled up. Winces. So it's not just the *Advertiser* now, then. Somehow Columbo's sensationalist article looks worse on the bigger screen. It's cleverly crafted, he'll give the hack that much; there's just enough genuine detail buried under the wild theories to give the whole thing a veneer of substance.

'It's got to be a leak, sir. It's bloody annoying, but you know it happens in every high-profile enquiry—'

'I *know* it's a damn leak. We can find the bastard responsible and hang him by his gonads later. What I'm struggling with is why the MIT is discussing runes and spells and bloody Vikings in the first place!'

'The symbols were noted at both scenes, sir. We took advice on what they were and their potential relevance to our investigation. As we do in every enquiry.'

'Maybe. But we don't let ourselves be papped talking to an expert on witchcraft about them!'

Hunt retrieves the tablet, enlarges the photograph. Turns it round again so Mahler sees it. 'Christ, man, couldn't you see where they'd go with it after all the stuff in the papers about the new course she's running at UHI? The pair of you look like you're walk-ons in a bad horror film. All you need is a couple of vampire bats flying around.'

'We were *papped* at a funeral. Where it's customary to wear black, yes? How were we supposed to know some bastard with a telephoto lens—'

'You're supposed to have your wits about you, that's how! If you don't know how our journo pals operate by now . . .' Hunt pushes the tablet aside, waves an irritated hand at Mahler. 'This line of enquiry ends now, is that clear? No more woo-woo stuff about Viking runes and seal women and God knows what else.'

'Sir—'

'No more! You're looking for a local guy Fleming had a serious falling-out with, not some nutter with a pointy hat and a broomstick. And as for Isla Stewart – well, good luck finding someone to talk to you about her now with all this spooky crap flying around.'

Several responses Mahler could make to that assertion. He opts for the one least likely to get him suspended.

'Alex Fleming was found with a pocketful of occult symbols. The girl wore a bracelet with those symbols and thought she was some sort of . . . of seal whisperer. Two murders, twenty years apart – and we're supposed to believe that's just coincidence? I don't like the link any more than you do, but we can't just ignore it!'

Hunt exhales slowly, as though he's experimenting with a new meditation technique. Glares at Mahler with the look of a man who's just found something unspeakable in his dinner. 'Enough. Just . . . go.'

'Sir?'

Another careful exhalation. 'Leave Andy Black and Fergie in charge of things at this end, and get yourself on the first flight back to Kirkwall. This whole enquiry's turning into a grade-A clusterfuck, and your face is right in the middle of it – so go up to Orkney and sort this out. With no more input from Anna Murray and her weirdo pal, understood?'

Mahler weighs up a range of possible responses. Settles for the only one he trusts himself to give. 'Sir.'

He leaves, makes his way downstairs to update Fergie. And finds him outside the MIT room with Amir Riaz and what looks suspiciously like a party pack of Harry Gow doughnuts.

'You do know you two are behaving like walking clichés?'

'Ach, it's the boy's birthday,' Fergie tells him: 'And we were just having a wee debrief about our joint op the other day. Unofficial, like.' Some odd note in Fergie's voice, there. And in spite of the doughnuts, Amir doesn't look particularly celebratory.

'I see. Well, the Chief's asked me to pass on his congratulations to the MIT, and I'm happy to include your team in that, Amir. Picking up Frankie Mason was a great result for everyone involved.'

God, he's channelling Chae Hunt. No wonder Amir's giving

him an odd look. 'Anyway, it went well. So, er, enjoy your doughnuts.'

'Yeah. Thanks.' Amir takes the box, starts to walk away. Turns back. 'That Harkness guy, Lukas. What did you make of him?'

'I can't say I took to him particularly. But he seemed very . . . driven. Very results-oriented. It's what Gartcosh specialises in, I'm guessing.'

'Yeah.' Amir nods. 'Yeah, that's what I thought. See you two around.' He raises a hand in farewell and heads back down the hall to the OCCT room.

Mahler starts to say something, but Fergie shrugs. 'Don't ask me. The way he was talking, it sounded like he'd got his arse kicked over something. But if Ken . . . er, if the Chief's handing out pats on the back, it won't be that. Maybe he's just having a bad day?'

'Aren't we all. And can we please remember not to refer to the Chief by that particular nickname?' Though given some of the others Mahler's heard, comparing Chae Hunt to Barbie's plastic boyfriend is the lesser of several evils.

'Sorry, boss.' Fergie attempts a repentant look. 'So, am I still heading to Kirkwall tomorrow?'

Christ, he'd asked Fergie to go at the morning briefing, hadn't he? Mahler shakes his head. 'Get the team together, Fergie. There's been a change of plan.'

57

There are several options in front of Mahler when he gets back to his flat, all of which would make his life a little better at this point. Apologising to Anna and his mother would be one, except that neither of them are returning his calls. And frankly he doesn't blame them.

Even joining the rest of the MIT for a drink at MacGregor's isn't completely out of the question; he's wary of alcohol as a rule, wary of the loss of control it inevitably brings. But tonight, drinking away the memory of the past twenty-four hours feels dangerously like a rational choice to make. Which is precisely why he doesn't do it.

Instead, he throws some things into a travel bag for his morning flight to Kirkwall, and pulls on his running gear. Heads out round his usual route, adding an extra circuit of the Islands until his heart is pounding and his shirt is sticking to him.

Home and showered, he puts Julie Fowlis on the music system and takes out the last of his grandfather's whisky from the monstrous Art Deco drinks cabinet his mother had insisted he needed in his life. He mouths a silent apology to his grandfather, pours a couple of fingers and drinks it down like medicine, while Julie swears she'll find him somewhere in the dark.

Finally, Mahler picks up the hardback Anna had sent him on

Orcadian folklore, before he'd taken a wrecking ball to their relationship. Stupidity, self-destructiveness, or some lethal combination of the two? Not that it matters, given the result.

He pours another finger of whisky, stretches out on the couch and opens the book at the driest chapter he can find. Sleep still won't come easily, he knows that, but at least he's giving it all the help he can. After a couple of pages, he's starting to drift off.

He puts the book down on the coffee table, thinks about getting up and going through to the bedroom. Sets off *Somewhere* again instead, and closes his eyes to listen one more time.

It's the faintest of sounds that wakes him. Just a click, followed by a barely-there creak in the hallway. Then silence. But not an empty one; whoever's entered his flat is standing there, unmoving. Suppressing their breathing. Assessing whether it's safe to proceed?

Whoever it is, they're good, he'll give them that; if he'd been asleep in bed, Mahler doubts if he'd have heard them. But even with the whisky, sleeping on the couch is only borderline comfortable. And he knows his flat well enough to feel the subtle alteration in atmosphere the intruder's brought with them.

He makes himself remain motionless. Keeps his breathing regular as he hears the door to his bedroom being nudged gently open. His phone's on the coffee table, but he doesn't reach for it yet. Whatever's going on here, it isn't a burglary. Not a normal one, at least.

Mahler eases himself off the couch, pushes the throw and cushion together to approximate the shape of a body sleeping there. It won't fool anyone for more than a few seconds, but he's hoping that's all he'll need.

He waits until his eyes grow accustomed to the dark. Calms his breathing again and takes a couple of cautious steps away from the door as he hears the intruder come out into the hall again.

Looking for him? Got to be, Mahler realises. Another creak, louder this time, as the bathroom door is opened. Then light footsteps coming down the hall. Stopping. The door opening slowly inwards as the figure of a man comes into view—

The anger comes out of nowhere, a vast, adrenaline surge of it powering him forward. He shoots out an arm, grabs the intruder by the neck and lands a blow to the side of his head with his other hand. Feels it connect and reaches for the man's wrist, forcing the arm back and up. *On the floor. Now.*

He pushes his foot hard against the intruder's knee. Hears a grunt of pain, and pushes harder. It should have been enough to bring them down – it almost is. But the intruder arches his back, twists sideways, and gets a punch into Mahler's ribs.

Trained, then; the man's move was too quick, too smooth to be anything else. Which begs a whole new series of questions. If Mahler ever gets the chance to ask them.

He staggers, losing his grip on the intruder as he fights to keep his balance. His height gives him a slight advantage, but if he lets himself be put on the floor, everything changes. Mahler pivots, jabs at the man's solar plexus, aiming fast and hard. But the intruder backs away quickly, his hands raised. He retreats towards the door, flicks the light switch. Pulls off his ski mask and grins at the look on Mahler's face.

'You're fast,' Harkness tells him. 'Angry, too. Excellent.'

He's breathing heavily, and the cut above his eyebrow is bleeding, but he looks far too amused for Mahler's liking. 'Shall we stop now, before we damage each other too badly?'

'You broke into my damn flat.' Mahler's winded and his ribs are throbbing, but right now the thought of damaging Harkness is not without attraction. He gestures towards the middle of the room. 'Over there, hands where I can see them. Tell me what you want, then leave. Preferably without the macho bullshit.'

'Fair enough.' Harkness looks round, spies the near-empty bottle of Lagavulin on the coffee table, but Mahler's there before him. He picks it up, locks it away in the cabinet. Crosses his arms and waits.

Harkness shrugs. 'Not very hospitable, are you? Never mind. To business, then. Let's talk about that little triumph your merry band of misfits managed to pull off. The one that's likely screwed up any chance of us finding the real movers and shakers behind this brotherhood set-up – yes, it's part of what Absinthe was looking into. What the hell did you think you were doing, sticking your nose in there?'

'We had no idea it impinged on Absinthe. We received intel that needed to be acted on urgently and set up a joint operation with local OCCT. One you were informed of—'

'Do I look like I keep office hours to you? By the time I got your sodding email, your clown show was already underway.' Harkness glares at him. 'You'd no authority to sign this off, Mahler. Not you, not your boss.'

'And yet we disrupted a Class A drug-supply chain. Kept God knows how much of the stuff off the streets. And got our hands on the men behind Liam Gerrity's murder. If you call that a little triumph—'

'Who did you get? McMonagle? The Styles brothers? Did you fuck! You got Frankie fucking Mason, whose IQ barely makes it into double digits. He's a foot soldier, Lukas. A disposable. A big fat zero.'

'Who tortured and killed Gerrity with Eddie Ross. Damn right we got him. Damn right we're enjoying that—'

'And big players like the Brotherhood just carry on as normal.' A weary contempt in the look Harkness gives him. 'Yes, they're real. Big enough and efficient enough to make the Styles brothers' operation look like a bloody playgroup. Give them a couple of days, and they'll have a whole new route set up – and that stuff you're so chuffed at taking off the streets? There'll be just as much again back out there next week. But sure, enjoy your moment of glory.'

'You pulled this stunt to tell me that? Seriously?'

'Not entirely. Your operation was bloody irritating, but there was an undeniable . . . slickness to the way you ran it. Sometimes that attracts attention in unexpected quarters.'

Harkness makes a show of looking at the trio of commendations in a discreet frame above Mahler's work station in the corner of the room. 'Your bosses at the Met rated you, you know. Word is, you'd have made DCI a lot sooner if you'd stayed at Charing Cross.'

'I had responsibilities here.'

Harkness nods. 'Your mother, yes. Still, she's doing much better now, isn't she? At the moment. Then there's your little academic friend—'

Mahler takes a step towards him. Sees the flicker of satisfaction on Harkness's face, and stops. The man's testing him, somehow. Pushing for a reaction. Why?

'You know I could call this in.'

'You could,' Harkness agrees. 'But you won't. Because I haven't come just to kick your arse, richly deserved although that is. I've come to offer you a job.'

58

Mahler stares at Harkness. Replays that last sentence in his head and tries to turn it into something that makes sense.

'With OCCT?'

Harkness makes a non-committal gesture. 'We can discuss specifics later. For now all I need to know is whether you're interested in expanding your horizons.'

'Meaning . . .?'

'Don't be dense. You're smart, you're fit, and you think on your feet. Usually. These are . . . transferable skills, shall we say.'

So that's it. Mahler looks Harkness up and down. Allows himself to be briefly flattered at being head-hunted by a genuine spook. And shakes his head. 'Tempting. But my horizons suit me just fine, thanks.'

Annoyance. And a flicker of disbelief on Harkness's face. 'You're wasted here, man. Seriously, this is as far as you want to go? DCI in Nessieland?'

'Maybe not. But the job I'm doing right now gives me enough of a clear conscience to let me sleep at night. I somehow doubt working for you would do the same.'

Harkness shakes his head. 'Trust me, you're making a mistake. This is a one-time only offer.'

'I'll take that chance.' Mahler crosses to the door, pushes it wide. 'Now, if you don't want to take a chance on whether I'll call this in, I suggest—'

Harkness shoots out a hand, grips Mahler by the throat. Slams him against the wall with the casual ease of someone who's done it before. Many times. 'Not a good idea. Take it as a friendly warning.'

'Acting like a Bond villain counts as friendly?'

'Trust me on that one.' A razor-wire smile flickers. Dies. 'Right then, this is how the rest of this mess plays out. Two of my team will be here tomorrow morning to interview Mason and Ross. It's not connected with your enquiry, it won't take long, and your lot will keep their nose out until we're done. Is that clear?'

Mahler starts to say something, but Harkness shakes his head. 'Not up for discussion. You've got your collars for Liam Gerrity's murder so be happy with that. And leave the grown-ups to salvage something from this almighty fuck-up.'

Something off, here. Something *badly* off. Mahler briefly considers not taking the shot in the dark he's contemplating. And goes for it anyway.

'The Holland connection. That's what this whole "mopping-up" crap was about, isn't it? Nothing to do with Cazza MacKay – you were on a fishing trip, pure and simple. Gerrity was just collateral damage.' Suddenly the car he'd seen at HQ late one evening makes perfect sense. 'Why couldn't we just have worked together on any of this?'

'Not your business, matey. Not any longer. So get your paperwork ready for the Fiscal and move on. We clear?'

At Mahler's nod, steps back. Looks him up and down. Nods. 'Good. Needless to say, I was never here and this conversation didn't happen. In the meantime, keep your fucking nose out of things above your pay grade.'

Harkness goes out into the hallway, makes his way to the door. Turns back to look at Mahler. 'Like I said, you've attracted attention, Lukas. Your name's come up in conversation a couple of times at Tulliallan, for example – nothing major, just a few mentions in passing. Better make sure it continues to be for the right reasons, yeah?'

The door closes behind him. Mahler walks to the window, watches Harkness walk out of the entrance. As he crosses towards the river, a taxi pulls up and Harkness gets inside. Mahler thinks briefly about checking the plate, then realises how completely pointless it would be. He doubts that's a genuine taxi, and he very much doubts those are its original plates.

The Holland connection. He'd used Gerrity's phrase to get a reaction from Harkness, and it had worked. Harkness's expression had stayed completely neutral, apart from a momentary flicker of something so unexpected, Mahler almost missed it.

Relief.

Relief, because *Holland* isn't the connection to McMonagle or the Styles brothers or even the bloody Brotherhood Harkness was looking for; they were hunting for a man, not a location.

A man whose name Mahler had first come across two years earlier during a murder enquiry that's still unsolved, still waiting for that elusive final breakthrough; he and Fergie had come so close to tracking him down back then, only to be told by the powers-that-be at the Crime Campus that no such man existed.

A man Mahler suspects is the real force behind organised crime's incursions into the Highland area.

A man who'd organised at least one brutal murder and a string of arson attacks, covering his tracks with an expertise that tells Mahler he's been doing it for a long, long time.

A man called Hollander.

59

Orkney

The sun is bright enough for midsummer when Mahler lands in Kirkwall. But there's a winter bite in the air, a rawness that catches in his throat and makes him grateful for his heavy over-coat, even on the short walk to the terminal.

With a storm due to arrive by early evening, the concourse is all but deserted. The Avis clerk gives him a doubtful look as she hands over a set of keys.

'If you're heading anywhere off Mainland, I wouldn't leave it too long – they've already cancelled a couple of ferry sailings this lunchtime,' she warns him. 'Don't be out near the water later on, if you can help it. And check with Radio Orkney for road closures.'

Mahler assures her he'll be careful, switches his mobile on and heads outside to pick up his hire car. He's only halfway there when the call from Craig Falconer at CAHID comes in.

'Lukas, great, I caught you – listen, have you looked at my report on the skeletal remains yet?'

'Only briefly.' He'd glanced at it during the flight, and put it aside until he could concentrate on it fully. But there's an edge of excitement in Falconer's voice that's making him regret that now. 'Craig, if there's something I need to know—'

'The bone pit. I said in my email that I'd asked for some

supplementary research on the material we found there, if you recall. Well, the results came through today – and boy, do they make interesting reading.'

'Go on.'

A definite hint of smugness in Falconer's voice now. 'Yep – some interesting organic matter we wanted an expert opinion on. So we spoke nicely to our friends at the Hutton Institute. Go us, huh?'

'Soil forensics?' The twist between his shoulder blades pulls a little tighter. The Hutton Institute is world-renowned for the breadth of its expertise. And the assistance its expert witnesses have provided to governments and law enforcement agencies across the globe. 'Enough teasing, Craig. What did they find?'

'Hold on.' Rapid tapping on a keyboard at the other end of the line. 'Report's on its way to you now. But the short version is, their tests revealed traces of *Hyoscyamus niger,* better known as black henbane. *Conium maculatum*, or hemlock. And *Atropa belladonna*, known as—'

'Deadly nightshade, yes. It's highly toxic, isn't it?'

'According to my forensic toxicology pal, they all are. And the chances of all three of them occurring naturally in that location and in those concentrations, are frankly minimal.'

Falconer sighs, the earlier smugness dropping from his voice. 'Got to hand it to you, Lukas – right now, your investigations are cornering the market in weird. I can't tell you what killed these women – given the condition of the remains, there's no way we'll ever know for sure. But if I had to pick a cause of death, I'd say it's highly likely those women were all poisoned.'

'Poisoned?' Whatever Mahler had been expecting, it wasn't that. 'With those toxins?'

'That'd be a reasonable assumption, yes – but I'm not done with the weird stuff yet. Something about that combination

271

nagged at me, so I did a bit of digging. Turns out they were common ingredients in a funky medieval concoction known as witches' flying salve.'

Witches. Flying. Mahler exhales, massages the area of tension building at his right temple. 'I know I'll regret asking, but why flying?'

'Ah.' The smugness is back in Falconer's voice. 'Some of the sources are a bit dodgy, you understand, and it would depend on the precise quantities of the toxins involved, but basically, transdermal absorption of mixtures like these could produce psychotropic effects including intense hallucinations, feelings of euphoria, and a feeling of being able to fly. In other words, you'd have the trip of your life – if it didn't kill you, that is.'

'And this stuff was absorbed through the skin?'

'In a salve or ointment, yes. I'll stick all this in an email and send it over, but I thought you'd have questions – and you know I'm always happy to talk weird stuff with you.'

'I wish I could say the same. But thanks.'

A pull at the back of his neck as he ends the call and finds his hire car. *Weird stuff.* Exactly what this case needs, he thinks. More weird.

He unlocks the car, chucks his jacket in the back and sends an urgent email to Marco McVinish. The pathologist's report had mentioned the same toxins as Falconer, but he hadn't established how they were administered. But what if someone had managed to concoct a modern-day version of the witches' salve? If they'd overpowered Alex first, could that be how—

Another call. Another number flashing up on his screen. When he answers, Gudrun's practically shouting in his ear.

'Lukas, you're here in Kirkwall, yes? Fergie told me. Good. Can you meet me in Judith Glue's?'

'Right now? Gudrun, I've only just arrived, and—'

'Now, please.' She's stopped shouting, but the urgency in her voice is unmistakable. 'I have news about those runes you found. And that house.'

60

Kirkwall Police Station

Tony reads through the overtime figures, makes a last-minute correction, and sends them through for processing. He doubts HQ will be impressed with this month's increase, but they're not in any position to object; dealing with the Sandisquoy enquiry is eating up resources, even if his budget must look like a drop in the ocean compared to Lukas Mahler's MIT guys.

The enquiry's taking its toll on Tony's team. Taking its toll on him too, he supposes. Folks don't really turn grey overnight, he knows that, but he's convinced his short pepper and salt crop is sporting a hell of a lot more salt these days. And the under-eye bags that greet him in the bathroom mirror every morning bear depressing witness to how little sleep he's currently getting by on.

Not that any of his team are faring much better. They've adapted, because they're in the Job, and that's what they do; they put on their calm, professional faces and go out to deal with things none of them had ever expected to see, not in their entire careers. What they'd seen at Sandisquoy had been . . . no, he won't call it evil. Not a word he uses. Not a concept he believes in.

But it had affected them all in different ways, he can't deny that. Spreading through the station like a bloody virus. Forcing them to adapt to the sound of constantly ringing phones, the journos doorstepping folk like wee Colin McAvoy, hassling the desk staff—

Phones. The phones aren't ringing.

Tony closes his laptop. Sits up straight. Listens out for the sounds from the front desk, the sounds his ears are so attuned to now that he has to force himself not to simply insert them into the sudden silence. When that doesn't happen, when the front desk world stays silent, Tony's up and moving towards his office door, hand reaching for his baton—

No one behind the desk. No lights blinking on any of the phones. No bloody lights anywhere. What the—?

Movement in the corner. Tony turns. Starts to call out. And stares at the hunched form of Murdo Sangster, his desk sergeant, huddled in the tiny space between the copier and the filing cabinet.

'Bloody hell, Murdo.' Tony's racing heart slows to something approaching normal as he walks over to see what the problem is. 'What's happened, electrics had a meltdown? We'll need—'

The words die in his throat as Murdo looks up at him. He's unshaven, puffy-faced, his uniform stained and crumpled as though he's been on a three-day bender. But it's the look in his eyes that makes Tony take a half-step backwards as Murdo holds out his phone towards him.

'It's not the electrics. I just . . . everything was too bloody bright, that's all. So I pulled the plug.'

'You pulled—'

'Joyce's nursing home rang.' Murdo sounds as though the words are being pulled from him, and Tony flinches, guessing what surely must be coming. 'They told me she . . . she . . .' He shudders, lets the mobile fall to the floor. 'Her heart gave out, so it's over now. All of it.'

Ah, Christ. 'I'm sorry, man. God, that's . . . I'm sorry.' Tony stretches out a hand to help him out of the tiny space, but Murdo shrinks away, shaking his head.

'Not yet! Not until I've said my piece.' He takes in a ragged breath. 'Joyce is gone, Tony. She . . . doesn't need me anymore. I don't have to protect her anymore.'

'Protect her?'

'From what we did that night. From the whole damn *weight* of knowing what we'd done. How we could never put it right.'

A slow heaviness forms in Tony's guts. Heaviness, and the sick suspicion that however bad his day's been up to that point, it's about to get a whole lot worse. 'Murdo, man, you're not making any sense. Look, you've had a shock – come out of there, and we'll get the doc in to see you—'

'You're not listening to me! You need to listen to me, Tony. You need me to tell the truth about it all.'

Murdo pulls his feet in, clasps his hands around his knees. Starts a slow, rhythmic rocking that sets every nerve in Tony's body jangling. 'Just give me a minute, eh? A wee bit more time before I tell you how it happened that night near the headland.'

No. *No.* Voices coming closer. The sound of swing doors opening behind them as Tony stares down at his desk sergeant. His *friend*. And tells himself whatever Murdo's talking about, it can't be *that* thing. Not that.

'How what happened, Murdo?' Keeping his voice calm, his face composed as the pair of uniformed officers reach them. 'What is it you think you did?'

Murdo stops rocking. Scrubs his hand across his eyes. And looks up at Tony.

'I killed her, of course. I killed Isla Stewart. And I hid her body at Sandisquoy.'

61

Kirkwall

When Mahler arrives at Judith Glue's, Gudrun's waiting at the back of the café. She manages a smile and wave of greeting for him, but Mahler doesn't miss the way she uses both hands to guide her large cappuccino to her mouth.

'I haven't got long, I'm afraid,' he warns. 'My flight was delayed, and I'm due at Burgh Road shortly.'

Gudrun shakes her head. 'I have meetings also, but this won't take long. And it's important, I think.' She opens her rucksack and takes out a slim, cloth-bound book. 'We talked a little about the seal runes last time, yes? I asked you to send me the images of what was found with the Sandisquoy woman.'

Hell. 'You did – Gudrun, I'm sorry. Now that there's been a positive identification of the remains, the enquiry's moved onto a different footing, and—'

'Things have been so busy for you, I can see this in your face,' she tells him. 'It's not a problem. Because after our talk, I have been busy too. I talked to some people about local history. Looked around in the library a little. And I found this, misfiled in the reference section for Scandinavian mythology. I'd say I came across it by accident, but now . . .' Her shrug holds more than a hint of nervousness as she passes him the book. 'Maybe I'm starting to believe in *wyrd* – in fate – a little myself.'

Mahler takes the book. Neither the author's name nor the title, *Folk Tales of the Orkney Isles*, mean anything to him at first. But the cover image, embossed into the cloth, is a gaunt Victorian building standing alone at the edge of a rocky coastline.

'This is Eliza Rattray's book?'

'Marsetter was her mother's maiden name,' Gudrun tells him. 'Please, look at the page I've marked for you.'

Mahler opens it at the bookmarked page. Stares at the illustration directly beneath the chapter number. 'Bind-runes?'

Gudrun nods. 'Not every chapter has them. But this story comes from Viking times. It talks about a *vǫlva*, a seeress, who lived on these islands. She was not a nice person, this seeress. She was said to worship *Selkolla*, a seal demon who took the form of a woman, and—'

'A seal demon.' Mahler stares at her. Tries to tell himself he's wrong about where she's going with this. 'Gudrun, this had better not be heading into supernatural territory—'

She produces a withering look. And what he suspects is an Icelandic swear word.

'She wore a cloak of seal skins, this seeress. She gathered a group of followers – a coven, you would maybe call it – and taught them how to fly, according to this story. No one knows where she was buried, but it's said her followers kept it as a sort of shrine, burying their most honoured dead with her in turn. And those women taught their daughters what they'd learned.' Gudrun leans forward, taps the bind-rune illustration.

'Where did Eliza get this bind-rune from, Lukas? How did she know to put it with this story?' He starts to say something, but she holds up her hand. 'I know, I know – but what if her followers are still around? A secret thing, a thing maybe this young girl stumbled on and couldn't be allowed to talk about? What if—'

'Okay, that's it.' Mahler shakes his head, gets to his feet.

'Gudrun, the rune connection is . . . interesting. But that's where it ends. Twenty years ago, a young woman was brutally murdered – beaten to death, in all likelihood, by some evil but all-too-human bastard. That's who I'm going to bring to justice, Gudrun, not some gang of modern-day witches. And certainly not some bloody Viking seal demon!'

'That's not—'

'No!'

A scraping of chairs. Mahler looks round in time to see the last couple leave the café, casting nervous glances behind them as they leave. He exhales, brings his voice down to something approaching its normal level.

'No more, Gudrun. No more runes, no more myths and folk tales, no more digging into this like some sort of Icelandic Miss Marple. This is an ongoing police investigation, and—'

Tony Armstrong's number flashes onto his mobile. Mahler answers. Listens. Starts to say something a couple of times. Stops. When Armstrong finishes speaking, Mahler tells him he's on his way.

'Bad news?'

Mahler puts the phone away. 'I'm beginning to wonder if there's any other kind. Take care, Gudrun. And no more amateur detective work. Please.'

The duty medical officer has agreed Murdo Sangster's fit to undergo an initial interview, but Mahler's not convinced. The man's recovered from his earlier breakdown, but his expression is remote, disconnected, as though only part of him is there in the room with them.

'You've said you don't want a solicitor with you at this time. Or your union representative. Is that still the case?'

'It is.'

Armstrong starts to say something, but Sangster holds up a

hand. 'My choice, Tony. I've waited twenty years for this to be over, and I'm tired. Let me tell it my way, aye?' He looks across at Mahler. 'If you still have questions once I'm done, I'll answer anything you want.'

At Mahler's nod, Sangster lets out a long, slow breath. 'Okay, then. It was the year I got accepted for the force. Joyce's brother Ewan was back from uni – he was a second year medic, doing really well by all accounts. One of his pals was playing in a band at the Ferry Inn in Stromness, so we went over to see them perform.' He shakes his head at the memory. 'They weren't that great – bloody terrible, in fact – but we still enjoyed ourselves. It was one of those nights, you know? One of those really good nights you get sometimes.'

'You were celebrating. Enjoying a few drinks. And then?' Mahler has a sudden bleak certainty that he knows where this is going, but he needs Sangster to say the words himself. 'What happened then?'

Sangster stares down at his hands, his shoulders hunched. When he raises his head, his face looks ten years older. 'Then I got in the car to drive us home. And yes, I knew I was over the limit. But the roads were quieter in those days – I know it's not an excuse, but they were. We didn't meet a soul on the way, until we got to Sandisquoy headland. Then the girl . . .' He swallows, shakes his head. 'You have to believe me – she came out of nowhere, running like an axe-murderer was on her tail. There was no chance of avoiding her, none!'

'Isla,' Armstrong snaps. 'Christ, Murdo, at least give her back her name. The girl you killed . . .' He frowns, breaks off. 'Hold on. You were driving home from Stromness with Joyce and Ewan. So what were you doing at Sandisquoy – hell of a detour, isn't it?'

'We were taking the back roads. Just in case.'

No. Something in Sangster's face, then. Some tormented,

hidden thing. Mahler leans forward. 'You said you want this to be over, but there's something you're not telling us. What is it, Murdo?'

'They were on the way to Birsay,' Armstrong's talking to Mahler, but it's Sangster's face he's watching. 'It's where you lived back then, isn't it? But that only makes sense if you were going to be dropped off first. If someone else was driving. Someone like Ewan.'

Sangster bends his head, his shoulders hunching further as the silence stretches out. Finally, he nods. 'Doesn't matter now, does it? They're both gone, him and Joyce. He tried to help her, though – Ewan did everything he could, I need you to believe that.'

Everything except call an ambulance. The words hang in the air, unspoken. Mahler nods. 'What happened then?'

'She died.' Sangster heaves a long, shuddering sigh. 'Died on the road while we stood there watching. And what we did was wrong, so wrong – but the lassie was dead, and there was no bringing her back. We were in a blind panic, all of us! Then . . . then Joyce remembered the underground room at Sandisquoy.'

'How did she know about it?'

'Joyce's ma was friends with Eliza Rattray,' Sangster tells them. 'Kept an eye on her house if she went away, popped in now and again to check she was okay. She even talked about having written a book with her once, though I don't know if that's true. That's how we knew where . . . where to put her. Eliza was in hospital and the house was empty. So we let ourselves in with her ma's key, and we did what we had to do.'

And Isla's bracelet? When Mahler asks about it, Sangster looks blankly at him. 'Fell off, probably. That or it got broken while we were moving her.'

Mahler nods. 'So Eliza died, and Alex Fleming bought the

house. You panicked then, didn't you? If Alex found the chamber—'

A weary headshake. 'It wasn't me,' Sangster tells him. 'I get why you'd think that, but there was no one left who knew about the chamber by then – even if Fleming found it, what would link her to us? And by then, Joyce was ill, and she wasn't going to get better. And as long as I lasted until she'd gone, I didn't give a damn what happened after that.'

He wipes a hand across his mouth. Raises haggard eyes to meet theirs. 'It's always there, you know – like a video, stuck inside my head. The sound of her hitting the bonnet. The . . . the blood. That awful bubbling in her throat, when—' Sangster draws a ragged breath, turns to Mahler. 'She spoke to me. Her mouth was all bloody, and her eyes . . .' He shudders at the memory. 'I was trying not to be sick, so I wasn't sure I'd heard her—'

'What? What did Isla say, Murdo?'

'She said . . .' Sangster scrubs at his mouth again. 'She said, "I saw her face. I called her, and she came".'

62

Orkney

There are formalities to be completed, paperwork to be put in order. Debriefs to be arranged and meetings to be scheduled with Cath McAvoy, the Fiscal. And of course, the inevitable holding statement to be compiled for Media Liaison. And Mahler can't face any of it. He leaves Tony Armstrong to set everything in motion, goes back to his car and drives out of Kirkwall.

It's a pleasant little place, the kind of place he could enjoy wandering round at any other time, but even in the islands' tiny capital, there are more people around than he can cope with right now. Sometimes Mahler suspects the tally of people he can cope with, even on his best days, is gradually reducing. And this is very far from one of his best days.

He stops at a petrol station, grabs a sandwich and takeaway coffee, and finds a near-deserted car park by the shore, a little way out of Finstown. The first time he'd come to Orkney, the sea had been a deep, jewel-bright blue, but in mid-November the water is a chill, dark pewter.

Mahler opens the sandwich, peers at its innards, and opts for the coffee instead as he walks along the shoreline. The wind feels as though it's scouring the skin from his face, but after the interview room's desiccating heat, it's almost pleasant.

I saw her face. I called her, and she came. Isla Stewart's final words are lodged inside his head, resisting all his attempts to make sense of them. Who had she called? *Who?*

He drains the coffee, looks round for a bin. He'll have to go back into Kirkwall in a little while, he knows that. Check on Armstrong's progress, report in to the Chief. But for the moment, minimal phone reception by the water means—

Buzzing in his pocket. Reminding him that minimal doesn't mean zero. Mahler pulls out his phone to see Fergie's number flashing on the display.

'Boss, you still in Kirkwall? Better head back there sharp-ish, if not.'

More grimness in Fergie's voice than he's heard in a long time. Mahler's stomach clenches in anticipation; whatever Fergie's got for him now, it's nothing good.

'Just outside Finstown, but it won't take long to get back.' He turns around, starts to head for the car. 'What's happened?'

'I did more digging on Fleming – Shawcross got the wrong victim, boss. Ruth Osborne was an only child, and her husband's sister died when she was a kid. Whoever Fleming was sleeping with, it must have been—'

Mahler stops dead. Stares at the BMW he's heading for on auto-pilot instead of his hire car. The one at the other end of the car park. He swears, about-turns, but the phone signal's dying; he catches something about *Alison* and *Kate*, and the call drops.

More swearing. He's running now, waiting for *no service* to disappear. A single bar pops up briefly as he gets to the car. Before he can ring Fergie, a message preview flashes up:

Flying salve plants grow at Sandisquoy. Going to get evidence.

Ms Marple

This time he swears loudly enough to scare a scavenging gull into flight. Getting evidence from a crime scene. The crime scene where Colin McAvoy had disturbed an intruder and earned himself a stay in hospital. She's sent a photo as well – a selfie posing with the plants, no doubt – but it's not downloading.

Mahler glances at the time stamp. Tight, but if he leaves now . . . He can call Fergie back once he's found Gudrun, read her the riot act about playing amateur detective again, and still get back to Kirkwall to assist Tony Armstrong. He types up a text ready to send once he gets a signal, and sets out for Sandisquoy.

It's only three-thirty, but the light is already failing, the wide Orcadian skies closing in around him as he drives through Finstown and out onto the coast road. By the time the headland comes into view, the sea and gunmetal skies are merging, the landscape slowly emptying of colour.

He rounds the final bend in the road, and Sandisquoy appears, bleak and solitary at the foot of its long, rutted track. It's not old by Orkney standards, Mahler knows that, but the half-dark is playing with his perception of the house, distorting its stark angles into odd, unsettling shapes. Not for the first time, he wonders if anyone could live there for long and still retain their sanity.

He pulls off the road, kills the engine. There's enough of a signal here for him to send the first text. And to see the image sent from Gudrun's phone, the one he hadn't been able to download earlier.

The one showing her lying on a stone floor, eyes closed, face ghost-pale.

Mahler exhales slowly. Pushes back the sickness rising in his gut. He should hold off until he can call for back-up, of course he should; he has no idea what he might be walking into, what he might be dealing with. But if Gudrun's badly hurt—

Mahler gets out, stuffs a pair of nitrile gloves into one pocket and shoe covers in the other, and sets off down the track.

Halfway there, he stops. A car is parked at the side of the house, but it's not the one he'd been expecting, and the scenario he's been constructing in his head abruptly falls apart. To be replaced by an even less welcome one.

Mahler pulls out his mobile, checks for a signal as he walks up to the door. Nothing yet, but he taps out another message to accompany the first, hits *send*. Even now, he's hoping he's got this wrong. Hoping there's no way what's going through his mind can possibly be true.

He pushes the door, watches it swing open. He steps inside, moves slowly along the hall, checking each room in turn. Not calling out, because there's no point; whoever's here knows exactly who he is. And why he's come.

No sign of Gudrun or her attacker. Once the ground floor's clear, he heads upstairs, works his way through the rooms in turn until he reaches Alex Fleming's attic studio. Mahler knows the room by now, knows the impact of its stark white space after the gloom on every other floor, but its chill brilliance still stops him in his tracks when he pushes the door wide.

An empty brilliance now, though; the film of dust coating the wooden floorboards is undisturbed, telling him no one's been here recently. And the twitch between his shoulders is stronger than ever, a bright stab of urgency driving him back downstairs. To the one place he realises he's overlooked.

The entrance to the passage had been closed earlier, Mahler's sure of it. Now it's standing open. He takes a step towards it. Stops. It's cold there, colder than it ought to be, even allowing for the empty, unheated house. And a distant high-pitched cry draws ragged fingernails down his back. *Seals. The damn seals.* But he shouldn't be able to hear them, not here. Not unless—

The signal icon's back on his mobile display; only one bar, but it'll have to be enough. Mahler brings up his message, hits *send*. And starts to turn, too late, as the air displaces behind him.

Something thuds into the back of his neck, forcing him to his knees.

Heavy breathing. Movement. Something rough being forced over his head.

Another blow.

Then nothing.

63

Sandisquoy
Two Days Before the End

He walks through the house like a king walking through his palace. No fear now of the sounds half heard in the darkness of the night, no fear of what he's glimpsed in the shadows. Ridiculous that he'd ever allowed himself to get so low. How could he ever have believed that anything here could harm him?

The booze, he thinks. It must have been the booze. How often had he told himself to quit? But he'd been weak, then, thinking he needed its crutch to get him through the long Orcadian nights. Thinking he needed to lock away the knowledge of the man he'd been, the history he'd carried with him for so long. How could he ever have believed he'd be satisfied with that?

He goes upstairs to his studio, walks to the stack of canvasses piled against the furthest wall. They're better than he'd thought, he can see that now. Not as good as the ones he'd produced in the heat of that parched London summer of 2008, of course; he thinks they may have been the best he's ever done. But they'd been a little too faithful to their subject matter; a smoking gun, you might say, if suspicion had ever fallen his way. So once he'd made up his mind to move here, he'd made himself destroy them all.

One of the most painful decisions of his life, that. It still gets him now sometimes, if he's honest. But moving to the other end of the country, he'd needed to hire a firm to transport his belongings, and he couldn't rid himself of the mental image of a pair of careless removal men smashing open a crate containing his greatest treasures, and the canvasses spilling out in front of them. And what he'd created once, he could do again, he knows that now. Even if he'll have to be more discreet than ever, now he'll be flying solo.

He reaches behind the final canvas, lifts the loose piece of wooden flooring. Takes out the little bag of carved bones he'd taken from the withered thing in the chamber. He doesn't know if their strange markings mean anything, and frankly, he doesn't care. As soon as he'd set eyes on them, he'd known they were a sign. A call to action, if you like. And at last, he's finally ready to answer that call again. It'll be harder working alone, without the tricks of the Job to cover his tracks. Without the special bond he'd had back then. Harder, but safer. And ultimately, more satisfying.

Sanctuary. He'd thought that's what this place had offered him, but he'd been wrong. The house had known him, somehow. Known what he was, and offered him a straightforward choice: carry on hiding in the shadows, cursing the seal-things in the bay and drinking himself to death. Or be the man he was always meant to be.

The killer he was always meant to be.

64

Mahler opens his eyes to darkness.

Not the near-instant totality of black, whose suddenness is the last thing he remembers. This dark is faded, uneven patches of grey light bleeding through it like sun through cheap linen, and it smells of sweat and ozone. There's something wrong with his face, some odd shrouded heaviness against his skin, and a smell like rotting vegetation. He's cold, too, colder than he's ever been. And he can't move his arms. Or his legs.

Bit by bit, as memory returns, he starts to understand the reality of where he is. And what's been done to him.

The passageway. The seals' distant, high-pitched cries. Christ, how could he have been so stupid?

The sound of footsteps, moving across the shingle. He strains to listen as they come closer, gets the final confirmation he needs. As the footsteps halt in front of him, he sucks in the salt and ozone air, moistens his dry lips.

'You didn't need the hood. I'd worked out it was you.' A little late, but he'd got there.

Silence. Then there are hands on his shoulders, yanking the hood upwards and off. He blinks, tries to clear his vision; right until the last minute, he'd been hoping he'd got it wrong, but the face bending over him is the one he's expecting to see.

Liz Clarke, the first Witchfinder victim, that's what Fergie had been trying to tell him.

Liz Clarke's sister.

'I'm sorry.' Cath McAvoy straightens, rises. 'This isn't where I expected us to end up, Lukas. I need you to believe that.'

'And yet here we are. So, when did you pick up the Doric accent – was it when you switched from Kate to Cath, or when you studied law at Aberdeen?'

A shrug. 'I needed to make sure no one connected me with Liz's shy wee sister. Anyway, our mam was from Inverurie, so I was just going back to my roots, really.'

The shingle crunches under her feet as she takes a half-step backwards. 'You had a chance to save yourself, you know. If you'd stepped back, right at the beginning . . . DCIs aren't meant to be this hands-on, are they? And with your personal connection to Fleming . . .' Cath shakes her head. 'You shouldn't have been anywhere near this case, Lukas. You know that, don't you? Think of all the folk who've been hurt because of your pig-headedness.'

'It's been mentioned.' And she's right, he realises. Matt. Colin. Gudrun. *Gudrun.* He runs his tongue over his lips again. 'You took a chance sending me that photo. Is Gudrun . . . is she okay?'

An impatient nod. 'I needed to bring you out here, and she was on hand – don't worry, I gave her a wee dose of something to make her sleep and dumped her in the chamber, that's all. I've no reason to want her dead.'

'Unlike me, I assume. Why re-enact Alex's murder, though? Why not just chuck me in the sea and make me disappear?'

He catches her expression. And answers his own question. 'You *want* me to be found like he was – the Witchfinder link's been established, but you want it hammered home. And Alex had to die because he let you down. Promised to find your sister's killer, took advantage of you when you were vulnerable. But Alex failed you – he failed you, then he just moved on. Then—'

'That's the best you can come up with?' She gives him a bright, angry smile. 'Do better, Lukas. It shouldn't be that hard. Not for you.'

'Help me out, then.' Trying to ignore the strange numbness creeping into his limbs. Trying not to think about the texts he'd sent, the ones he isn't sure had managed to get through. 'Help me understand, Cath. You want justice for your sister, yes? You want her killer found. But—'

'I know who killed my sister! It took me years to put it all together, but when I did . . . I wanted pain for him, Lukas. I wanted suffering, and fear. I wanted *death*. And that's what I gave him.'

'No.' He tries to shake his head, forgetting he can't move. 'You think Alex was the Witchfinder killer? Cath, that's crazy. You *know* it can't have been him—'

'I have proof. It's in a paper file in a case at the bottom of my wardrobe – and a memory stick in my office safe, with Fleming's dying declaration on it.' Cath's mouth twists in a bitter smile. 'He thought telling the truth would save him, I suppose. Thought I'd take him in to Tony after he confessed.' She folds her arms, gives Mahler a look he can't decipher. 'Fleming killed those women, Lukas. He killed them all. But you know that, don't you? Because he didn't work alone. He couldn't have – he needed an accomplice.' A coldness settles on her face. 'Or maybe an apprentice.'

It takes him a moment to put her words together and work out what she means. *Who* she means.

'No!' Mahler tries to shake his head, winces as the strap pulls around his neck. For God's sake, you can't believe—'

'He was your friend. Your *mentor*. That's what you told

me, isn't it? Took me a while to work it out, but once I did, everything made sense.' A brief almost-smile lifts one corner of her mouth. 'I nearly didn't recognise Alex, you know that? He'd got fat and old – and if I hadn't been going to a meeting at the Community Centre that day, I'd never have seen him. Enough to make you believe in fate, I—' She breaks off, turns as if startled by something.

'What's wrong?'

'Nothing.' She frowns, rubs her eyes. 'Nothing. I've mailed another memory stick to the media, and one to each of the other victim's families. Should be enough to stir things up a bit, don't you think?'

'Whatever proof you think you've got, it's wrong. Alex wasn't a killer, and neither am I. You *know* that, damn it!'

The flicker of uncertainty on her face gives him a moment of hope, but it's gone the next second.

Cath shakes her head, gives him a grimly satisfied smile. 'Nice try, but it all fits. I don't expect a confession from you, don't worry – once those memory sticks are out there, it won't take much for folk to start joining the dots.' She frowns, bends towards him. 'How are you feeling, by the way?' She tilts his head up, checks his pupils. 'I gave you something to . . . to make things a bit easier for you.'

'The witches' salve. I assume it made us easier to handle, too.'

He can feel the vagueness creeping into his brain, matching the heaviness in his limbs. There's something else, too; strange flickering colours dancing in and out of his vision. And an odd fluttering in his chest. *Deadly nightshade and black henbane. Maybe a little mandrake on the side.* 'How did you know about that?'

He stumbles over his words; the stuff she's given him is spreading through his system like a virus. *Keep talking.* He has to keep talking. Keep himself *alive.*

Cath's mouth twists in a smile. 'You can call it fate, if you like. I followed Fleming to find out where he lived, and when I saw the house . . . Don't you feel it? This place is *old*, Lukas. Old, and powerful. I stood on the headland that day, and I felt it call to me.' She glances back at the house, still smiling. 'So I did my research. Hit the library, and found everything I needed.'

'Eliza Rattray's book. Cath, they're just folk tales, for God's sake!'

A shrug. 'The power here is real enough. Who's to say whether it comes from the Viking priestess and the women they buried with her, or the place itself? And the witches' salve – you know *that's* real enough, don't you? You can feel it working through you, I can see it in your face.'

'Tony knows I'm here.' Slurring his words. Focus. *Focus*. 'I . . . I sent a text—'

'To his mobile, yes. Which he seems very carelessly to have misplaced after I dropped in to see him about Murdo.' She glances up at the darkening sky, and back at him. 'You're tiring now, aren't you? Try not to fight it, Lukas. It shouldn't be long.'

'No! Cath, don't do this. Please.'

His body feels oddly weightless, as though the belt round his neck is the only thing tethering him to the ground. Floating. *Flying* . . . His head fills with a nightmare image of him choking on his own vomit as his oesophagus slowly shuts down. He forces down the sourness in his throat. 'It's not too late to stop this.'

'Of course it is.' A hint of impatience in the look she gives him. 'Can't guarantee it will be painless for you – didn't look that way for Fleming – but it should be fairly quick. And your death . . . your death will give those women the justice they were denied.'

She strips off her gloves, puts them in the clear plastic bag at her feet and stuffs it in her rucksack.

'Right, time for me to leave. I've got a booking on the last ferry to Aberdeen, and after that . . . well, we'll see what happens, won't we? I've a few wee changes in mind to make to my appearance. And I know a few folk who can organise fresh ID for me, if it comes to that.' Her mouth quirks in a grim smile. 'Cops and lawyers always do, don't they? Maybe we all live a little too close to the dark side.'

She reaches for her rucksack. Misses. Frowns, as though she's trying to work something out. And there's something odd about her expression—

'Cath, what is it? What's wrong?'

She stares down at her hands. Raises them to her face. Inhales. And her mouth falls open, her eyes wide and disbelieving as she holds them out in front of her.

The salve. It's all over her gloves. And she's been touching her face while we've been talking. Touching her eyes, her mouth—

'Cath, don't panic. You'll get a signal in the garden. Go and call 999—'

Inside his head, he's shouting at her. But only inside his head; his tongue feels thick and stupid in his mouth, and his voice is a rusty croak.

Mahler watches her eyes slide past him, fix on an empty patch of shingle a couple of metres away. Hears her scream. Sees her shake her head, once. Twice. And then she's running, flying across the shingle towards the darkening horizon. Plunging into the ink-dark sea.

As the shock of the icy water makes contact with her skin, Cath cries out. A moment later, a line of sleek dark heads break the surface as a pod of curious seals bob closer. Mahler manages to shout her name, just once, and Cath turns her head; turns to look at him, he thinks, until he realises her eyes are fixed on something just beyond his field of vision. And then she disappears.

She reappears almost immediately, her mouth open as though she's trying to scream. Mahler tries to call her name again, but it's getting harder and harder to keep his vision clear of the darkness creeping in around him. And his voice is failing, lost in the bleak sound of the seals' urgent keening as Cath dips out of sight once more.

As he closes his eyes, the sleek dark heads begin to swim away.

65

Police sirens, wailing through the dark towards him.

Vehicles rumbling down a rutted track.

Stopping. Doors opening and slamming shut.

Footsteps hurrying over shingle.

Shouting.

Coming closer.

Lights.

Lights, so blindingly bright they feel as though they're burning through his eyelids. Mahler winces at the brightness, tries to turn his head away, but there are faces bending over him now. Frowning, exchanging glances. Talking in calm, professional voices that don't quite match the worried looks they're giving him.

A momentary tightness round his neck, and then it's gone. He slumps forward, but there are arms supporting him, voices telling him to stay with them, the ambulance is on its way—

Cath. Cath in the water!

Reaching out to grab an arm with fingers that won't move. Trying to shout with a voice that's barely a whisper as the faces above him start to blur. The last thing he hears is the keening of the seals as his rescuers signal to whatever's rumbling down the track towards them.

More lights. And more faces, drifting in and out of focus. Mahler floats in a hallucinogenic haze, his thoughts untethered, aimless. Some part of him understands that he's been taken to hospital; *the Balfour*, he thinks. The *Balfour in Kirkwall*. But then the pastel walls he glimpses seem to melt away, and he's back at Sandisquoy. At times his body feels weightless, a thing without substance riding the thermals above the headland. At others, he's lashed to the pier, his cries for help swallowed in the sound of the sea crashing over the shingle as darkness falls. And death is waiting for him there; he sees it floating on the edges of his vision. Waiting for the light to fail—

'Lukas, can you hear me? Lukas?'

An Orcadian accent; kind, tinged with faint professional concern. He opens his eyes to see one of the white-coated figures he recalls from earlier bending over him. The doctor smiles, straightens up.

'Just having a wee bad dream there, I think.' She unclips the chart from the foot of his bed, runs her eye over it. 'How's your throat feeling today?'

'Like I swallowed a razor blade.' He sits up, reaches for the water by his bed and takes a sip, bracing himself for the ground-glass sensation as the liquid hits. 'How long—'

'Two days,' the consultant tells him. 'You were a wee bit confused for most of yesterday, though. Your throat will be a bit uncomfortable, so try to rest your voice as much as you can. But your partner's here and desperate to see you, if you're feeling up to visitors.'

'My . . .' He manages a nod. Waits as she crosses to the door and calls a name Mahler won't let himself believe until Anna walks into the room.

'Fergie told me.' She closes the door, pulls a chair next to the bed. Opens her bag and dumps a small gift-wrapped package on the bed with half a dozen brightly coloured envelopes.

'Get well cards,' she tells him. 'There's one from Fergie and the MIT, and a Mr Hunt? Oh, and something from Gudrun.'

'How is she?'

'A bit shaken up, obviously. But happily singing your praises to anyone who'll listen. I, on the other hand . . .'

The look she gives him could blister paint. 'You do know what almost happened out there, don't you? How close you came to—' Her voice catches on the last syllable. She swallows, looks away. 'Bloody hell, Goth Boy. Bloody *hell*.'

'Anna, don't. Please.' He reaches for her hand, feels her fingers curl round his. 'I . . . I can't believe you're here. *Partner*.'

A faint flush at that. 'It's the only way I could get in to see you. And "girlfriend" makes me sound about fifteen, so—'

'Partner sounds bloody good to me.' He puts his arms round her, breathes in her citrus and honeysuckle scent. 'I owe you more apologies than I can count. What I said at Mina's funeral—'

The dryness in his throat explodes into a series of harsh, wracking coughs. Anna grabs the water by his bed, guides it to his mouth. Shakes her head when he tries to speak.

'You're not supposed to talk too much. And there's a fierce-looking policeman pacing up and down outside – the doc only sneaked me in first because I told her I had to catch the next flight back.'

'And do you?'

'Afraid so. I've a couple of appointments I need to keep, but I had to come and see you.' Her hand tightens around his. 'You're not still in any sort of danger, are you? Fergie seemed worried when he dropped the cards off to me.'

He shakes his head. There will be questions to answer, though: about Gudrun, about Cath. About Alex. His stomach clenches. 'Nothing like that. I promise.'

Her hand tightens around his. 'Good. Because you matter to me, Goth Boy. You know that, don't you?' She leans in to kiss him, then straightens up. 'I'll tell your mam you're on the mend – so don't make a liar of me, okay? Look after yourself, get better, and I'll see you back in Inverness.'

'Anna, wait.' Holding onto her hand as she gets up to go. 'There are things I need to say. Should have said much earlier.'

'Me too. But not here, and not like this. Look, I really need to go. I'm sorry.'

Mahler watches her leave, listens to the sound of her fading footsteps. And tells himself he'd imagined that odd discomfort on her face.

He reaches for more water, takes a quick, uncomfortable sip. And looks up to see Tony Armstrong's bulky frame appear in the doorway.

'Doc said I could have a quick word, as long as I didn't tire you out.' He crosses to the chair Anna's just vacated, sits down and gives Mahler a quick, assessing glance. 'Looking and sounding better than when they brought you in, for sure. If wee Colin hadn't picked up your text when he did . . . well, you were damn lucky, that's all.'

'I'm grateful.' Mahler risks more water, winces. 'Did you find . . . Has Cath's body been recovered?'

A head shake. 'It's the North Sea, Lukas. In November.' Armstrong scrubs a weary hand over his face. 'Christ, I can't believe we're talking about her like this. I've been in the Job for over twenty years, and this is the first time I've felt like none of it makes sense.' He looks across at Mahler.

'This isn't an official visit – the docs would have my hide if I tried to statement you right now, and there's . . . well, procedures to be gone through.'

Procedures. Yes, Mahler knows just how many procedures and investigations and enquiries will be heading his way as soon as he's declared fit, he has no illusions about that.

At his nod, Armstrong glances at him. Exhales slowly. And asks the question he's been leading up to since he arrived.

'You told the paramedics that when Cath ran into the sea, it looked like she was trying to get away from someone. But we carried out intensive searches of the area – you and Gudrun were the only people anywhere near the locus, apart from Cath. So who was she running from, Lukas?'

Mahler runs his tongue over his dry lips. 'The witches' salve. Cath had it on her hands, her face. It must have affected her. Affected what she saw, the same as—'

'What do you mean?'

I saw her face. I called her, and she came.

Mahler draws in a ragged breath. Exhales. And slowly shakes his head. 'Sorry, I'm still a bit confused. I can't be sure of anything at the moment.'

'Aye.' Armstrong looks him up and down, sighs. 'Aye, fair enough. God knows, you were well out of it when we found you. Look, get some rest, and concentrate on getting well right now.' He gets to his feet, raises a hand in awkward farewell. 'Take care, eh? Time enough for this when you're fit.'

Mahler leans back against the pillows, lets his eyes close as Armstrong leaves. For a moment, he tries to pull his thoughts together, tries to get a fix on everything that happened. But the memories feel vague, untethered, and he can't tie any of it down. And maybe he doesn't even want to.

Because right at the end, when Cath had run into the water, she'd looked back at the empty patch of shingle. At something just behind him, Mahler thinks, something over to the right and on the furthest edge of his vision. And for a moment, Mahler had managed to turn his head a fraction. Had turned his head, and seen—

No. Nothing was what he'd seen in the formless dark. Nothing moving. Nothing that looked like a tall female shape, wrapped in a sealskin cloak, drifting across the shingle towards the ink-black water.

Nothing.

66

Three Days Later

'You should still be on sick leave.' Chae Hunt closes the file on his desk, pushes it to one side and looks across at Mahler. 'I have a stack of medical paperwork *this* high telling me to keep your arse out of HQ for another seven days, and yet here you are.'

'It was only a recommendation, sir. And the sooner I've been fully debriefed, the sooner we can forward plan for all the ram-ifications of the events on Orkney.'

'Can't argue with that, I suppose.' Though Hunt's expression suggests he's sorely tempted to try. 'You know this won't be a simple in-house debrief, don't you? Cath McAvoy's death means—'

'I know what it means, sir.' It means his actions will be under scrutiny from the moment he identified Alex Fleming's body at Sandisquoy, with all the disciplinary consequences that could entail. 'I'm prepared for that.'

Hunt raises an eyebrow. 'You *think* you're prepared. Trust me, unless you've been through something like it . . .' He shakes his head. 'Tony Armstrong's lot recovered that file and memory stick from Cath McAvoy's office. There's enough for the Met to action a case review, but a lot of it's circumstantial stuff. And Fleming's confession was obviously under duress—'

'Of course. But I think he did it, sir.' Hard to say the words aloud; hard even now, when he's had days to think it over. To revisit the events of that summer, look at them again with the eyes of an experienced DI. And come to a devastating conclusion.

'Cath was right – Alex Fleming killed those women. And he wasn't acting alone, she was right about that too. She just had the wrong person down as his accomplice.'

Hunt folds his arms, leans back. 'I'm listening.'

'Right from the start, Fleming's choice of alias bothered me,' Mahler tells Hunt. 'I could understand the need to move away and make a fresh start if he'd undergone a mental and physical collapse. But why pick a name from your traumatic past, if you were desperate to get away from it? Yes, there was the physical resemblance with Billy Spencer, but it seemed oddly callous to steal a former colleague's name. Particularly when Matt Shawcross said Spencer's death had contributed to Fleming's breakdown.'

A nod from Hunt. 'Go on.'

'Before I went to Kirkwall, I asked Fergie to do some digging into Spencer. It turns out he and Fleming had lived in the same street, growing up. They went to the same schools, hung out together – got into some minor trouble, but nothing that resulted in a record. Which was odd because I don't remember he and Alex ever showing any sign that they knew each other beyond being friendly work colleagues.'

'Might just have been keeping things professional,' Hunt offers, and Mahler nods.

'I thought so too. Until we turned up a couple of old news reports about three murders that took place in the late nineties in the Dartford area. Three young women, killed half a dozen streets away from where Fleming and Spencer lived. There were no occult symbols found with the bodies, but they were posed in humiliating positions. And they were remarkably forensically clean – as though the killer, or killers, knew what they were doing.'

'Christ. Fleming and Spencer were spoken to, presumably, during the enquiry?'

'And eliminated,' Mahler tells him. 'But the murders were never solved. And with advances in forensic technology since then—'

'Aye.' Hunt nods slowly. 'It's all circumstantial, but if you're talking some sort of *folie à deux,* like Ian Brady and Myra Hindley . . . They knew each other a long time, didn't they? So when Spencer died in that car accident, that was what forced Fleming to stop killing?'

'It affected him – we know that. And with Spencer gone, he'd lost his back-up – if he'd continued alone, he would have had no one to tidy up the scene with him. Maybe it was a risk he realised he couldn't afford to take. But I suspect the urge to kill never quite left him.'

And moving to somewhere like Sandisquoy . . . Mahler had seen Fleming's eerie paintings as evidence of a fragile mind, tormented by the house's oppressive atmosphere. But now he wonders if it had simply been the darkness inside Fleming, clamouring for release.

Hunt grunts in agreement. 'If he did intend a relaunch, thank God it never got beyond the planning stage on Orkney. Looks like our pals in the Met are going to be busy for a while, though.' A corner of his mouth twists in a brief half-smile. 'Ah well, a trouble shared, and all that.

'We'll have plenty to keep us going at our end too. Fortunately, we'll have an extra pair of hands soon to help us out – I spoke to June Wallace today, and she's been passed as fit to return to work. Which means I won't be two key personnel down when the brown stuff from all this hits the fan.'

'Sir?' Mahler has a sudden, sick certainty he knows where this is going. 'Sir, if we're talking disciplinary, I should speak to HR—'

Hunt holds up his hand. 'Because you realise this is all one big bloody mess? Yes, thank you, I *know* what the formalities are, and how long it's all likely to take. Which is why your sick leave is hereby reinstated as of now – no, you will *not* argue the toss with me, Lukas, not over this – to be followed by the week of annual leave you're due to take by the end of this month. Are we clear?'

'Sir, I didn't request any leave—'

'Nevertheless, you're taking it. While June and I put our heads together and see how the hell we sort this out. Or I could just send you for mandatory, open-ended counselling – and believe me, I could make a damn good case for it.'

He leans back, folds his arms. And gives Mahler the kind of smile even June Wallace would be hard pressed to match. 'What's it going to be?'

It's still late autumn according to the calendar, but there's already a winter chill in the air. As Mahler walks along the river to meet Anna, most of the trees are bare, and the water has a swollen, angry look. By the time he gets to Eden Court, the cathedral clock has already struck half past and there's no sign of Anna. But then she's coming down Ness Walk towards him – *hurrying* towards him, her cheeks flushed, her emerald scarf bright against the November greyness.

'Sorry,' she tells him when she draws level. 'Not too late, am I? There was a call I had to take, and then I got talking to Lorna—' She looks closely at him, frowns. And produces an Icelandic-sounding curse he suspects she's picked up from Gudrun.

'Forget lunch. You don't look well enough to sit through a restaurant meal. Are you sure you shouldn't still be on sick leave? Because—'

'I *am* on sick leave. As of today. After that . . .' His bark of laughter is harsh enough for a couple walking past to glance at him. 'After that, Christ knows. I've been stupid, Anna – stupid, and bloody pig-headed. And a woman died because of it. Which isn't anything you should have to hear, but—'

'Stop that.' She softens the words with a smile, but there's a whisper of steel behind them. 'We talked about this whole "being close" thing, didn't we? Let's see if we can get it right this time.'

Anna loops her arm through his and guides him to the café at the rear of Eden Court, where she orders soup and sandwiches and steers him to a booth. And listens as Mahler tells her about Alex Fleming, the man he thought he'd known. And the monster he'd turned out to be.

'Alex *was* decent to me,' he finishes. 'Matt was right, I did look up to him. So when I should have been stepping back and letting Fergie handle things, I couldn't let it go . . . and maybe I missed things, Anna. Things I should have seen, things I *would* have seen if I hadn't had this image of saint bloody Alex stuck in my fucking mind.'

Silence. A long silence, before she takes his hand and covers it with both of hers. 'Okay. So, here's the thing – I can't give you absolution here. You said you made mistakes on Orkney, and it's not for me to say what should happen to you because of that. But I *do* know you can't beat yourself up for not seeing a monster when you looked at Fleming. Because no one did, Lukas. *No one.* Everyone in the Met saw exactly what he wanted them to see. Yes?'

He starts to say something, but Anna shakes her head. 'Hold on. You won't like this, but I think your boss is right. You need to be on sick leave a bit longer, and you need time away from work afterwards – *real* time, Lukas, not the odd weekend. Which sort of ties in with something I wanted to talk to you about anyway. About a new project I'm putting together.'

And there it is again, that odd discomfort in her face he'd seen on Orkney. Something hard and heavy starts to form inside his gut. 'The visiting lectureship in Reykjavik, the one you talked about at Mina's funeral. You're going to go for it, aren't you?'

'Not that one, no. But a couple of other opportunities have come up since then – one in Dublin, one in Cologne. They would only be for six months because no one knows what's happening with Brexit, but they're really interesting, Lukas. Particularly the Cologne one.'

Cologne. Of course, it would have to be there. 'When would you go?'

'Next term, if everything works out okay,' Anna tells him. 'But I'd want to spend a few days there first to get the feel of the place. I can't go until the hearing's over, of course. But if Jamie's appeal is dismissed—'

'*When* the appeal is dismissed.'

'*When* his appeal is dismissed, I thought I could find someone whose German is way better than mine – a detective, for example, who really needs to take a break – and persuade him to come with me.' Anna's smiling, but there's a hint of uncertainty in her voice. 'What do you think, Lukas?'

Cologne. Ancient Roman settlement on the Rhine and free imperial city, dominated by its stunning medieval cathedral. Birthplace of kings and statesmen, writers and artists. And Jochen Friedrich Mahler.

Wyrd, Gudrun had called the rune he'd been drawn to; fate, working itself out, no matter what. Mahler can't quite bring himself to believe in that. But with so much of his career hanging in the balance, perhaps this could be a chance to exorcise his father's malign ghost for good.

'As luck would have it,' Mahler tells Anna, 'I have just the person in mind.'

67

Edinburgh Evening Chronicle, **Wednesday 16 November**
  BREAKING NEWS
  "EXPLOSION" AT HIGH COURT

Reports are coming in that streets surrounding Parliament House have been sealed off following an "explosion" at the High Court of the Justiciary.

Images posted on social media appear to show damage to the side entrance of the building and to a GeoAmey vehicle, which had been in the process of transferring prisoners to the court.

Emergency services including the Scottish Fire and Rescue Service (SFRS) are in attendance.

It is not known if there are any casualties.

Edinburgh Evening Chronicle, **Thursday 17 November**
PRISONER ESCAPES AFTER HIGH COURT FIRE

A prisoner is on the run after escaping security at the High Court of the Justiciary yesterday afternoon, it has emerged. The building had been evacuated following unconfirmed reports of an explosion, and appliances from the Scottish Fire and Rescue Services despatched to the scene. However, the fire now appears to have been confined to a small area surrounding the side entrance to the building, and investigations are now underway to determine whether this may have been intended as a diversion to enable the prisoner's escape.

James Gordon, 38, had been due to attend an appeal hearing for his conviction in the 2014 murder of TV presenter Morven Murray.

He is described as 5' 11", of stocky build, with scarring to the left side of his face and brown hair. Members of the public are advised not to approach Gordon but contact the police immediately.

68

Edinburgh
Early December

Waiting for the phone call, he's nervous.

He's not a man who does nervous, not normally. Nervous is for the people around him, the little people. Some folk take a look at his good suits and expensive lifestyle and call him arrogant – not to his face, of course. Not if they want their own features to stay the way they're currently arranged. But he's heard the whispers, just the same. Only they're wrong.

Self-confident, sure. You have to walk the talk, don't you? He'd learned that in a hard school, a long time ago; fee-paying, as it happened, though he's damn sure his parents would have hauled him off to the nearest comprehensive if they'd known the sort of career his expensive education would eventually equip him for. Or the kind of people he'd end up mixing with. But arrogant . . . with the kind of man whose call he's waiting for right now, displaying any sort of arrogance would be a mistake. Possibly the last he'd ever make.

When his mobile buzzes on his desk, he doesn't flinch, not exactly. But he sits up straighter before answering and moves his chair a little closer to the wall.

'Good morning. My package will be ready for collection this evening, I understand?'

The voice on the other end is calm, almost benevolent. But he's not stupid enough to think that means anything. 'Of course. It took a little longer than anticipated, but getting the . . . the necessary paperwork together for an extra component—'

'Understood. The agreed fee will include a small bonus in recognition. I like to acknowledge good working relationships, wherever possible.'

'Thank you.' He runs his tongue over his dry lips. 'Unfortunately, there's been a slight complication. The package was damaged slightly during collection.'

'Damaged.' Enough of a chill in that single word to make him grateful this isn't a face-to-face encounter. 'How badly?'

'We were able to make some temporary repairs. The package wasn't in the best condition, and we had to move quickly. But I assure you, it's ready for shipping now.'

Not in the best condition – that's one way of putting it, he supposes. Internal bleeding, concussion and broken ribs would be another. But James Gordon's been certified out of danger now. Medically, at least.

'Good. It would be a shame if I needed to revise the terms of our agreement.'

'Mr Hollander, I assure you that won't be necessary—'

'I'm glad to hear it. And you know of course not to use that name again. Yes?'

'Of course.'

Christ, that was stupid of him. Even if he suspects that name is only one of several identities belonging to the man on the other end of the line. 'I'm sorry. I just . . . I'm confused, I suppose. I can't see what benefit this particular package is going to bring you. Or how you're going to use it.'

Silence. A long silence, giving him plenty time to think about the likely consequences of what he's just said.

'Understandable.' No anger in Hollander's voice, thank God;

if anything, he sounds faintly amused. 'Perfectly understandable – because, you know, I haven't actually decided yet. Our asset at Divisional HQ is still on stand-by, yes?'

Asset. Christ, the man sounds like a bad spy novel. Not for the first time, he wonders whether this association might end up costing him more than he's willing to lose, in spite of its undeniable financial benefits. But he's not naïve enough to think there's any way for him to walk away from this unscathed. At least, not as things stand.

'As you instructed.' He moistens his dry lips again. 'Do you anticipate a need for involvement from that quarter, then?'

'Anticipate?' Something non-standard in the man's pronunciation, something that hints at a first language other than English, in spite of his current alias. 'Not immediately. But if Lukas Mahler can't be dissuaded from any further . . . irritation, I will be forced to reconsider.'

Glossary

I never actually planned to do this. But three books into Lukas's story, I'm delighted to say that he's acquiring a healthy following, not just in the UK, but also across the pond.

Quite a few US readers have been asking if I could do a quick guide to some of the police ranks and terminology used throughout the series – and with a steadily growing cast, I thought it might be fun to add a little *Who's Who* and glossary as well.

Hope this helps!

Police Scotland Terminology/Locations

RANKS
As per other UK police forces. So a **DCI** is a Detective Chief Inspector, a **DI** a Detective Inspector, and so on.

MIT
Major Investigation Team – leads the investigation of all murder inquiries and large-scale and complex criminal investigations. Lukas's team is based in Inverness, but all teams can be deployed to locations throughout Scotland as needed.

SIO
Senior Investigating Officer.

OCCT
Organised Crime and Counter Terrorism Unit. Seriously not to be messed with.

GARTCOSH
Police Scotland's very imposing Crime Campus, opened near Glasgow in 2014. Houses various specialist and analytical departments as well as the Crown Office & Procurator Fiscal Service.

TULLIALLAN
Police Scotland's training college, similar to Hendon in London.

BURNETT ROAD
Where the *real* policing happens, according to the officers who work there. Cells, interview rooms and more uniforms than you can shake a stick at. (Though you probably shouldn't do that.)

N DIV HQ
Administrative headquarters of Police Scotland, N Division (Highlands & Islands). Convenient for Raigmore Hospital and a 24-hour Tesco. Where the easily bored 'Bang-Bang Boys' (Armed Response Unit) and Mahler's MIT hang out.

PROCURATOR FISCAL
In Scotland, the fiscal/PF investigates all sudden and suspicious deaths (similar to the role of a coroner elsewhere). They also conduct fatal accident inquiries and handle criminal complaints against the police, and form part of the **COPFS** – Crown Office and Procurator Fiscal Service.

(CRIME) SCENE EXAMINER

Hard-working, meticulous, friendly (as long as you don't mention *CSI*). They work for the Scottish Police Authority, carrying out scene examination, recording and evidence-gathering.

Recurring Characters

INVERNESS

Capital of the Highlands, aka 'The Sneck' 'Sneckie' to its inhabitants (I don't know why, before you ask). Population around 70,000, it became a city at the millennium, something it's still coming to terms with. Still known as 'the town' to older residents.

(Acting) DCI LUKAS MAHLER

Native Invernessian, slowly re-adjusting after years spent in foreign climes (Catholic boys' boarding school, Cambridge, Metropolitan Police). Don't call him a pretty boy in a sharp suit, and don't diss *Runrig*.

(Acting) DI IAIN 'FERGIE' FERGUSON

Sidekick. Proud owner of the most disreputable set of wheels ever to (dis)grace Police Scotland North Division's car park. Never met an item of baked goods he didn't like.

DC 'SKIVEY' PETE NOBLE

Gingerish IT nerd – think Shaggy from Scooby Doo, and you wouldn't be a million miles away. Nurses a semi-secret passion for Naz.

DC NAZREEN KHAN

Smart, ambitious, Glaswegian. Going places. Destined to break Pete's heart.

DC 'BIG GARY' MCALLISTER
Not the shiniest set of handcuffs in the MIT.

DI ANDY BLACK
Leather-jacketed dark horse.

DCI JUNE 'BRAVEHEART' WALLACE
Lukas's former boss, currently on sick leave. Definitely no truth
in the rumour she once took down a pair of muggers with only
a can of Irn-Bru and a miniature cheese-grater. Definitely not.

ANNA MURRAY
Coffee addict, historian and reluctant TV talking head. Particu-
lar interest in the witch persecutions in 17th century Scotland.
Based at the University of the Highlands & Islands (UHI)
Centre for History in Dornoch.

CHAE HUNT
Chief Superintendent, impressively smooth and unlined of
forehead and burnished of complexion for a man approaching
the big 5-O. Known as 'Ken' or 'Plastic Man' and rumoured
to have his medical aesthetics (Botox) consultant on speed-dial.
Not a fan of Lukas Mahler.

CAZZA (CARL) MACKAY
Small-time former villain and semi-retired dodgy businessman.
Despite his reputation, Cazza probably never even lived up to
Mahler's description of him as a Poundland *mafioso*. Though
he does still keep a couple of useful-looking hard men on his
payroll. You never know when you might need some knuckle-
dragging muscle, right?

HOLLANDER
Watch this space.

Invernessian and Scots Expressions

AYE, RIGHT
Like the English 'Yeah, right.' With a *lot* more attitude.

MANNIES/WIFIES
Universal but particularly Highland, for men/women. Often preceded by 'wee'.

FURRY BOOTS TOWN
Aberdeen, so called because the Doric dialect frequently switches an initial 'wh' or 'h' for an 'f' sound. So 'Where are you from?' becomes. 'Furr aboot ur ye fae?' (approximately – I'm not a Doric speaker!)

CLUSTERBOURACH
A *'bùrach'* is just a big mess (think teenager's bedroom), so this is just a milder version of the English 'clusterf..k'

THRAWN
Translates as 'stubborn', but honestly, that doesn't come close. Inject a megadose of attitude, then you're getting there.

PEEDIE
Orcadian word meaning little. Like Scots 'wee'. And no, I haven't overburdened this book with cod Orcadian, because I know how much it grates when people attempt to reproduce speech patterns/dialects they're not familiar with. Trust me on this.

Acknowledgements

This book was begun when the world was relatively normal, and completed when it was anything but. Halfway through, I pretty much ripped it up and started again, and I think it's a better book because of it – but boy, was it 'a sair fecht', as they say.

I've visited Orkney many times, and right from my first visit I knew I wanted to set a story there. But it took a visit to the creepiest holiday flat ever to fix the opening scenes of *In The Blood* in my mind. This book carries on a couple of the themes from book two, but if you notice a distinctly more spooky vibe this time round, that's probably why!

I hope Orkney folk will not take it amiss that I've borrowed the name of probably the most famous victim of the Orkney witch trials, poor Alison Balfour, for this book. Like Janet Horne, who featured in *What Lies Buried*, her story is utterly harrowing (the Orkney Heritage Society, https://www.orkneycommunities.co.uk/, has some excellent information on Alison and the many other victims if you're interested in reading up on this). And if you're lucky enough to visit the islands, can I recommend you take a short walk up from Kirkwall cathedral to the monument on the green at Gallows Ha' – it's unostentatious but somehow really fitting:

Thanks are due, as always, to Martin, who put up with my wild-eyed, wild-haired self during lockdown and kept the coffee flowing. To Alison Bonomi at LBA Books and my amazing new editor at Orion, Lucy Frederick, who patiently dug away at the roughest of rough drafts with me until we found some decent foundations to build on. To Ian Anderson, 'Staggie' fan and scene examiner with the Scottish Police Authority, whose procedural advice on transporting a body from Orkney was invaluable. To Professor Niamh Nic Daeid, who kindly kept me right on the properties and likely effects of the infamous 'witches' ointment'; and not least to lovely Lilja Sigurðardóttir, who cheerfully supplied all the Icelandic curse words I could ever need – and no, you *don't* need them translated – but *vinkona* just means girlfriend (not in the romantic sense).

Following feedback from across the pond, I've included a short character list and glossary this time round – hope you enjoy them! And if you're interested in learning more about the Lukas Mahler series, you can find me on:

Twitter:	twitter.com/HighlandWriter
or my blog here:	margaretmortonkirk.wordpress.com/
or Facebook:	facebook.com/MargaretKirkAuthor/

Credits

Orion Fiction would like to thank everyone at Orion who worked on the publication of *In The Blood* in the UK.

Editorial
Lucy Frederick

Copy editor
Clare Wallis

Proof reader
Linda Joyce

Audio
Paul Stark
Amber Bates

Contracts
Anne Goddard
Paul Bulos
Jake Alderson

Production
Ruth Sharvell

Publicity
Will O'Mullane

Design
Debbie Holmes
Joanna Ridley
Nick May

Editorial Management
Charlie Panayiotou
Jane Hughes
Alice Davis

Finance
Jasdip Nandra
Afeera Ahmed
Elizabeth Beaumont
Sue Baker

Sales
Jennifer Wilson
Esther Waters
Victoria Laws
Rachael Hum
Ellie Kyrke-Smith
Frances Doyle
Georgina Cutler

Discover the first DI Lukas Mahler mystery . . .
SHADOW MAN

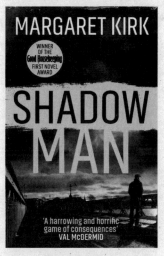

Two sisters
Just before her wedding day, Morven Murray, queen of daytime TV, is found murdered. All eyes are on her sister Anna, who was heard arguing with her hours before she was killed.

Two murders
On the other side of Inverness, police informant Kevin Ramsay is killed in a gangland-style execution. But what exactly did he know?

One killer?
As ex-Met Detective Inspector Lukas Mahler digs deeper into both cases, he discovers that Morven's life was closer to the Inverness underworld than anyone imagined. Caught in a deadly game of cat and mouse, is Lukas hunting one killer, or two?

'A harrowing and horrific game of consequences'
VAL McDERMID

**And don't miss DI Lukas Mahler struggling
to put the pieces together in . . .**

WHAT LIES BURIED

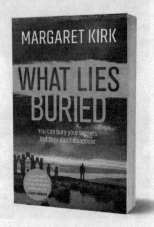

**A missing child. A seventy-year-old murder. And a
killer who's still on the loose.**

Ten-year-old Erin is missing; taken in broad daylight during
a friend's birthday party. With no witnesses and no leads, DI
Lukas Mahler races against time to find her. But is it already too
late for Erin – and will her abductor stop at one stolen child?

And the discovery of human remains on a construction site
near Inverness confronts Mahler's team with a cold case from
the 1940s.

With his team stretched to the limit, Mahler's hunt for Erin's
abductor takes him from Inverness to the Lake District. And
decades-old family secrets link both cases in a shocking final
twist . . .

'Tartan Noir at its very best . . .'
DAILY MAIL